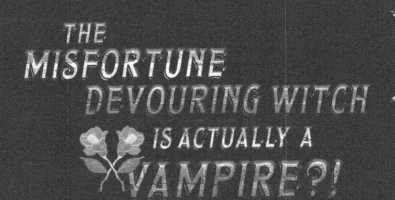

THE MISFORTUNE DEVOURING WITCH IS ACTUALLY A VAMPIRE?!

BY KIIRO HIMAWARI
ILLUSTRATED BY KIBIURA

Cross
to
World

The Misfortune Devouring Witch is Actually a Vampire?!
Kiiro Himawari

Translation by Amber Tamosaitis

Illustration by Kibiura
Title Design by A.M. Perrone
Editing by Robert Fox
Proofreading by Charis Messier
Book Design by A.M. Perrone

The Misfortune Devouring Witch is Actually a Vampire?!
© 2018 by Kiiro Himawari
English translation rights reserved by
Cross Infinite World.

English translation ©2019 Cross Infinite World

Cross Infinite World
contact@crossinfworld.com
www.crossinfworld.com

Published in the United States of America

Visit us at www.crossinfworld.com
Facebook.com/crossinfworld
Twitter.com/crossinfworld
crossinfiniteworld.tumblr.com

First Digital Edition: January 2020
First Print Edition: October 2020

ISBN-13: 978-1-945341-43-4

TABLE OF CONTENTS

Chapter 1: First Case, First Reward

THERE is a witch who devours the misfortunes of others. She lives alone in a dank and dreary manor and has yet to receive a single visitor.

Her manor lies in a narrow alley not far off a bustling main street, one that floods with ladies in dresses the color of the recently melted snow. Yet the stillness that pervades her alley makes it feel like another world entirely.

It was into that world that a tall blond man walked, his eyes on the handwritten map he carried, checking each building along the way before finally reaching his destination: an old two-story house with ivy winding its way up the brick walls. A small signboard was perched next to the wooden front door.

"'The Witch of the East's Apothecary,' eh? I'm not sure if that's charming or suspect…"

The colored glass window inlaid into the door was fogged over, obscuring the inside from view. The windows were all covered with flowery lace curtains, making the sign's presence the only hint that the shop was open for business. Ernest knocked and then tried to peer through the curtains. After waiting for a few moments with no response, he opened the door.

"If she put the sign out, that must mean the shop's open for business, right?"

He was so excited, it made him feel like a child. But why wouldn't he be? He was about to meet a witch from a distant land, one who could devour the misfortunes of others.

The door lurched open with a creak, followed by the resonant chiming of a bell. The shop was completely dark, despite the fact that it was the middle of the day. As his eyes adjusted to the dark, a unique floral aroma overtook his senses.

He took in the shop filled with the sort of things one would expect from a witch's shop: jars crammed with plants, frogs preserved in alcohol, unfamiliar powders, and tomes written in a foreign script. There were several shelves, a counter, and a door into another room, but it was on a couch in that back room next to a small window where Ernest's gaze finally landed.

There sat a petite girl with jet-black hair who couldn't have been more than fifteen or sixteen.

Her otherwise straight hair was disheveled on one side, as if she had slept on it. While most of her clothes were very much in the Hylantian-style, the shawl-like garment covering her shoulders appeared to be Eastern

"Good day, m'lady…or perhaps I should say, 'good morning.'"

The girl's eyes popped open, shocked by the young man's sudden appearance. Her body went rigid, making her look like a frightened cat. But the stoic expression she wore eclipsed any hint of the anxiety she was feeling inside.

Ernest flashed her a smile, and she rushed to sit up straight.

"A customer? I beg your pardon."

Embarrassed that she had been caught napping on the job, she took her place behind the counter. The single tuft of hair that bobbed atop her head gave her otherwise subdued demeanor a subtle charm.

Her eyes, festooned by long lashes, were the same arresting black as her hair, a feature so rare it made it clear she wasn't from Hylant. She was cute now, but would surely grow into a beautiful woman in her own right.

"How can I help you?"

"Ah, yes…I'm Ernest Travis Selden, an attendant to the royal family. By that, I mean I do various jobs for the benefit of our country," Ernest said, using simple words for this careless girl whom he had caught napping on the job.

"Are you…a nobleman?"

"Yes, I hold the title of count. Might I ask your name?"

"How rude of me. I am Yuuri. Yuuri Watoh. Pleasure to make your acquaintance, Count Selden."

Ernest was familiar with the Watoh name. The head of Watoh Company himself was the one who suggested Ernest visit the witch's shop. Watoh Company was well-known as a purveyor of goods from the East, catering especially to the desires of the nobility and the royal family. The head of the company hailed from the East himself, so it should have been no surprise that this girl shared the same last name.

"You're such a big girl to be helping out in the shop like this. Are you a relative of the Watohs?" he inquired, intending his first words to be a compliment.

But the petite girl went silent, her lips in a pout and her cheeks red, clearly not amused.

"I heard the witch here is an expert in Eastern medicine? Is she here?"

"That would be me," the scowling girl said curtly.

"Come again…?"

"I am the witch you seek. My grandmother previously held that title, but as she's passed away, I am all that's left."

"*You're* the 'Misfortune Devouring Witch'?"

"I don't care for that title. …And just so you know, I'm nineteen. You don't need to talk down to me like a child."

The Misfortune Devouring Witch is Actually a Vampire?!

Ernest stood opposite Yuuri, his eyes fixed on her. Nineteen? By Hylantian customs, that made her an adult.

Sensing his doubt, Yuuri turned away with a loud "hmph" added for good measure.

"…My apologies, m'lady. Please accept this letter of introduction the head of Watoh Company wrote on my behalf," he said, setting the letter on the counter. He hoped it'd be enough to convince her to help him. Yuuri took her time in reading the letter and ensuring the seal was the genuine article before finally looking back up at Ernest.

"So, you want to learn about medicinal herbs from the East, specifically those from Xingka?"

Xingka was the largest country on the eastern continent, and the continent's leading power in economics, cultural influence, and medicine.

"Yes. I'm not at liberty to go into detail, but I desperately need books on Eastern herbal medicine. I could order them through Watoh Company, but it would take too long." Ernest was acting at the behest of the royal family and thus, discretion was paramount.

"So that's why Watoh Company sent you to me?"

"I'm afraid so."

"Would you mind having a seat over there then? Many of my books are shelved and it will take me some time to find the ones you require," Yuuri said, indicating the couch beneath the window. There was a table next to it with a teacup and a book written in an unfamiliar script on it. Yuuri shelved the book, cleaned up the remnants of her tea, and headed for the back.

She returned a short time later, accompanied by a gentle flowery aroma. She was struggling to balance a tray with two teacups on it, a sight which did little to convince Ernest she really was nineteen.

"….Here you go. It's jasmine tea, a Xingkaese specialty."

"So that's where that flowery aroma was coming from. …Is your family from Xingka?"

"No, my family is from Hinomoto, which is further east. Watoh Company is heavily involved in trade in that region and much of Hinomoto's medical knowledge comes from Xingka anyway, so we learn Xingkaese growing up."

Hinomoto was a small island country, east of the eastern continent, and the farthest place on the planet from the western continents.

"Hinomoto, eh? I've only ever seen it on the map. What is the customary way of drinking tea there?"

"Support the base of the cup with your left hand and wrap your right hand around the cup. It's not boiling hot, so take your time and allow the cup to warm your hands," Yuuri explained, demonstrating the gesture as she spoke.

Ernest wrapped his hands around the dainty teacup as she instructed and lifted it to his lips. The tea had a strong fragrance and smooth taste, but it left a slightly bitter aftertaste. It was subtle in flavor, completely different from the black tea he normally drank.

"...It's good. The flowery aroma is strong."

"Normally, jasmine tea is made using low-quality tea leaves and so the aroma is meant to obscure its weak taste. But here, it's imported by the aristocracy, and is made using higher quality leaves instead."

"It seems the royal family, and subsequently the nobles, have taken a liking to Eastern goods. They seem to have developed a great respect and affinity for your culture."

"I am pleased to hear that. ...If you'll excuse me, I'll see to your books."

Yuuri curtsied and headed for the back room. She was so polite and proper, and yet still painfully unaware of the hair sticking up on top of her head. The corners of Ernest's lips twitched into a smile.

"You might want to take a look in the mirror first. Your hair has wound itself into a most charming state."

He knew it was rude, but he couldn't help himself. She froze and her free hand wandered to the top of her head. With a gasp, she rushed out of the room.

"Looks like I made her mad again..." he sighed. He wasn't normally one to tease young women. And yet, something inside pushed him to tease this young witch he had only just met.

Yuuri returned with an arm full of books just as he was finishing his tea. "Several of these books are hard to find, so please be sure you return them to me."

"Of course. And thank you. When I return, I'll see to it you are compensated accordingly. ...Until next time, my little witch."

Yuuri clearly resented being called little. She was seething.

And that was how Ernest Travis Selden met the mysterious witch

The Misfortune Devouring Witch is Actually a Vampire?!

from a distant land, Yuuri Watoh.

🍎 🍎 🍎

ONLY three days after his first visit, Ernest once again found himself at the witch's door.

The jangling of the bell over the door gave him away. Imagining the look on the witch's face when she saw him back so soon excited him. But Yuuri was nowhere to be found.

"How can she be so careless...?"

Last time she was sleeping, now she was missing. As both a shopkeeper and a woman living alone, she was frighteningly negligent.

A rattling sound shook Ernest from his thoughts. It was coming from an interior door that had been left ajar. The area seemed to be part of her private living quarters. Undeterred, Ernest headed toward the sound.

Peering inside, he spotted her right away. She was perched atop a ladder, her back to him, reading a book. She wore a jacket with a different pattern from the other day and her hair was as shiny as ever.

She evidently wasn't expecting any customers. The books that once lined an entire section of shelving were now in piles on the floor. Ernest couldn't be sure whether she was looking for one in particular or just going through them all, but either way, she was so immersed in reading that she hadn't even heard the bell.

"Hey, Miss Witch! How's it going?"

"Eek!"

He hadn't meant to scare her, but he thought it would be creepy of him to just stand there silently watching her. Still, the sound of his voice caught Yuuri off guard and she lost her balance. Both she and the book she was holding came toppling off the ladder.

Ernest charged in and caught her. Even as the ladder and book came tumbling after her, he still managed to catch the petite witch with surprising ease. She refused to look at him after he set her down.

"That was close. Are you all right?"

Even with her back turned, he could see her ears glowing bright red. If he said something about it, he knew she would only grow cross with him. He decided to let it go for the time being.

"I'm terribly sorry. Are you hurt?" Yuuri finally turned in his direction. Her eyes were still downcast as she looked him over to make sure he hadn't been injured.

"I'm fine. And I should be the one to apologize. I hadn't meant to frighten you. Why were you reading back here with the door unlocked?"

"I wasn't originally. When you came to borrow those books, it made me realize I should organize my collection…so…"

"Haha! So, you started going through them and got caught up reading!"

So she *was* reading instead of minding her shop. His laughter finally got her to look directly at him. And, as he feared, she was mad.

"ANYWAY, why have you come to see me today?"

"…Well, it may take a while to explain, do you have the time?"

Yuuri led Ernest to a couch like the one he had sat on last time and pulled a chair over for herself that looked like it came from her dining table. She prepared a different kind of tea for him this time as well.

"It's about the books you lent me. A colleague of mine who's proficient in Xingkaese was supposed to translate them for me, but says he can't understand them."

"What?"

He had borrowed these books, knowing they were written in Xingkaese. How foolish he sounded now, complaining he couldn't understand them.

"I was baffled at first, but I suppose it does make sense. He works as a civil servant, so I expect it was a bit much for him to understand the text of a specialized medical book, even in his own language."

"So, even though he can speak enough to manage diplomatic exchanges, he doesn't know enough to read medical texts?"

With her dainty hands clasped around the teacup, Yuuri took a sip. Ernest mimicked her elegant, practiced movements. Finished with his tea, he decided to move on to the main topic at hand.

"You don't talk much, do you?"

"…I guess not. I don't go out very often."

"That's the impression I've gotten. You're a sharp girl, so you must understand that I haven't been forthcoming for a reason. We're willing to reward you handsomely if you'll assist us."

"To be completely honest, I do not wish to involve myself in anything troublesome. But, seeing as the head of Watoh Company himself has commanded me to help you, I suppose I cannot refuse."

"I'm sorry to get you caught up in all of this, Miss Yuuri. But I must ask that you keep this matter between us."

With that out of the way, Ernest began to divulge the matter he was investigating:

It all started a month prior when the Queen fell ill at a welcome reception for a dignitary from Xingka. Her breathing remained ragged and her eyes bloodshot for hours after the ceremony.

"The Queen has always had a delicate constitution that waxed and waned with the seasons, so we believed there was no immediate cause for concern. And yet…"

A week ago, the Queen once again collapsed. The only known similarities between the two incidents were the Xingkaese tea the Queen drank and the maid who had prepared it for her. But a lot of people drank the tea brought by the ambassador and they were fine. This particular maid had been taught how to prepare the tea by the ambassador and his wife, so she was the one asked to do so this time as well.

The maid was quickly taken into custody and put through an intense investigation, but her story remained the same. She maintained complete innocence.

"The Queen has complete faith in this particular maid. She has ordered that this matter not be made public, convinced that there must be some misunderstanding."

"So the Queen's maid and the tea from Xingka are the two common threads."

"Yes. Many of the maids also drank the tea, including the one in question. The only person who collapsed was the Queen. So it's not unreasonable to believe her responsible, yes?"

Assuming that no poison had been detected in either the tea or the cup it had been served in.

"Have you considered the possibility that a poison unknown to the doctors of your country could have been used?"

"We have. We searched the maid's belongings and tested the cup for anything that could be a poison, but we found nothing. Since makeup from the East, particularly from Xingka, has become popular here, we've also been evaluating the possibility that a poison could have been smuggled in under the guise of being makeup as well."

The investigation hadn't firmly settled on Eastern poisons being the definitive cause. They were merely assessing each possibility,

"I understand. So you would like me to summarize all of the Eastern poisons that could impact the respiratory system. Could you give me ten days?"

"Yes, thank you, we would be incredibly grateful." Ernest's generous grin made Yuuri blush. She told him she rarely ventured outside and hardly interacted with anyone beyond her family, so it made sense that she would be unaccustomed to interacting with others.

"By the way, do you have special powers or something?" he asked.

"What do you mean?"

"Like the power to rid yourself of wicked men?"

Everyone called her either the "Witch Who Preyed Upon Misfortunes" or the "Misfortune Devouring Witch," but in person, she wasn't the least bit imposing. Her lack of vigilance began to worry him.

"People call me a witch because I brew potions and treat their maladies. I'm more akin to a doctor. I have no mystical powers." Her answer was matter-of-fact, and yet, she looked as if she would burst into tears.

"Shouldn't you be a little more careful then? I mean, if I just grabbed your hair right now, you wouldn't be able to get away." Ernest would only have to take a step from the couch and the girl would be his. But the girl didn't seem to be afraid.

As soon as Ernest touched her hair, Yuuri balled her hands into fists and glared at him. "Let go of my hair. If you do anything untoward, I won't help you."

Her anger was no more frightening than a kitten's yowl to Ernest. It actually made him want to see more of her reaction. But he felt he owed her a word of warning for her lack of vigilance.

"If I genuinely wished to harm you, I would have done it long before now. You really should be more careful about keeping your shop locked."

"No one ever comes to my shop. They're so afraid of me, they do not dare...so there is no danger. Your concern is unnecessary; please let it go."

"But, what about me? I'm here."

"Your work brought you here."

"Really? Still, I urge you to use caution while bad men such as myself lurk about, dear lady witch."

Ernest left the shop and the witch with her cheeks red and her head hanging low.

❦ ❦ ❦

SCARCELY three days had passed before Ernest returned to the shop.

Yuuri had heeded his warning and was there to greet him when he arrived. And yet, every time he came within striking distance, she quickly moved away. His excessive demonstration the other day had now turned her into a full-on frightened feline.

While Ernest usually only visited the witch for business matters, she fascinated him so much that he decided to visit her on his day off.

"It is a pleasure to see you again, m'lord, but our agreed upon deadline has not yet come."

"...True, but since you're open for business anyway, I thought it might be all right for a customer such as myself to stop in."

"A customer? You've never actually bought anything from me! Just stopping in to tease an innocent woman does not a customer make!"

"Hahaha, I suppose you're right. So, what are you up to?"

The cold look in her eyes told him not to bother her, that she was busy, but he ignored it.

"I'm blending tea. It's been quite popular as of late," Yuuri said as she weighed tea leaves and flower petals atop a scale covered with a thin paper. There was a porcelain pot small enough to fit in the palm of one's hand on the counter, likely also for sale.

"I see..."

Tea from Xingka was extremely popular among aristocratic women, but, as it was still rather scarce in Hylant, it was far from affordable for commoners. Ernest tried picturing a noblewoman deigning to visit the sketchy little shop, but couldn't.

"You actually get customers here?"

"How rude! They may not actually visit my shop, but...I have to make money somehow!"

"So you don't get customers then."

"Watoh Company informs me of their customers' ailments and I mix the tea for them to sell as their own. The product is extremely popular now that people have heard it is mixed by someone trained in the East...."

The shelf was lined with many similarly packaged tea mixes, making Ernest think that while the witch herself had no business, her sales under the Watoh Company name enabled her to sell enough to get by. He felt like he finally had some sort of grasp of Yuuri's relationship to the company, as well as how a shop that sold nothing managed to stay open.

"I see, so you aren't just slacking off all the time! Think you could spare some jasmine flower tea for a weary nobleman?"

"This isn't a cafe, you know!"

"All right then, you finish that up and we'll go to an actual cafe. I have to make it up to you after being so mean. Do you like sweets?"

The word "sweets" caught her attention. She gazed through the lace curtains out the window, then shook her head.

"...I can't go outside, and besides, I was warned to be wary of wicked men."

Her expression darkened as she gazed outside. Ernest had to admit to himself that he hadn't seen many foreigners about town, so her reluctance was understandable.

At the same time, on the wall behind the counter hung a feminine-looking jacket and a parasol, both serving as ample proof that she did actually leave the shop. So why couldn't she go to a cafe with Ernest?

"Aw, you're no fun. But why not? It's so nice out. And I'm not really a wicked man."

"I don't care for sunny weather."

"Would you prefer we go on a rainy day then?"

"I don't care for rainy days either."

"You don't care for anything!" Ernest groaned, plopping down on the sofa by the window.

Yuuri pouted, realizing he was unlikely to leave anytime soon. Finally she relented and went to make some tea. She emerged a short time later with the tea Ernest requested.

"So, how is the work for us coming along?"

"I'll have what you need in plenty of time, as long as Your Lordship stops interfering with my work," Yuuri said sarcastically as she returned to mixing the tea.

"You're such a hard worker. …So I've been wondering, is that robe from Hinomoto?"

"Yes. It's a *haori*, which is a Hinomotoese-style of outerwear. It was a gift, but I'm afraid wearing it in town will make me stick out, so I primarily wear it around the shop."

Ernest found himself rather curious about who exactly had given Yuuri the red *haori*. Could it have been from the president of Watoh Company himself or maybe someone else she knew. Another employee of the company? In any case, the red of the *haori* complemented her black hair so perfectly that whoever gave it to her must have known her well. This was only Ernest's fifth visit to the shop, but each time she wore a *haori* of a different color, so he assumed she had quite a selection.

Ernest had so much he wanted to ask her beyond who gave her the *haori*. How was she related to Watoh Company exactly? He knew about her grandmother, but what of the rest of her family?

"Are those flowers native to Hinomoto?" he asked, indicating the white and gold flowers dotted vividly against the red background of the *haori*. The slender petals reminded him of dahlias or perhaps marguerite daisies, but they were a bit different.

"They're chrysanthemums… In the East, you can even get tea made from them. Here, have a look."

Yuuri placed something puffy and amber colored on a small plate and handed it to Ernest. It didn't look anything like the flower pattern on her shirt, likely because it was being dried out to be used in tea.

"Is something wrong?" Ernest asked, noticing Yuuri was staring silently at the chrysanthemum.

"Have there been any developments with the tea incident?"

"The royal doctor has ordered that no one consume it until his evaluation is complete, seeing as it has caused the Queen to collapse twice."

"Couldn't you give me a little longer before deciding whether or not it was actually the tea?"

"Possibly, but the tea is so popular. If it got out that tea the ambassador brought caused the Queen to collapse, it could lead to a diplomatic breakdown or even war."

"I see. But still, you've asked me to look into this."

"Well, we did come to you for a third-party opinion. Perhaps you should have a look."

"Really?"

"Though that would require you getting more heavily involved…"

Ernest pulled a bulky envelope from his shirt pocket and laid it on the table.

"Miss Yuuri, I don't believe we've actually gone into detail regarding your compensation, have we?" Ernest asked, fixing her with a serious gaze for once.

"I don't suppose we have. And since this job will take me ten days, it is an important matter."

"Then please accept this as your advance."

Yuuri took the envelope and peered inside. She found the envelope filled with more bills than a man at the prime of his working life could hope to make, even over the course of several months.

"What is this? Hush money? …Do I really appear to be in such dire straits? Or perhaps you see me as a woman with loose lips. Either way, I don't care for the implication."

Her normally sullen demeanor seemed to be at least partially the result of an embarrassment she was struggling to hide. But in this moment, her displeasure was clearly the result of her irritation at the contents of the envelope. She took pride in the work she did, and thanks to her work ties with Watoh Company, she clearly was holding her own.

"Oh…it appears I've offended you."

"If you're truly that concerned, then why not just threaten to have me rolled up in a mat and tossed into the sea if I speak a word of this to anyone."

"How could I say something so dreadful to such an impressionable young woman? Am I to understand you do not require payment…?"

He meant her no harm. But he was hoping that the hush money would at least constitute a confidentiality agreement of some sort with her.

"…Well…what if I were to share my secret with you? It could be a trade of sorts. You would know my weakness. And I would be forced to keep your confidence, correct?"

She was clever. If she accepted the money in exchange for her silence, she was locking herself into a contract. But by revealing a weakness of her own, she was in a way encouraging him to protect her. With both of them knowing each other's secrets, they were bound by a shared trust, neither able to divulge the other's secret without having their own exposed. Though he didn't like the thought of her being so suspicious of him.

Still, this secret had piqued his curiosity. So he gave a deep nod and flashed a wicked grin.

Though the idea was hers, Yuuri found her thoughts difficult to convey, starting and stopping over and over again. Ernest waited patiently.

"I-If you truly want my expertise, simple money will not do. You need to offer something of greater significance...something like blood."

"Blood? I'm not sure I like where this is headed."

Try as she might to sound self-assured, her voice wavered. "I am the descendant of vampires. I must drink blood at least once every three months. If I am able to receive the blood of another, that would be compensation enough for me. ...That is my secret."

At any other time, Ernest would have laughed at what she told him. But Yuuri appeared to be on the verge of tears. If he laughed at her now, he could be sure she would never smile upon him.

And I so desperately want to see that smile.

Whether it was anger or embarrassment, Yuuri was certainly an expressive woman. But Ernest had yet to see her smile even once. So, even as dubious as it all sounded, he was willing to take his chances.

"Perhaps that is the source of your otherworldly beauty. All right, that should be fine. How much blood do you require?"

"I only need a little, about as much as what falls from a tiny cut."

Ernest removed his tie clip and used the pin to prick his index finger. After a few seconds, vivid crimson blossomed on his skin.

"Have a taste."

Yuuri said she needed to drink blood, and yet she looked afraid. Ernest pressed his finger to those rose-colored lips of hers. As she began to lick the blood on her lips, her expression went slack, as if she were intoxicated.

The timid, wavering Yuuri disappeared, as if she never existed, replaced now by a ravenous woman, wildly lapping up the blood. But the wound was tiny, born only from a pin prick, and so the flow quickly ceased.

No sooner had Ernest pulled his finger away than did Yuuri's lips find their way to the base of his thumb. She bared her fangs and sank them into his flesh.

"…Ah!" Ernest tensed up at the sudden pain, causing Yuuri to come to her senses.

"I'm so sorry! I-I…"

"I don't mind. That couldn't have been enough. Were you that hungry?"

Yuuri burst into tears, clearly dismayed at seeing the pain she had caused him. But he could see now that she had been telling the truth. Her canine teeth were sharp, though not unthinkably so for a human, and she completely changed when she drank his blood.

He heaved a deep sigh and lovingly gazed upon her as she fed. Her tears were heartbreakingly beautiful.

That alone made Ernest feel that fulfilling her request was of the utmost importance, and that other questions, such as what exactly she was, could wait.

When she finally finished, Yuuri fell back, her expression sluggish and dazed. Ernest pulled her close to him, embracing her. Yuuri did not try to pull away, instead choosing to lean into him.

It was something she likely otherwise would never have done.

"What do you normally do for sustenance?"

He wasn't sure he could handle it if she had drunk the blood of another man. It now felt like such an important task to him.

She was cautious before, like a skittish cat that would run at the first sign of trouble. But now here she was, curling up in his lap of her own free will. This defenseless side of her only made him want to protect her more.

"…I don't know. This…was my first time…" Yuuri drifted off midsentence.

Ernest now overflowed with concern for the girl who had once threatened him for simply touching her hair.

"First time? Miss Yuuri…? What do you mean? Are you all right? Don't go falling asleep like a baby after its bottle on me!"

He shook her gently, but she would not wake. He resigned himself to serving as her pillow for the time being.

"M'lady, I do not think you appreciate me enough. If I weren't the gentleman that I am, it would have been you and not I that was the prey here."

He felt entitled to at least kiss the top of her head, but thought better of it. They remained like that for over an hour, until she awoke, screaming at him.

🦇 🦇 🦇

YUURI shrieked and retreated to the other end of the couch.

Her memories of what had happened came flooding back and she quickly apologized, her cheeks bright red. Her expression rolled from one emotion to the next, and Ernest teased her, causing her to become even angrier.

Yuuri noticed the bite marks her feeding frenzy had left and ran off to fetch supplies to treat Ernest's wounds. By the time she returned, she had finally calmed down.

"I'm so sorry. That must hurt..." she said meekly, attending to his wounds with a disinfectant-soaked cotton cloth. She then carefully applied an ointment with a fragrant herbal aroma.

"The bleeding's stopped, so it's fine. I won't become your servant or something because of the bite, will I?"

"Not at all. But the open wound is at risk of infection, so it's best to disinfect it."

The sight of her little hands feverishly attending to his made Ernest smile. It did hurt, but her attention afterward more than made up for it. He felt an odd sense of pride knowing that the evidence of her secret resided on his left hand, hidden just below a bandage.

After replacing the now cold tea from earlier with a fresh batch, Yuuri brought a chair from the dining room and sat across from Ernest. He suggested she join him on the couch, as it was meant to seat three people, but she merely shook her head. It was clear that she was over any desire to be that close to Ernest for the time being. He realized that pain was the price he would have to pay to see her true self. He lamented the fact that she really was like a skittish cat, only wanting to be handled if food was involved.

"...So, please tell me more. What are you, really?"

"...I'm the descendent of the vampires of Hinomoto."

"You said your grandmother was the 'witch' before you. Was she a vampire as well?"

Yuuri gulped and nodded. "My grandmother was a vampire, but

my father lacks any vampiric characteristics. While my blood may be diluted, I am much like my grandmother—our ancestral blood flows strong in me."

"So it's a sort of atavism, where those traits skipped your father's generation and made a return in you? ...So what of your parents? Are they still alive?"

"Yes. The head of Watoh Company is my father. I don't look much like him, do I?"

The head of Watoh Company was the one who told Ernest about the witch's shop. He looked different from most people in Hylant, but his olive-brown hair and eyes were a far cry from the deep ebony of Yuuri's. Ernest had suspected they might be related, but they certainly didn't look enough alike to suggest they were father and daughter.

"Ever since I was a little girl, I've been able to see well in the dark, but that also means I have a hard time in bright places. And my teeth are sharp... If you asked my Hylantian mother, she'd tell you I'm a monster. My mere existence tore our family apart," Yuuri rattled off these words with the same disinterest one might with a shopping list.

But Ernest sensed something deeper in her apathy, as if she were trying to keep her fragile heart from breaking. After all, her mother couldn't bring herself to accept that her daughter looked nothing like her beloved husband, couldn't bear the light, and loved the dark. "Unconditional love" apparently meant nothing to her.

"Is that why you live here alone...?"

"I've lived here since I was little. But I had my grandparents with me, so I wasn't lonely..."

But now she was alone. Her contact with her father seemed mostly perfunctory, so she was more or less alone.

"I see...then it's decided!"

"What is?"

"I will keep your secret. But if you ever need anything, all you need do is ask."

In the beginning, it was likely just his fascination with the strange girl from a foreign land. But after seeing the expression on her face as she became intoxicated off his blood, one he was sure she never intended another to see, he resolved himself to become her source of sustenance.

"No, really, I'm all right. I don't want someone hanging around, treating me like a circus attraction. Please leave me alone."

"You said you were only going to try my blood, but you drank a lot of it. Was it that good?"

"......"

Yuuri stared at his left hand, wrapped in the bandages she'd painstakingly applied.

"And here I went and gave you an advance and yet, you're still so cold toward me. I thought I'd give you more if you were honest with me, but…" He was only trying to tease her and act put off, but she continued staring at his hand.

"Aren't you afraid? You're not repulsed by all of this?"

The one quaking in fear and disgust was Yuuri.

"You have to feed once every few months, but you won't hurt anyone beyond that, correct?"

"I don't think so. My grandmother lived her life in peace alongside my Hylantian grandfather."

Now that he had served in the same capacity, it was clear to Ernest that Yuuri's grandfather had been the one to provide blood to her grandmother.

It seemed one thing Yuuri herself was unaware of was that vampires were said to have the ability to charm their prey. Ernest decided he didn't mind, as long as he was the one and only person she used that ability on.

"Well then, there's no need for me to be afraid, is there?"

"You're an odd man. Well, I suppose, until we tire of each other, you're welcome here anytime."

He was sure the line about tiring of each other was more for her benefit than his. Until recently, she didn't know Ernest. And even now, he still seemed like a passing presence in her world. Despite his affable nature, she was still cautious of him. Her words were meant to soften the blow, should that day come when he abandoned her.

Too bad for her. I have no plans of going anywhere. And I rarely tire easily of anyone or anything that strikes my interest.

And so, he willingly became the sole food source for Yuuri Watoh.

ERNEST visited the witch's shop once more, one day before he was scheduled to. Perhaps it was because of the secret that they'd bonded over, but she didn't threaten him or try to run him off as she had before.

"Afternoon, Miss Witch. How's the job coming along?"

"Oh, it's almost done. I can bring it to you if you'll wait here for a moment."

"No need to worry, I'll come for that tomorrow. I have some of the tea in question with me and thought you might like to see it."

A doctor who served the nobility was now in charge of securing the tea and testing it for poison. With his permission, Ernest was allowed enough for one pot, and so he placed it into a small flask and brought it with him.

Yuuri brought out a small saucer and they shifted the bottle's contents onto it. She squished up the tea leaves with her bare hands and smelled them to ensure they were in fact tea.

"...Was it all right to do that? Do you suspect the tea leaves themselves might be poisoned?"

Naturally, Ernest wouldn't have given the tea to her if he did not think it safe, but it was clear that she had some suspicions of her own.

"Many people drank it and did not fall ill, and Xingka is a friendly nation, so they wouldn't knowingly mix poison into it, right?"

"That's true..."

Yuuri brought out a pair of tweezers and sifted through the tea leaves one by one. As Ernest looked more closely, he realized there were light yellow and red bits mixed in with the brown leaves. Once she finished sifting, Yuuri wrote several words on a sheet of paper.

"This tea is what we call flowering tea. The jasmine tea you love, Count, is also generally considered a flower tea," Yuuri explained in response to Ernest's confused head tilt.

Flowering teas like jasmine tea were a common delicacy in Xingka and came in many varieties. Some were made by simply mixing the flower petals directly into their cup, while others relied on a premade bundle of dried flower petals and tea leaves.

The tea the ambassador had brought as a gift was indeed flowering tea, as was the tea mix Yuuri had prepared for Watoh Company a few days earlier.

"This mix has a lot of petals, don't you think?"

Now that the tea leaves and other pieces were separated, it was clear that the light yellow and red bits were dried flower petals. There was an especially high concentration of the light yellow petals.

"These are chrysanthemum petals."

"Oh, yes, like the ones you showed me the other day, right? …Does that mean something to you?"

"Just that, maybe, the Queen wasn't poisoned."

Yuuri clearly wasn't one for jokes, yet Ernest found this hard to believe after seeing the Queen collapse firsthand. How could it be anything but poison?

"She wasn't poisoned?"

"You've never heard of someone falling ill because of something they ate or drank?"

Yuuri held out a Hylantian medical journal. It was opened to a page discussing people who, as soon as certain foods touched their lips, broke out into hives and had trouble breathing. And though they hadn't been able to prove this was the cause, it was believed to be linked to several deaths.

"The tea leaves themselves are the same in Xingka as they are in Hylant. The difference is that, here in Hylant, we don't normally blend chrysanthemums into our tea."

She handed Ernest another book. This one he recognized. It was one of the medical books he had borrowed from her originally, but returned after being unable to translate the text. There was a picture of a chrysanthemum on the page she had bookmarked.

"Here. I only translated the section about chrysanthemums."

Indeed, she had exclusively translated the pages describing the chrysanthemum and its effects, color, and characteristics. At the very end was a warning that chrysanthemums could cause hives, itchiness, or, in severe cases, asphyxiation, in some people.

"There are many foods that can cause this condition, both in Hylant and the East as well. And it isn't just food. Makeup has also been linked to similar illnesses."

"So you're saying it's not a poisoning! Have we wasted all this time trying to research poisonous plants?"

"No, I am not willing to assert that much yet. Just that, your people should explore other possibilities outside of a targeted poisoning…and that, if this is the cause, it explains a lot."

Those words were clearly her honest opinion.

Ernest also had his doubts about this being caused by poison. They hadn't been able to detect any in the Queen's tea or on her cup, so he had at least suspected it was not a poison common to Hylant. Poison was just one possible explanation, so they couldn't rule out the other possibilities just yet.

"May I borrow this book? I'd like to hear what the royal physician has to say on the subject."

"Of course. I thought you might ask."

"If you're right, then both the Queen and the maid will be spared. It would be a matter of happenstance and not the maid's fault."

The maid had insisted she had no reason nor desire to poison the queen. Since the Queen's faith in her was so great, she had only been placed under house arrest for the duration of the investigation. It was fortunate that the matter had been kept quiet.

"Still, it's important to remember that, even though no one meant for this to happen, substances that can cause these types of reactions are still considered poisons by many."

"You are right. People who know about the Queen's weakness to such substances, such as yourself, could use it against her…"

If trade with the East continued to increase and flowering teas continued to increase in popularity, there was no guarantee something like this wouldn't happen again. Only a small amount of chrysanthemum petals had been in the tea that caused the Queen to collapse. A larger amount could kill her. In order to prevent that from happening, palace servants and cooks would need to be made aware, at the very least. But who needed to know beyond that? And how much should be revealed? And then, there was the one person who knew every last detail, and probably shouldn't.

"What are you scheming?"

Yuuri was a commoner and thus, one of the last people who should know the Queen had such a weakness.

Ernest was carefully considering how he could ensure her silence. "Ah, well, I'm a bad man, so I must be planning something nefarious. Do you really want to know what I'm thinking?"

"…Is it about how you're going to roll me in a bamboo mat and toss me into the ocean?"

"Of course not! What a horrid thing to say! You're the daughter of a wealthy merchant; you must have more faith in your position and our relationship than that. And let's not forget we have our secret to bind us."

"That is true."

She had unwittingly stumbled onto this royal family secret. And being as clever as she was, she likely understood the danger that entailed. If the king or queen were the malicious sort, it wouldn't be unthinkable for them to want to silence her. And yet, she discussed the matter with such detachment, as if someone else were in the danger she currently found herself.

"My, you're in quite a bit of trouble, aren't you, my little witch?"

The mother that bore her wanted nothing to do with her. The grandmother that had lovingly raised her was dead. She was truly alone in the world. And yet her flagrant disregard for her own life troubled Ernest.

If only you could boost your social status, eh? ...It won't be easy though...

Ernest smiled to himself. He knew if he told her how he intended to protect her, she would throw him out in a panic. He would be heartbroken if she did, so he elected to keep it to himself for now, at least until she asked him.

❦ ❦ ❦

ERNEST Travis Selden was one of King Rodrick the Second's closest friends. And at that moment, he was in a confidential meeting with the king, queen, and the royal physician in a room just outside the palace.

"Everything the count said was correct."

King Rodrick nodded along as the physician spoke.

They conducted an investigation into whether the Queen had this reaction to small amounts of chrysanthemums that were consumed in other ways. It was a dangerous experiment, but Queen Adeline had insisted on it to prove the innocence of her trusted servant.

"I see. So, Ernest, or should we say, Watoh's daughter, was correct."

Hylant's young king sat in an ornate chair, resting his chin in his hands. At twenty-eight, he was only one year older than Ernest, and the two shared a relationship that was one part lord and retainer, one part close friends. The two had traveled together quite often in Rodrick's days as the crown prince.

"Please extend her my sincere gratitude as well. It is due to her efforts that my dear maid's innocence was brought to light."

Adeline had suffered greatly out of fear over some unknown malevolence. Though her health still wasn't completely restored, she appeared to have relaxed upon hearing she hadn't been deliberately poisoned.

"I am grateful we've determined the cause, but I still have some concerns."

Likely chief among those concerns was how much information about the queen's affliction to divulge. They would only tell the staff that needed to know. And to those precious few, only the fact that chrysanthemums might cause her a rash.

Their other concern was Yuuri. They trusted Ernest's assessment of her, as he seemed to have come to understand Yuuri, and yet…

"Are you certain that this Yuuri Watoh will indeed keep this matter confidential?"

"You can trust her, Your Majesty."

"It does not sit well with me to doubt the one who has been so generous in aiding us… What to do with her…?"

The king had not come to know Yuuri the way Ernest had, and so he was forced to treat her with suspicion. But Ernest had anticipated the king would not trust her so easily and had planned for that possibility.

"If that is your concern, why not make her one of our own then?"

"You mean through an award or honorary title? But then the public would want to know why…"

The people had been told the queen's collapse was merely due to poor constitution, so rewarding someone for finding a cause was out of the question.

"No, I was actually thinking of making her my wife."

"What?!" Rodrick had lifted his head and was gaping at Ernest.

"If she were to marry into the nobility, it would then be her responsibility to serve the royal family and maintain their confidence. She will keep your secret. I stake my life on it."

Yuuri's father may not be nobility, but their family had riches that rivaled any noble. And it was common for wealthy merchants to try to marry their daughters off to nobles (generous dowry and all). Marrying Yuuri would be a simple matter.

"U-Uh...that is unfair to Watoh's daughter. And no matter the reason, I cannot force her to marry you."

"Of course not. I would never dream of asking you to compel a woman who does not love me to marry me just for the secrecy of the royal family. But listen to me. She has all the charm of an aloof cat..."

"Ernest, you cad! So you prefer women who are cold on the outside!" Rodrick shook his head in his hands, long familiar with his friend's antics.

"I suppose you could say it was love at first sight."

"So do you think Miss Watoh feels the same?" The king glanced curiously at Ernest, already having guessed what he was thinking.

"Definitely...well, maybe."

"I wish I knew where you derived your confidence from. Well, I suppose now you need to ask your potential bride-to-be and her father. If she accepts, you'll have my blessing. Considering the influence he has as a merchant, Watoh's lack of status should not be an issue."

"You have my gratitude."

"That poor girl has my pity though, as does anyone who has caught the eye of an odd man like yourself. Who knows what other shenanigans you'll pull her into?"

Ernest was shocked by Rodrick's words. Yuuri's reticence was what led him to tease her. If she would be warmer toward him, he would gladly whisper sweet nothings into her ear. The thought made him laugh.

"Even your laugh makes me shudder..."

What a cruel thing to say. He was well-aware everyone believed his smile to mean he was plotting something.

It seemed as if all the loose ends in Ernest's plans to make everyone happy had been tied up nicely. Queen Adeline was equally pleased that, if Ernest married Yuuri, she would be able to thank the girl in person.

"Well, I believe we're done here. I'm off to inform my little witch of everything we've decided."

And with that, Ernest once again set off for the witch's shop.

BY the time Ernest reached Yuuri's shop, the sun was beginning to set. The pleasant dinnertime aroma of meats and spices filled the streets.

"Well, good evening."

"Good evening, Count."

Yuuri lit the oil lamps as she met Ernest at the door.

"I apologize for coming after hours, but I have some news to share."

He took his usual seat on the couch, but this time, she sat down next to him. She pretended to be annoyed, saying she just sat next to him because it was inconvenient to keep bringing out the chair.

Ernest first reported the results of the investigation and the maid's return to her station. He also shared the royal couple's gratitude for Yuuri's role in finding the cause.

"I see. Knowing that the maid has been allowed to return is thanks enough for me."

"Miss Yuuri, I still must ask—"

"Ask what?"

"Which title is correct? Are you the 'Misfortune Devouring Witch' or the 'Witch Who Preys Upon Misfortune'?"

Yuuri told him she hated that moniker, period.

But Ernest had another thought. Perhaps the grandmother who had raised and trained her was the one who preyed on the misfortune of others.

"She devoured them, yes. As a young woman, my grandmother served this town by helping people solve their problems, thus devouring those troubles and bringing people good fortune. They gave her that name as a sign of their affection. But..."

Even in the dim orange light, he could see her expression darken.

"But as time went on, the ordinary citizens turned toward more modern medicine and the era of the witch came to a close. She was forgotten." But the name somehow managed to persist, taking on a life of its own. Because of that, no one dared enter the witch's shop, spawning a vicious cycle.

"I see. I believe your grandmother would be proud of the way you helped us. You have my deepest gratitude."

Yuuri looked genuinely surprised for once, the corners of her eyes softening.

"Did you just smile?"

"I can smile just fine, thank you very much. I am not a doll."

Ernest instantly regretted pointing it out to her. Her bright red cheeks swelled.

"You're positively adorable when you're angry, but I hope to make you smile more often. After all, I am your treasured food source. Oh yes, and I wouldn't mind hearing you call me by my name for once."

"No."

"I thought you might say that. You're so obstinate!"

Ernest sighed. At this rate, he wouldn't get her to agree to marry him anytime soon.

On the other hand, nothing worth having is easily gained.

"Well, I can be just as stubborn as you, so I expect we make a fine pair." Ernest laughed while Yuuri's annoyance only grew.

Chapter 2: The Love Letter and the Cabinet Trap

YUURI startled awake from a nightmare, her throat dry, the room mired in shadows.

From the second-floor window of her bedroom, she could just glimpse the sky through the spaces between other houses. As she peeled back the heavy curtain, she noticed the eastern sky just beginning to lighten. It was still early for her to be up, but she doubted she could fall back asleep.

"Lord…Ernest…" She tried to give voice to the name she could never say in front of him. The blond young noble was a frequent feature in her dreams as of late. He was the source of both her nightmares and her thirst. And the only one who could quell either.

"If only I could learn to endure this thirst on my own," she muttered softly. There was no one else around to hear her and yet she wanted, no, needed, to let those words have form.

What a cruel man! Why is he so nice to me? How irresponsible!

Yuuri was different from everyone else. She had received so many of her grandmother's vampiric qualities and now that she had reached maturation, she would need to drink the blood of others, just as her grandmother had drank her grandfather's blood. But that desire hadn't come right when she reached maturity. By the time it did, her grandparents were gone and she was left unsure of how to handle it.

Unable to bear it any longer, she'd asked for blood as compensation for the unique request of her family's knowledge.

If only he had returned her request with laughter or disdain like any normal person would have, her craving wouldn't have grown so strong. She might have resented him in the moment, but they'd both be better off in the long run.

But Ernest was not the type to do as others would expect. He had an annoying knack for doing just the opposite.

Yuuri's memory of the event was hazy after Ernest had offered her his index finger. The sweet intoxicating scent just below the skin was burnt into her mind. Not a second after his blood touched her lips, she became an animal, and try as she might to stop herself, she couldn't. That change terrified her and she burst into tears. But she knew, now that she had tasted it, she couldn't live without Ernest's blood.

Suddenly, Yuuri missed her grandmother terribly.

"Oh Grandmother, Grandfather, what should I do? I've made a horrible mistake…"

The dawning sun drifted behind the clouds, chasing away the lingering traces of night with gentle rays. The light was dull enough not to overwhelm her eyes.

"All right."

If the sun's rays were too bright, Yuuri became sleepy and wanted to sink into the shadows. Early mornings were the time she had the most energy.

She changed out of her nightgown, washed her face, and gnawed on some toast. When Yuuri did actually leave the sanctity of her home, she chose a Hylantian-style jacket over the comfort of her usual *haori*. Even in her best efforts to blend in, with her distinct features, she already stood out enough.

Once she was dressed, she posted a sign that read "Will Return Shortly" by the door, though she doubted anyone would actually come during her absence.

There was only one visitor the sign might apply to, and he was an oddball who cared little for holidays or closures anyway. And yet she prayed that very visitor would find his way to her as she shut and locked the door.

Yuuri pulled her hat low over her face and carried a parasol for extra protection, despite the overcast sky. She approached a large road where horse-drawn carriages dashed to and fro.

She bought a flower bouquet to leave for her grandparents before approaching the stagecoach boarding area. A passing carriage stopped abruptly and Ernest suddenly popped his head out.

"Miss Yuuri!"

He leapt out and strode over to her. The young nobleman wore a tailored suit, with his blond hair covered by a hat, and he carried an intricately crafted cane, all of which painted the features of a posh noble as Ernest flashed Yuuri his usual easy smile. His clear blue eyes shone with a mischievous glint in the early dawn.

He was a close friend of the king. Some viewed his appearance and mannerisms as befitting of a lighthearted gentleman, while others saw him as insincere and disconnected.

Yuuri could never bring herself to ask the bright, handsome young man why he chose to spend his days off with a dismal witch like her. She was the one who told him he could come, yet she feared he'd soon tire of her.

"Good morning, m'lord."

"I was a bit taken aback to see you outside during the daytime."

"How rude. I can handle shopping at the very least. And where might you be off to?"

Ernest gave her a snarky grin, as if to imply she should know. His flippant attitude did irk her at times. "I have the day off. And since the weather is so pleasant...I thought I might invite you out to spend it with me."

Yuuri told him she hated sunny days as much as rainy ones, so cloudy days must have seemed the only logical conclusion for what she did enjoy. She especially hated this uncanny confidence and know-it-all attitude of his.

"I'm sorry, but I'm on an errand of my own."

"So you're awaiting a coach? Why not let me take you? Come now, I insist!" Ernest snatched Yuuri's parasol and grabbed her hand before she had time to refuse him.

"Huh, wha—wait!" Neither her objections nor her stern glare seemed to faze him. He was so swift that Yuuri was in the carriage seat before she realized it.

"Now then, where to?"

"My grandmother's grave. It's atop a hill past the harbor."

"All the way out there?"

Ernest quickly relayed her directions to the coachman and they were off. The hill on the far side of the harbor was home to a church as well as a graveyard. The hill had a breathtaking view, and it was a popular resting place for the nobility and the equally well-off.

"Your grandmother wasn't involved with international trade like the rest of your family, was she?"

"She wasn't. I heard my great-grandfather brought his family here from Hinomoto, but sailing regularly was difficult for a man, let alone a woman, so the family business skipped over her to my father."

Sailing between countries was a large part of a merchant's job. Not only that, but leading a life at sea, surrounded by men as rough as the seas they sailed, was likely difficult for a woman. It was easy to see why Yuuri's grandmother had passed on inheriting the family business.

"...I see. Wouldn't the family have urged her to take on a husband who could have succeeded the business then?"

Ernest was right. Most merchant families would select a skilled employee with stellar business acumen to marry their daughter and take over the business. But vampires were not the most versed in modern social standards.

"My grandfather was a gardener who worked for the Watoh family, but he had no sense for business."

Yuuri's grandfather was a gardener, but his inability to speak a foreign language or handle complex math made him a poor choice to succeed the family business. He remained a gardener until just before he passed away.

Since Yuuri's grandfather had been unable to take over, her father was groomed as a successor from a young age. Sailing alongside her great-grandfather, he learned the skills of the trade.

"So your grandmother married for love. Were her parents all right with that?"

"My grandparents weren't part of the nobility, so outside of having an heir to take on the business, I don't think it mattered as much."

Yuuri's heart pounded in her chest. If this conversation continued, she might have to explain other vampiric customs to Ernest.

"Ahh. If you're going to pay your respects, may I join you?"

"...Very well."

Honestly, she didn't want to tell him about her grandparents. But, unable to find a good reason to refuse, she relented.

❦ ❦ ❦

THEY jostled about in the carriage over the next hour before it broke onto the seaside road. The dismal weather and thick clouds made it difficult to see too far ahead, but the lack of sunshine suited Yuuri just fine.

"Mind if I open the window?"

After only an hour of travel, the air outside the windows had changed considerably. The salty aroma of sea air danced about the carriage.

"Is that the harbor? Look at the huge boats docked there."

Ernest was pointing at the two large boats docked in the harbor, flanked by several smaller vessels. Products for trade were stored in warehouses neatly built along the shoreline. Several of the storehouses belonged to Watoh Company.

The coastal road eventually gave way to a hilly incline. The carriage came to a stop in front of a stunning church, leaving its passengers to make the remainder of the journey on foot. Ernest leapt out first and instinctively offered Yuuri his hand.

Just how many ladies has he helped out of this carriage...?

Yuuri wasn't quite sure what to make of Ernest and his eccentricities, his behaviors and mannerisms were very refined. He was especially gentle in his treatment of women, which made Yuuri suspect that he wasn't exactly inexperienced with them.

Meanwhile, Yuuri was a naïve, socially awkward shut-in. Being a vampire aside, she had always struggled with social mores. Her chest tightened upon realizing the difference between them, and she began to resent him for it.

Ernest reached up to help Yuuri down. Despite her resentment, she took his hand. Her mind desperately wanted to pull away, but some other part of her, the human part, was completely entranced by him.

So she held his hand as they climbed the hill to her grandparents' graves.

No matter how sullen she became, Ernest continued to offer her the same gentle smile. That patience only irritated her further.

The Misfortune Devouring Witch is Actually a Vampire?!

The hilltop had a view of the ocean and a quaint little graveyard nestled under a large weeping willow. Yuuri headed straight to where her family rest.

"June, H.E. 751…and July of the same year? You had so much loss in such a short time," Ernest murmured in shock as he read the dates etched into the gravestone.

"Yes, but they both lived to a ripe old age, so I believe that, as long as they're together in Heaven, they're both happy," Yuuri said, unable to think of anything else to say.

Her grandfather had died of illness. But her grandmother, who died shortly thereafter, had not succumbed to illness or old age. She had died of starvation, having lost her food source. But Yuuri did not see this as a sad thing. As a vampire, this was perhaps the greatest end one could wish for.

"I see…"

"Is something wrong?"

"No."

Ernest closed his eyes and offered a prayer to the pair. Yuuri placed the flowers she had bought and joined Ernest, closing her eyes as well.

Grandmother, Grandfather, I truly am a fool. Ernest is so good and kind. But someday, he too will leave me. So I can't…allow myself to fall for him.

She could never tell Ernest this. He was a good person.

If she went ahead and drank his blood and the day came that he could no longer sustain her, she would die.

She was the irresponsible one. For drinking his blood without telling him the truth. Wishing for him to stay with her solely because she would die without him was downright deplorable.

I'm so sorry, Grandmother. After all those times you warned me…

Vampires truly were awkward creatures. Awkward, yet devoted.

She was certain that her great-grandfather truly had wanted a son-in-law with a strong business acumen. Yet his daughter went and fell for a simple gardener. Vampire tradition dictated that once a vampire chose their partner, they were entwined for life. Her great-grandfather had been left no choice but to accept their decision, despite the difficulty this would cause him.

Thus, her grandmother had always harped on her to find someone she truly loved. Someone who could accept her for who she was, all of who she was.

But whenever Yuuri asked how to find the right person to fall in love with, her grandmother told her she couldn't answer that question. Still, she desperately wanted Yuuri to learn from her mistakes.

I'm so sorry, Grandmother. It looks like I'm a lost cause too. Yuuri continued her one-sided conversation with her grandmother in her thoughts.

Having said all that she needed to say, Yuuri slowly opened her eyes and glanced over at Ernest, who was still deep in prayer, his hands clasped in front of his chest.

"Count Selden…?"

"Hm? …Oh, done already?"

"Yes. I just wanted to let them know everything that has been going on."

"And did that 'everything' include me?" he teased.

Almost everything Yuuri shared with her grandparents was about him. About the case he'd assigned her, about how he treated her shop like a cafe…and about how he had offered her his blood.

He had been absolutely right, and yet his smug attitude, his know-it-all, "It did include me, didn't it?" irritated her so.

"Yes… I told them about how I've become acquainted with an odd nobleman as of late."

"Odd? …Ah well."

Ernest was so tolerant of all her idiosyncrasies, and yet she still struggled to be open with him. She instinctively pushed him away,

But she feared what would happen if she told him the truth, and what a weak person he might think her if he knew how greatly she depended on him now.

The two of them made their way back down the hill to where the carriage awaited them. When they reached the steps, he again offered Yuuri his hand. They walked hand in hand for a bit before Ernest came to a sudden stop.

Yuuri followed his gaze to see a young man in all black, down on his knees in silent prayer.

Ashes were scattered about his feet, as if he'd recently burned paper. He had likely delivered his thoughts to the departed by burning them on the scrap of paper, thus sending them along with the smoke to the hereafter.

Not wanting to disturb his silent ritual, Yuuri fell back a step to try and find another way down to the carriage.

"Joel? Joel Weller?" Ernest called out to the young man. The young man, his eyes moss green and his hair ash brown, stood up and slowly gazed at the pair. His mouth broke into a gentle smile as he recognized Ernest.

"Ah, Ernest. Fancy seeing you here. And who is this lovely lady with you…?"

"I've told you about my lovely little witch before, haven't I?"

"Yours? I do not belong to anyone!" Yuuri shoved his hand away, her face scarlet.

"Lady Yuuri, this is Baron Joel Weller." Ernest had intentionally ignored her outburst and moved the conversation along.

"Pleasure to meet you. I'm Yuuri Watoh," she greeted despite being irked with Ernest.

"So you're the famed daughter of Watoh Company. I've heard all about you from Ernest." Joel seemed like a decent man. Unlike so many others, he didn't leer at Yuuri, with her rare obsidian eyes and raven hair.

"Are the two of you friends?" she asked.

"We go all the way back to boarding school. Remember when I borrowed those medical books? He was the one who was going to try and translate them. He's a promising diplomat who's fairly proficient in Xingkaese. Or he's supposed to be…"

"Supposed to be? It wasn't my fault! Medicine isn't exactly my specialty, you know?"

Now it made sense why Yuuri's appearance didn't surprise Joel. As a diplomat proficient in Xingkaese, he likely dealt with people from the East on a daily basis.

"It's actually fortuitous to meet a witch from the East like this. I have something I'd like to ask your help with."

"You want my help?" Now Yuuri was taken aback.

"Yes. Actually, it's about my late father—"

"Hold it! All requests for the witch's help must come through me! Don't just dump your problems on her," Ernest said, cutting him off.

"Hey, don't just—ah!"

"Sorry, but please give us a moment." Ernest dragged Yuuri off, not releasing his hold on her until they were under the shade of a large tree.

"Miss Yuuri, you lack the knowledge of how things work and a fundamental cautiousness of the world. First of all, stop assuming that other men have your best interests at heart. You don't need to commit to helping him just yet."

If she shouldn't assume strange men had her best interest at heart, then what should she do about the strange man who made a habit of inviting himself into her shop?

She tilted her head and gave him a quizzical look.

"Uh, except for me, naturally. And you're always wary of me anyway. In this situation, you should do the opposite."

"Do the opposite?"

"For now, you should think of me as the only safe man in the world. All others should be suspect!"

Yuuri had no idea where he got the confidence for such declarations.

Clearly he had forgotten how he told her the second time they met that he was dangerous too. But, even though they still didn't know each other well, she was positive if she pointed this fact out to him, he would merely deflect with some eloquent comeback. Which was why Yuuri tried to change the subject rather than engage in a needless argument.

"...So are you saying I shouldn't even speak to other men for work? Even though I want to become a renowned witch who helps the people of this city like my grandmother?"

"Well, I'll be with you while you talk to this man, so it's all right. And if you do accept his request, I'll see to it you get proper compensation."

"Compensation...?" Yuuri stared into Ernest's blue eyes, now firm with his resolve. By compensation, it was clear he meant his own blood.

"You don't want mine? Would you prefer his instead? You know it's probably not a good idea to let your secret get around to too many people, right?"

No, Ernest's blood was the only blood she craved. She craved it so badly that just the suggestion of it suddenly made her mouth water.

"B-But what do you gain from all of this?"

"My, you are quite the difficult woman... Have you never heard of noblesse oblige? Also, it's natural for one friend to want to help another. But if you are going to help him, I insist on doing it with you, all right?"

Their negotiation settled, the pair returned to hear Joel's request.

The Misfortune Devouring Witch is Actually a Vampire?!

🍎 🍎 🍎

THE trio returned to the city in order to hear Joel's request in private. And since Ernest had appointed himself the go-between, he insisted on bringing them to his manor.

His manor was an elegant estate, resplendent with its own rose garden.

Yuuri might have lived a simple city life, but she was still the daughter of one the Five Great Merchants of Hylant. She wasn't as unaccustomed to vast mansions as one might expect.

"And here I had hoped Miss Yuuri and I would spend the day sampling the finest sweets at a local cafe. Joel, you owe me dearly for my boundless benevolence." Ernest lied, making it sound like he and Yuuri had been on a date.

"I beg your pardon for intruding on your afternoon date…"

"He's just teasing, we had no such plans, so please don't worry about it."

Joel looked nervously at the couple: Yuuri responded coolly while Ernest shook his head in absolute denial.

It was just about lunchtime when the trio arrived at the manor. They had finished lunch and were sitting down to tea when Joel finally brought up the topic he wanted to ask about.

"My adoptive father passed away over a year ago."

"Adoptive father?" Yuuri asked.

"Yes. The former Baron Weller and his Baroness were not blessed with children of their own, so they adopted me. It happened shortly after my mother passed away, so I was really quite lucky, but being thrust into the nobility and shipped off to boarding school so suddenly was overwhelming to say the least."

"Come to think of it, you were a cheeky little git when we first met."

If Joel and Ernest were indeed schoolmates, then Joel must have been twenty-seven as well. He seemed an affable gentleman by what Yuuri had seen so far, despite the fact that he hadn't been born a noble.

"Becoming a man and learning about the world tends to change a person, I believe. …Though it is a bit frightening how staunchly you refuse to change, Ernest. You were so fascinated with me in spite of my not being born a noble, or perhaps because of it."

Yuuri could easily picture what Ernest was like as a boy. He must have been a curious child, if the intense fascination with which he had stared at her and her garments the first time they met was any indication. He also had a mysterious charm that made him easy to get along with.

"Apologies for getting so off-topic."

"Not at all. Take your time…"

"Have you ever heard of a *funadansu*?"

"No, I can't say I have," Ernest jumped in before Yuuri could respond. She sighed, wishing he would just keep his mouth shut if he didn't know. Annoyed, she tried to explain what a *funadansu* was to him.

"It's an object similar to a safe and common in the East. It's used on boats to store one's valuables and built of wood so that, in the event the ship sinks, the *funadansu* will float while keeping the valuables secure."

"My adoptive father was a diplomat. While assigned to a post on the eastern continent, he received a *funadansu*."

According to Joel, most generations of the Weller barony had been diplomats as well.

Most furnishings from the East that were used to store one's everyday belongings were coveted as art pieces in the West. The *funadasu* was solid, airtight even, and its decorative metal fittings were beautiful. The ones crafted by artisans from Hinomoto were especially in high demand, and Watoh Company was more than happy to rise to the occasion. Even the *funadansu* which Baron Weller had received from a high-ranking Xingkaese official was made by a Hinomoto artisan.

"When he fell ill, my adoptive father pleaded with me to destroy the letter he had stored away in his *funadasu*. But try as I might, I could not get the *funadasu* open. His speech had declined so much, I couldn't even get him to explain it to me. I wasn't willing to risk destroying the *funadansu* either."

"But most *funadansu*—"

"Oh? Have you figured something out, Miss Yuuri?"

Yuuri glared at Ernest, irritated that he was needlessly running his mouth again.

"Count Selden, please be quiet for a moment. Baron Weller, the *funadansu* may have a mechanism, one that unlocks a hidden compartment."

"Heh, my adoptive mother has also suggested there might be a hidden drawer. I've tried several ways of finding it, with nothing to show for it. I had hoped that, with you being familiar with Eastern culture, maybe you would know a way…"

Joel was well-aware that there may be a hidden drawer, he just had no way of finding it. And that was about as much as Yuuri knew as well.

"I'm terribly sorry, but this is outside my area of expertise."

"…I see," Joel said, slumping his shoulders.

"Though I may know someone who can help you," Yuuri offered, disappointed that her grandmother's wisdom wouldn't be able to help this time. At least she knew someone experienced in Eastern craftsmanship.

"Oh, who's that?" Ernest asked, his eyes twinkling. He was more interested than Joel who had actually made the request.

"My older brother, Simon Watoh."

"Older brother, eh? Well I would definitely like to meet him."

Ernest's smile grew mischievous. A chill ran down Yuuri's back and she was sure that nothing good could come of this meeting.

Simon was the last person Yuuri wanted to introduce to anyone. As soon as she saw him she was ready to leave. And, just as she feared, as soon as her brother came up, Ernest, that meddlesome ball of curiosity, insisted on coming along.

Heaving a big sigh, Yuuri relented to take them both to the main headquarters of Watoh Company.

※ ※ ※

WATOH Company's headquarters were in the wealthiest part of the city, just off the main road.

Yuuri normally never went anywhere near the family manor where her mother resided, but she did occasionally visit the company office. The company's best-selling products were the teas Yuuri mixed, sold under the auspices of being from an Eastern brewer made with Western ingredients. It was the exact same as the tea Yuuri sold in her own shop, but with no customers aside from Ernest, who always drank jasmine tea, she had no sales numbers for comparison.

The doorman standing in front of the building recognized Yuuri and readily opened the door for them. The vast entrance was adorned with an ornate chandelier. Eastern-style vases dotted the room and scrolls hung on the walls. Yuuri's companions were awestruck at the sight.

"Welcome back, miss. And fond salutations to your friends." The older man who served as Simon's adviser appeared. Welcoming Yuuri back as if this were still her home was a small kindness he always offered her.

Yuuri gave a tiny nod. "I apologize for disturbing your work. Where is my brother?"

"Lord Simon is in his office."

"Is he busy today?" They had, after all, shown up unannounced. If he had clients scheduled, they'd either be forced to wait or come back another time.

"I'll need to confer with him. Please wait here for the time being," the elder man said, guiding them to a side room normally used for business dealings before disappearing to find Simon. Moments later, he returned, carrying a tray of tea and confections. Both Ernest, who'd learned from the copious amounts of tea he drank at Yuuri's shop, and Joel, who worked as a diplomat, deftly managed the handleless teacups.

"Yuuri!" a slender man exclaimed as he charged into the room. With chestnut hair and grey-blue eyes, Simon's petite stature was the only thing he had in common with his sister.

His clothes were all that gave away his Hinomoto ancestry. He wore *hakama*, traditional Hinomoto trousers, as part of his daily attire. And he was clearly the one sending Yuuri *haori*.

He immediately rushed toward his little sister, causing her to hide behind Ernest.

"I'm terribly sorry for disturbing you at work...and, I, uhm, brought visitors with me..." He could see that Yuuri was clearly afraid of him, and like a scolded dog, he pulled away.

"Sorry, it's just you never come and see me. Now then..." he said, turning his gaze to the two young men.

"This is Count Selden and this is Baron Weller. They need your help," she introduced from behind Ernest.

"I'm Yuuri's older brother, Simon. Pleasure to meet you. Count Selden, I hear you have been taking particularly good care of my sister, yes?" Simon began his introduction with the affable politeness one would expect of a businessman. But as he broached the topic of Ernest, his words became sharp and his eyes began to narrow. Yuuri's fears had been right on the mark: there was no way these two would get along.

"Not at all. As it happens, I am the one in her debt. And please call me Ernest, my esteemed big brother!"

"What?! I'm afraid you are further on in years than I, Count Selden!"

The Misfortune Devouring Witch is Actually a Vampire?!

"S-S-Simon! These are our guests! And noblemen at that..."

Watoh Company certainly wielded its own influence among the nobility, but at the end of the day, the Watohs were still commoners. Ernest, on the other hand, was the head of a prestigious noble family and a close friend of King Rodrick. Ernest might be a playful sort of man, particularly with Yuuri, but such inconsiderate words in standard polite society were not allowed. The fact that the Watoh family heir would speak with such unbridled distaste to someone, especially during the first meeting, left Yuuri mortified.

And Ernest, grinning wildly with a surprising amount of composure, was of little comfort to her. "Miss Yuuri, it's all right. I'm not upset in the least. Lord Simon was just worried about you."

Rising to his provocations, Simon was shaking, his hands clenched into fists.

"By the way, Lord Simon, are those clothes of yours from Hinomoto?"

"Yes, they are! I am of Hinomoto descent, and so are my clothes!" Simon's face was scarlet as he could scarcely answer the question, embarrassed at how his opponent baited him.

"So you must be the one who sends her all those *haori*. They suit her very well. I especially like the vivid blue one with the red flowers on it."

The tension in Simon's face disappeared at the mention of Yuuri's *haori*. "The camellia one? I agree. I picked it out for her myself when I was in Hinomoto."

"Uhm, Simon, perhaps we should get to the real reason we've come today. The baron here has something he'd like to ask you about..." Yuuri suspected it was now or never if she wanted to guide the discussion back to the baron's request while her brother was still in a good mood.

"Hm? Ah, yes, my apologies."

"Baron Weller has a *funadansu* in his possession, but has asked for help in finding its hidden compartment."

"A *funadansu*?"

"Yes. He received it from a Xingkaese diplomat, but it's of Hinomotoese craftsmanship."

"There are certain principles guiding Hinomoto trap construction. If I can take a look at it, I could figure it out with ease!" Simon was an avid collector of works of art and craftsmanship from Hinomoto.

When he first began negotiations with Xingka and Hinomoto, he took an interest in local fashions. As his interests deepened, he began wearing *hakama* even when he was at work.

"Really? Thank you very much, Lord Simon!" Joel was overjoyed at Simon's easy confidence.

Still, if his adoptive father didn't want the letter found, then perhaps that's how it should stay?

Yuuri couldn't help but wonder why Joel was so desperate to find the letter. Perhaps he had an idea of what might be written within it. But Yuuri doubted disclosing what the deceased had wanted destroyed was the right thing to do.

Still, Joel's serious demeanor suggested he wasn't searching for the letter out of mere curiosity. And she was hesitant to butt into another family's affairs. So, in the end, Yuuri decided not to ask him.

Simon agreed to pay Baron Weller a visit in three days' time and with that, they brought the conversation to a close.

They had been so engrossed in their discussion that the sun was beginning its descent before they realized it. Just as the three visitors prepared to take their leave, Simon hurried to stop Yuuri.

"Yuuri, why don't you stay for dinner? We can eat out somewhere; we don't have to dine in the manor."

"N-no, I can't...I have plans."

She avoided being alone with Simon at all costs. She knew he worried about her living all alone and wished nothing more than for her to come live with him. Yuuri felt she must be a horrible sort of person for being so cold to someone who only held the best of intentions.

"Plans? You don't mean with the esteemed count here, do you?!"

"No! And anyway, it's none of your business. What if she says something...?" She felt guilty, but in the end, she turned him down.

"Let Mother say whatever she likes—it doesn't matter to me!"

"...And I hate to see you two fight!"

"But that won't happen, I promise!"

"If you keep covering for me, she'll turn that same icy glare on you, Simon."

Simon always wore the *hakama*, so as not to lose touch with his Hinomoto roots. Each time he visited the country, he brought his sister back beautiful clothes. Though Yuuri appreciated his kindness, she couldn't reciprocate.

"I'm sorry, Simon," Yuuri said, leaving the room before he could object further.

Before boarding her carriage, Yuuri bowed to the two men who had accompanied her. "I am so terribly sorry both of you had to see that."

"I'll see you home," Ernest said, looking unusually worried.

The pair parted with Joel and rode the rest of the way to Yuuri's shop in silence. Yuuri could tell Ernest's silence was out of concern for her. But what she really wanted was for him to comfort her.

"Can I tell you something?" Yuuri asked as he walked her into her shop.

"I assumed you didn't feel much like talking, so I remained silent, but of course. I always want to hear more about you," Ernest said, taking his usual seat on the couch.

Yuuri sat down next to him and began to explain her relationship with her brother. While she did not look like either of her parents due to the atavism, Simon was the spitting image of their mother. Their mother showered Simon with as much love as she did Yuuri with hate. Due to his mother's influence, the young Simon began to hate Yuuri as well. It seemed a natural progression, with Yuuri living at her grandmother's, the siblings rarely saw each other. But as he grew, he recognized the cruelness in his mother's heart, and his treatment of Yuuri began to change. Yuuri, still a child then, was simply grateful for her brother's sudden kindness.

This harmony didn't last.

One day, upon learning Simon had gone to their grandparents to see Yuuri, their mother rushed over there in a rage. Having almost forgotten her daughter, the look on Yuuri's mother's face when she saw her was one of rage and hatred. From that day on, Yuuri avoided Simon.

"You could see your mother lurking just behind your brother's eyes, couldn't you? Something like that?"

Yuuri bristled. Ernest was speaking the truth she'd sought to avoid.

Every time Yuuri and Simon got close, their mother went into a fit. That was true.

But the real reason Yuuri didn't want to spend time with Simon was because he reminded her of their mother. No matter how happy they were spending time together, it was her mother's piercing grey-blue eyes staring back at her, sending chills down her spine. Just as Yuuri's mother couldn't bring herself to love her, Yuuri couldn't manage to separate Simon from her mother. Because of that, she could never truly love him.

"If someone else is with me, it's all right. But when it's just the two of us, I never know what to talk to him about. I can't seem to relax around him. I'm sure it's some mixture of jealousy and hate."

Though they both had the same parents, they looked nothing alike. Their mother had given Simon all of her love. And for that, Yuuri both envied and hated Simon. And she hated herself for feeling that way.

"I see. But maybe you also care about your brother."

"Why do you say that?"

"Because you treasure the gifts he gives you. ...Now then..."

"...?"

Ernest pulled closer to Yuuri and took her hand.

Even in the dimly lit room, Yuuri's adaptive eyes could see the look on his face. She could tell he was planning to do something untoward, but she couldn't easily evade him.

"Now, what's the best way to comfort a lady in distress? Or rather, how much would you permit me?" He lifted her hand to his lips. Unsure of how to stop the thundering of her own heart, Yuuri merely froze. He lifted his other hand to caress her cheek. "You don't have to pull away."

He tilted her face up gently. But Yuuri pulled away, giving him a final warning. His heart sank.

"Please leave!"

Embarrassed at not being able to resist him right away, Yuuri stood up and moved away from Ernest. She chased him out of the shop before collapsing on the couch.

"'You should think of me as the only safe man in the world,'" she repeated what he had said to her earlier that day. "That was a big fat lie."

That lying count had drained the last of Yuuri's energy, leaving her too mentally exhausted to even consider her mother or brother.

❦ ❦ ❦

THREE days later, Ernest brought Yuuri to the Weller estate.

It was a dreadfully sunny day. The moment she stepped outside, the brilliance of the sun's light left her in a daze. Were it not for Ernest's carriage, she doubted she could have gone.

"You really can't handle the sun. Are you sure you aren't going to melt?"

"I just don't like the intense glare. Sorry to disappoint, but pleasant days are not my thing." Yuuri knew Ernest would laugh at the way her eyes squinted to dull the sun's glare, so she faced the other way. "Was it really necessary for you to come along? Just how many holidays do you get?"

"This concerns a colleague of mine. Of course I'd come along! I'm a stand-up guy, so I can leave my other tasks for now. And besides, I'm your go-between; I have to see this through!"

"…In other words, you're slacking off on your other duties," Yuuri deduced with deceptive ease, desperately trying to avoid reminding him of the tense way in which they had parted three days ago. That desperation was making her colder than ever towards Ernest.

They sat in the Weller family's parlor, awaiting both their host and Simon. Intent on not meeting Ernest's gaze, Yuuri let her eyes wander around the room. She began to study the portraits hanging on the walls. Her eyes settled upon a man and woman who seemed to be a couple.

"Huh? He looks like Joel." The gentleman in the portrait was in his forties, but his looks and demeanor closely resembled Joel's.

"…That was the former Baron Weller. My late husband."

The words came from an older woman, dressed in the standard black attire expected of a widow in mourning, complete with a necklace made out of fossilized jet gemstones. She was Joel's adoptive mother, Isabella Weller. Widows in Hylant were expected to wear their mourning attire for a considerably long time, so now, even a year after her husband's death, she was still clad in black.

The portrait must have been done many years ago. In it, Mrs. Weller was still blonde and beautiful, as opposed to the white-haired, wrinkly woman who stood before them now.

"Well hello, Lady Isabella."

"Good to see you, Count Selden. And is this the witch I've heard so much about?"

"I'm Yuuri Watoh."

As the wife of a diplomat, Isabella had met her fair share of people who looked like Yuuri while staying in Xingka, so she merely smiled and nodded at the girl's normally out-of-place appearance.

"Though you are our guests, I am the one in your debt. I hope Joel hasn't caused too much trouble on my behalf. If so, you have my apologies."

"Not at all."

"Joel is working so hard, even though we are not related by blood, so I suppose I shouldn't tease him."

They were not blood-related, which seemed all the more motivation for Joel to work his hardest to find the letter for her. He felt that, by finding the letter his adoptive father had tried to erase, he could repay his debt to her.

"Lady Isabella, if you find the letter, will you read it?"

Isabella gave a sad smile upon hearing Yuuri's question. "Yes. ... Do you think me a terrible wife for trying to find the letter my husband sought to hide?"

Was it wrong? Neither Isabella nor Joel seemed to be doing it out of nosiness. Yuuri continued to stare at Isabella without responding.

"So what do you think of our portrait? Count Selden, I know you were acquainted with the baron."

"He and Joel were a lot alike and I know, even now, Joel still tries to emulate him," Ernest said, unable to deny the similarities between them. Both he and Yuuri, who had just met Joel, could see how alike they were.

"My husband always said, 'it's easier to love a child who resembles you in some way.' And then he brought Joel home. As Joel grew, he came to look more and more like my late husband when he was young. They weren't related by blood, so I wonder why that was?"

That wasn't a question she wanted them to answer. It was clear that Isabella suspected Joel wasn't adopted, but in fact the former baron's illegitimate son.

"He hid it for all those years. So why the change of heart just before his death?" she muttered more to herself.

In other words, what purpose did divulging the dead man's secrets serve for Isabella and Joel? Yuuri, who already had reservations, was only beginning to feel more and more uneasy about the whole thing. She wondered if maybe Isabella would be happier not knowing.

Isabella stared at the portrait of her and her husband. Her eyes shimmered with a mixture of sadness and affection.

As a pair of voices approached the room, Isabella lifted a finger to her lips, as if to implore them to keep this conversation between them.

"Oh, Mother, so this is where you've been," Joel said as he entered the room, accompanied by two servants carrying the *funadansu* with Simon in tow.

"Yes. You were taking so long, I decided to chat with our guests."

"I'm sorry. Moving the *funadansu* proved to be more difficult than I expected."

Most *funadansu* were meant to be movable, but this one was especially large and required more than one person to carry it.

"I'm terribly sorry, you two. And Lord Simon, thank you for traveling all this way."

"Not at all. I'm ecstatic to see something so rare," Simon said, presenting Joel with a gift. Joel might not have been one of his clients yet, but a good businessman never missed the opportunity to seed a new customer. Shortly thereafter, Simon broached the topic of the rare Eastern treasure.

Yuuri sat silently next to Ernest, watching everything play out. Eventually, her eyes met Simon's.

"Yuuri...about the other day, I'm..."

"I was the one in the wrong. I..."

"You did nothing wrong! I...uh..."

The two of them became so embarrassed, they couldn't speak. Though they were siblings, the divide between them was still vast.

Yuuri knew her brother was only worried about her, living all alone as she did. She knew she couldn't run away forever, but she couldn't manage to figure out how to open up.

"Please do all you can to help the Weller family, Simon." Many thoughts raced through Yuuri's mind, but in the end, that was all she could think of to say.

Simon responded with a smile, showing that he was willing to do as she hoped.

🦇 🦇 🦇

THE cabinet sat on a table in the parlor. One by one, each drawer was removed and they peered inside. They all watched with rapt attention as Simon worked.

"The interior of this *funadansu* makes me think it was built for shipping."

"What's different about one built for shipping?" Joel asked.

"It's built much more practically. To open it, one would need to insert the right keys in the right order, for example. The antitheft design is complex, which means…"

Simon measured the width of the boards and knocked on the *funadansu*, listening for differences in the depth of sound. Wherever there were differences must be where the triggering mechanism was.

"Here it is." Simon had found his target on the side of the cabinet. The wood grain blended in perfectly, but sliding it up with enough force revealed it was a movable panel. The hidden compartment Joel had searched so long for proved an easy find for Simon.

"There we are," Simon said, feeling around inside the hidden space. The letter was indeed there. Joel took it and opened the envelope.

The envelope was unsealed and there were no stamps, meaning the former baron had never mailed it.

Ah, my dear Isabella,

Is there anything that could compare to thy beauty? The flowers of spring in full bloom? The glistening surface of the ocean in summer? Fall's harvest moon? But what of winter, our current season?

I can find nothing in the drab, colorless misery of winter that is worthy of your beauty. That is why I want nothing more than for your beauty to illuminate my frozen heart, every day.

Please forgive this flawed man, though his sins run deep.

"Is this a…love letter? The handwriting is absolutely Father's."

The envelope bulged with paper. There were at least ten pages. And every page was filled with romantic writings extolling his love for his not-yet wife in their younger days. Both Joel and Simon blushed while reading the flowery prose.

"Th-That's what the previous baron was hiding? Pfft! Hahaha!" Unable to contain himself, Ernest roared with laughter.

"Lord Ernest, please! You're being very rude!"

"I can't help it! Who wouldn't throw those out...! Haha!"

Despite Yuuri chastising him, Ernest grabbed his sides and chuckled. Joel could no longer hold his laughter in either. Simon lowered his head, but his shoulders were trembling.

"Mother?" Everyone looked to Isabella. She was trying to keep a straight face, but laughter was beginning to slip out.

"...I'm terribly sorry, everyone. I did not expect such a pleasant surprise. His letters were always so matter-of-fact and strictly business. I certainly never expected this!"

Though they had been together for decades, she was only just now seeing this side of her late husband. Though tears played at the corners of her eyes, it was Isabella's laughter that continued for several minutes.

"He truly loved me, didn't he?"

"Indeed. From long before you married right up until his death... always."

"And yet I doubted him and exposed the secret he desperately wanted kept."

"I'm sure he would forgive your laughter. He seemed like just that sort of man."

In the end, they learned nothing of Joel's real lineage. But discovering the secret depths of her husband's undying love surely bolstered Isabella's grieving heart.

Joel smiled, having seen his mother's reaction and his adoptive father's secret. And yet, for just a second, Yuuri noticed a darkness pass over his face. He was staring at the portrait of his adopted parents.

🦇 🦇 🦇

YUURI left the barony. Just as before, Ernest insisted on seeing her home. And instead of going on to his own home once she was inside, here he was again in his usual seat, drinking tea. She had hoped for some time to ponder the day's events on her own and hoped he would leave before long.

"Why the long face, my lady witch?"

"I was just wondering when you intended to leave?"

Ernest merely blinked and tilted his head at her curtness. Then he slammed his hands down as if he had just thought of something. "Let me see if I can guess what you're thinking."

"What's the point? I just told you!"

The only thing Yuuri was thinking about was how badly she wanted Ernest to go home. There was nothing else to guess. Sometimes words didn't seem to get through to him, so Yuuri strengthened her tone.

"I bet you're wondering what Joel burned up at that gravesite…aren't you?" Ernest guessed with a smug grin, as if he had it all figured out. He pretended not to have heard her when she clearly told him to go home.

"I-I'm not," Yuuri replied, shaking her head, insisting she was not speculating about the baron's personal affairs.

"It's all right. He can't expect us not to wonder. And he trusts us not to spread whatever we come up with."

"Could it have been the real letter revealing the circumstances of his birth?"

"Most likely. The baron had been married over thirty years, so Joel was likely a son born out of an affair. Apparently Joel was taken in shortly after his mother's passing."

Their conjecture was that, as Isabella had suspected, there was indeed a letter detailing the circumstances of Joel's birth. And that Joel had known how to access that hidden compartment all along. The bedridden baron, not realizing his wife was nearby, begged Joel to destroy that letter.

At first, Isabella remained unaware of the hidden compartment, and so Joel could go on pretending these were the ramblings of an old man in the throes of dementia. But then she looked into *funadansu* and learned of the hidden compartment and the triggering mechanism. So Joel burned the real letter before his adopted mother could read it and replaced it with a love letter from among his father's effects that seemed a good fit.

If Joel himself opened the hidden compartment for Isabella, she would suspect him of replacing the items within. That's why he needed an expert like Yuuri or Simon to find it for him, at least in front of her.

This was, of course, all Yuuri's speculation. But Ernest was Joel's good friend, and he had come to the same conclusion.

"Is it really all right to leave things this way?"

"Yes. What Joel wants is all that matters."

The deceased baron had loved his wife long before he married her and he loved her up until the end. That was all that anyone needed to know. It was the baron's wish, and Joel's.

"I don't really understand why he did what he did. I didn't say anything because it's not my place, but doesn't she have a right to know? What's the right thing to do?"

"What's most important is whatever gives the living their peace."

"Even if it means hiding the truth?"

Isabella had wanted to know the truth. With that in mind, it was hard to say Joel was right to lie.

"Good point."

"I..."

Yuuri had things she was hiding from Ernest, too. Something terribly important that she couldn't bring herself to say. Something she wanted hidden until after she died.

She decided if the lie was to protect someone, then it was all right.

She realized she was being impudent, but she hoped Ernest could forgive her.

🦇 🦇 🦇

SILENCE pervaded the space between them.

It always ended up that way if Ernest didn't start talking. Yuuri became uncomfortable and glanced over at him.

"Shall I give you your reward?" Ernest suddenly suggested. He had been the go-between and the one who offered to compensate Yuuri.

"But...I only took you to my brother. I didn't use any special knowledge I learned from my grandmother this time around," Yuuri said, though she wasn't very convincing. She wanted to refuse him, but Ernest had a way of getting the truth out of her.

Vampires and their descendants were said to be devoted creatures, but that didn't always mean they were open.

"But you worked hard. And you've kept my friend's confidence."

Yuuri remained frozen in place, still not convinced that this was all right,

"It's all right. Come here," Ernest beckoned, gently pulling the still motionless Yuuri into his lap.

They were at eye level with each other.

His shimmering blond hair, the standard for Hylantian nobility, and his blue eyes that shone like jewels really were different from Yuuri's. She hated looking him in the eye for that reason. But Ernest loved everything, including the parts of her that were different and even the parts of her that weren't human.

But she desperately wanted to hide those non-human aspects from him. She didn't want him to see how different she truly was.

"It's better if it's less visible, isn't it?"

Ernest swiftly undid his tie with one hand, unbuttoning the top button on his shirt and vest. His chest lay open and exposed.

She avoided the thick veins in his neck and looked toward his shoulder. Finally deciding where she would sink her teeth, she looked to him.

"Uhm, thank you for the meal, Count Selden."

"No, wait."

Ernest placed his index finger against Yuuri's lips. She began to feel anxious at this sudden redirection.

Hadn't he said it was time for her reward? Had she misunderstood?

"It's Ernest. Call me by my name. If I'm going to grant your wish, then I'd like you to grant one of mine." He ran his finger along her lips. Could he not see how much pain he caused her by dangling what she needed right in front of her, then snatching it away at the last second?

No matter how many times Yuuri swallowed her own spit, it was no replacement for the blood she craved. She had called his name so many times in her heart, but had so little practice saying it aloud.

Tearfully, Yuuri opened her mouth and finally gave voice to that unspoken name. "Lord Ernest, please, give me your blood."

His thin lips rose into an arc. His smug expression, overflowing with triumph, irritated her. Somehow, he always had the upper hand. "Go on, my sweet little vampire."

Planning where to bite, Yuuri pressed her lips against his shoulder before bearing her fangs and biting down. As soon as she did, the sweet taste of blood filled her mouth. Between the aroma that filled her nose and the taste of his blood as it pooled on her tongue, there was no substitute for what Ernest gave to her.

Her memories of that first bite, when she became intoxicated by his blood, were hazy at best. This was the first time that she had bitten and drank the blood of the man she was steadily coming to love while still in control of her thoughts.

Even as she hated herself for doing something so awful, she continued to suck his blood, tears streaming down her cheeks.

Several times throughout, Ernest shifted his body and she wondered if it was because it hurt or because it tickled. Either way, Yuuri was happy. He was enduring something unpleasant or even painful all because he cared about her.

Not even five minutes had passed before Yuuri lifted her face, satisfied, even as the blood continued to seep from Ernest's wounds. Her heart might have been satisfied, but her mind bore lingering regrets.

"…Let me treat your wound." Yuuri sat up and rose to reach for the first aid kit she had prepared.

"Miss Yuuri, why are you crying?" Ernest asked, pulling Yuuri back to him as she tried to pull away.

"Because I hate this. It isn't normal. And besides, I don't…want to hurt you, Lord Ernest…"

"Is it really so awful to drink a little of my blood?" Ernest asked, wiping away her tears with his fingers. He caressed her chin, then lifted it so he could gaze at her.

"Don't look at me!" Yuuri didn't want him to see her cry. But instead of pulling away from him, she clung to his chest, burying her face in his rumpled shirt and gripping it tight,

"But, if I told you it was fine, that should be more than enough, right?"

Yuuri shook her head vigorously. She was filled with happiness when she drank. But when it was over, regret swept in. She had become exactly what her mother feared she would: a hideous, blood-sucking monster.

"Lady Yuuri?"

Ernest stroked her hair. Rather than retreat from his touch, ashamed of what she was, she sank into his arms, quivering.

"I don't mind you getting all cozy like this with me. I just wish you wouldn't get mad at me when I tried it."

When Yuuri nodded, Ernest let out a sigh, and continued to stroke her hair.

Interlude: The Cold, the Key, and He

YUURI awoke to a knock on the shop's door.

She couldn't be sure what time it was in her drowsy state. But she assumed the sun must be high in the sky by the way its light broke through her thick curtains. Under normal circumstances, Yuuri would have been up long before now.

"Lady Yuuri? Are you home?"

There was only one oddball count who visited her shop on a regular basis. Cradling her throbbing head, chills wracked Yuuri's body as she dragged herself out of bed. She peered out her bedroom window, but a tarpaulin awning obscured her view of the shop door.

Yuuri never got sick, and yet the one time she did lined up exactly with Ernest's latest visit.

I'm so thirsty…but why so soon after my last drink?

Another knock sounded at the door, but in her current state, she needed to pretend she wasn't home. It hadn't even been a full month since Ernest had offered her his blood. But being sick had reawakened her thirst.

She was afraid if she saw him now, she would crave his blood, though she wasn't working on any cases from him to justify the reward.

After watching for some time, she finally saw Ernest walking away. The relief she felt was accompanied by pangs of loneliness as she slid back into bed.

Merely seeing Ernest filled her with an unquenchable thirst. She had a pitcher of water and a cup nearby, but she was so weak, she couldn't even manage to reach for them.

It was pointless anyway; water would not quench this thirst.

Yuuri closed her eyes, letting all sense of reality and the passage of time slip away.

🍎 🍎 🍎

IN her dreams, she saw Ernest gazing at her with a gentle look in his eyes.

"Are you all right? You have such a high fever."

His large hand caressed Yuuri's brow. It was cool and soothing. She didn't want him to stop.

"I think I've caught a cold. My head hurts, and I'm so thirsty."

"You need some water," Ernest said, glancing around the room before finally noticing the pitcher and cup.

Yuuri reached out from under her quilt and tugged on the hem of his pants. "No, wait…"

If Ernest hadn't been there, she could have lived with her thirst. But here he was. And since this was a dream, she felt she could ask whatever she wanted without fearing the consequences.

"You want blood? Is that it?"

"I do, yes… I'm so thirsty. I'm sure it's because I'm sick."

In her dreams, Yuuri could be open about what she wanted.

"I'll give you blood, but I'm putting it on your tab, okay? You'll have to do something for me in return."

Ernest loved to tease and provoke Yuuri, and yet, all she wanted right now was for him to be gentle and kind.

"Something for you…?"

Still dazed, Yuuri struggled to think of what Ernest would consider ample compensation. As a noble, no amount of money or goods she could prepare would satisfy him. He certainly wasn't hurting for money. Still, she racked her brain, trying to come up with something he would want that she actually had. Finally, the answer came to her.

"Would you like jasmine tea, Lord Ernest?" she ventured.

"Tea? No, that's not what I meant."

"But I thought…I mean, you never pay for it…"

He was always stopping by the shop and indulging in Yuuri's tea and snacks. Surely she was in the right to ask him to quench her thirst in return.

"Heh heh, I suppose I walked right into that one! Fair enough, if that's what it takes to get you better, I'll give you my blood."

An apple and cutting knife just happened to be lying on the table. Her dreams were being rather accommodating today, it seemed.

Ernest grabbed the knife and cut his left ring finger. It seemed as if anything Yuuri wanted in this dream would be granted to her. But she didn't want her desires to be the only ones satisfied. She wondered what she could do for Ernest.

If it was within my power, I'd give him anything he wanted. Anytime, anywhere, all he'd need to do is ask.

He pushed his finger into her mouth. Yuuri was happy she could taste blood, even in her dream, before her mind was swept away in blissful intoxication.

"What a wicked witch you are for testing my self-control like this. I might as well cast aside any claims of being a gentleman, right here and now."

Drunk on the sweet taste of his blood, Yuuri could no longer comprehend what Ernest was saying. All she could tell was that she had flummoxed him somehow. For some reason, his frustration amused her. Delighting at another's frustration was a wicked habit. Maybe Ernest was right: maybe Yuuri *was* a wicked witch.

🍎 🍎 🍎

THE room was dark when Yuuri awoke from her peaceful slumber. Her fever had subsided and with it, her ravenous thirst.

However, there was an oil lamp there, one she hadn't set out. Its gentle light illuminated the tall frame of a certain young man, casting his vast shadow against the wall.

"You're finally awake. How do you feel?"

What was he doing there? He frightened Yuuri so much that her heart skipped a beat and her mouth flapped open and shut.

Yuuri sat motionless on the bed as Ernest leaned in, gently touching his forehead to hers. They were so close.

"Your fever's still quite high. Have you eaten today?"

Yuuri kept quiet. She was feeling hot, her heart racing, but neither affliction was due to her cold. If she got sicker, it would all be Ernest's fault.

She glared at him once he finally pulled away.

"Why—how did you get into my house?"

"Oh, my Lady Yuuri, the lock on your door was so crude that it was easily undone by a simple wire," Ernest told her about his break in with a flourish. The illegality of his actions didn't seem to faze him.

He then recounted the events of his day to Yuuri. He had visited her shop that morning. He was about to leave since Yuuri hadn't answered, but then he sensed her spying on him from the second floor window.

"My keen Yuuri senses detected that you were ill, so I went to buy some fruit for you and came back."

He knocked again, letting her know he had come to check on her, but there was still no response. Out of genuine concern for her well-being, he was left with no choice but to break the lock.

"Rest assured, m'lady. While you slept, I enlisted the help of a locksmith to replace that shoddy old lock with a more secure one."

"Wh-Wh-Why would you just go and do something like that?"

Ernest twirled a key attached to a chain as he spoke. The key was a size bigger than the old one, and Yuuri rightly assumed it was her new key. "Why, because you're so reckless. I can't spend all my time worrying about you, can I?" he said as he set the key on her bedside table. He then grabbed the apple and knife, sat down in the chair next to her bed, and began peeling.

"So even nobles break the law?"

Yuuri found herself impressed at the skill with which he peeled the apple skin.

"'Tis just one of the many things one learns at boarding school," Ernest said drolly, setting the crescent-moon slices of apple on the plate as he finished with them. He popped one into Yuuri's mouth. "You need to eat something nutritious to help you get well."

A juicy burst of tart sweetness exploded in her mouth. She'd had no appetite the whole day, but readily devoured the apple slice that Ernest fed her.

An apple...? And Lord Ernest's finger...?

There had been an apple in her dream as well. And in that same dream, Ernest had slit his left ring finger. Here, in the real world, Ernest wore a bandage over that finger…

What…?

Yuuri suddenly became dizzy again and collapsed back onto the bed. The thought that her thirst had been sated only through Ernest hurting himself threatened her very sense of self. She closed her eyes, desperate for sleep to absolve her from this reality.

"Lady Yuuri? What's wrong? Are you all right?" Ernest asked, pressing his hand to her forehead. She slid beneath her duvet, desperate to hide from him.

"I am fine. I simply need a good night's sleep now…"

"Are you sure? I can come check on you tomorrow morning before I start work."

"Thank you. …Well, good night," Yuuri dismissed him, still concealed beneath the duvet.

Even though his visit brought with it a great deal of anxiety, she was still happy that Ernest came and cared about her.

For all the agitation Ernest's breaking in and changing her lock caused her, she had completely forgotten about it by the time she woke up.

Chapter 3: The Witch's True Love Potion

SUMMER, Yuuri's least favorite season, had arrived once more. It was hot and the sun was so bright, she couldn't bear to be outside. By the time she woke up, even the glare made her dizzy.

It would be another two months before summer reached its peak.

Living alone, Yuuri knew there was no way she could get by without leaving her home occasionally, even under the auspices of it being too hot. Meat and produce spoiled much faster in these conditions, so her trips to buy food became more frequent.

Yuuri struggled to balance her parasol and shopping basket as she made her way home from the morning bazaar. She was positive she hadn't bought too much at the bazaar, but after walking for some time, she realized just how heavy her basket was. It was an understandable miscalculation in this weather.

The road to her house was narrow and thus draped in the shadows of other buildings. She stopped for a moment to wipe the sweat away and rally her energy before starting off again. Gradually, her ivy-covered shop came into view.

When she finally reached her destination, she noticed a certain tall young man standing there, his arms crossed. He waved to her.

"Good morning, Miss Misfortune Devouring Witch. I've come to call on you once again."

Yuuri met Ernest's perfect smile with a stony face.

If he's going to show up, he could have at least offered to give me a ride home in his carriage, Yuuri sighed.

"Good morning, Count—oh, that's right. You don't like me calling you by your title."

Ernest was an attendant to the royal family with the title of count. Yet he was kind, lacking the haughtiness and unapproachability that plagued the nobility. On the other hand, he came off as very frivolous and vexing for his age. And his shimmering gold locks and sapphire eyes stood in sharp contrast to Yuuri's jet-black hair and eyes.

He seemed to glow in the sunlight, making the distance between him and Yuuri feel vaster than ever. She wondered whether he treated other girls the same way he treated her. Her social circle was so terribly small, she found it difficult to imagine their interactions. And what she did imagine proved too unpleasant, so she stopped.

"No, I don't. You promised to start calling me Ernest, so why won't you?" Ernest implored, playfully snatching away Yuuri's basket.

Yuuri used her freed hand to pull the key from around her neck, the one Ernest had gotten her the other day, and unlock the door.

"This heat wave seems to have come out of nowhere. At least you're dressed appropriately. You look nice today," he remarked as she stepped inside.

Yuuri was wearing an airy dress and her hair was pulled back with a ribbon made from the same cloth as a Hinomoto kimono. She always wore the *haori* her brother sent her around the house, but in this weather the *haori* was unnecessary. The ribbon was the only thing she wore from Hinomoto, and naturally it was a gift from her brother.

She should have been genuinely pleased at the compliment, but she instead lowered her head to hide her reddening cheeks. "Lord Ernest, what have you come for today?"

The shelves lined with jars of mysterious roots, frogs preserved in alcohol, and scrolls written in foreign script all seemed befitting of a witch's shop, but Ernest never came with the intent to buy such things.

"Shall we have some lemonade?" Ernest suggested, taking his usual seat on the couch after setting the shopping basket on the counter. He crossed his legs and made himself comfortable as if this were his home.

"This is a shop meant for paying customers, or have you forgotten?" Translation: this wasn't a cafe. But despite Yuuri scowling at him, he was unflappable, returning her glare with a broad grin.

"Now, Miss Yuuri, should you really say something like that to me of all people?"

"What do you mean?"

Yuuri had a bad feeling about this. His tone, his mischievous smile. He was planning something.

"The other day, while you were sleeping, I'm pretty sure I heard—"

"I-I didn't say anything! I don't remember anything! Just hush and I'll go get your lemonade!"

Yuuri had hoped he'd at least pretend to forget the words that had slipped from her when she was delirious with the fever. She grabbed her shopping basket and darted into the back. She stored the produce she had bought that morning in the pantry and set to work making lemonade. She already had some lemon syrup set aside, so she diluted it with water.

She had her own special lemonade recipe. After peeling the skin off the lemon, she sprinkled it with sugar and let it sit. Everyone had their own recipe, but Yuuri still worried that Ernest would mock her for having a childish palate. She gave it some thought, then added a mint leaf to the lemonade, hoping it would give the zesty drink a manly twist.

Yuuri set the lemonade glasses on a tray and ferried it out to Ernest. She had fled the room to avoid talking about what had happened, but Ernest seemed to have already forgotten about it as he casually accepted a glass. He really didn't seem like he wanted to cause Yuuri pain. But his mischievous nature and tendency to tease her made him hard to read. She sat next to Ernest, telling herself it was really just because there was nowhere else to sit.

"Ahh, there's nothing like lemonade on a hot day. This is delicious, Miss Yuuri."

Yuuri wondered just how long he had been standing outside waiting for her, because he must have been parched, as he drained the lemonade in one gulp.

"I've a favor to ask you. I need your help... Specifically, I need your insight."

The Misfortune Devouring Witch is Actually a Vampire?!

"Again?"

"Yes, again. I've found myself embroiled in another cumbersome situation. Do you know why this keeps happening to me?" Ernest stared at her with a serious expression.

"I don't. Nor am I certain that I can be of much help. But I can listen to what you have to say."

"Thank you. Will the usual...reward suffice?"

Yuuri emitted a soft gulp, then nodded once. She hoped he wouldn't be able to see her cheeks glowing scarlet in the dimly lit room.

"My good friend, a man by the name of Leonard who is a viscount's son, recently broke up with his fiancée. To put it bluntly, I'd like you to mediate the dispute between them. Will you help us?"

"I doubt I would be of much help in such matters. Do you really think I'm the best person to mediate a lovers' quarrel?" Matters of Eastern medicine and trade were the only two topics Yuuri was wholly confident within her scope of knowledge. She scarcely had a friend, let alone enough experience socially to mediate a dispute between lovers.

"You wouldn't happen to have a love potion for sale, would you?"

"L-Love potion?!" Yuuri nearly spat out her lemonade.

She was genuinely shocked at how casually he suggested the idea. She never would have expected that nonsense out of Ernest, and honestly, the suggestion irritated her. She downed the rest of her lemonade, hoping it would calm her nerves, then set the empty glass on the table.

"Magic potions are expensive! And the effects aren't permanent. I know of some that may alter a person's state temporarily. But a love forged under false pretenses will only hurt both parties in the long run," Yuuri said, angrily stating conventional wisdom despite her lack of social experience.

"All right. Then how about a potion to make someone speak their true feelings?"

"True feelings? There is such a thing as truth serum. Someone as involved with national security as yourself should know that much. But why would a little shop like mine carry something so potent?"

There was little difference in the fundamentals of Eastern and Hylantian medicine. If the medicine had a positive effect in one area, then there were bound to be side effects. And what was poisonous in one country was poisonous everywhere—the same applied to what was medicinal. Those principles were always the same.

The only major difference was what plants, animals, and minerals were available in each region.

"Well, that is quite the disappointing answer coming from a witch."

"Just so you know, that's not normally something a witch like myself would dabble in."

Ernest looked disappointed. Yuuri felt equally so. Because if she couldn't fulfill his request, she couldn't reap the sweet reward.

"This should come as no surprise, but I am not like the witches portrayed in fairy tales. I can't make miracles happen. I merely possess different medical and herbal knowledge from the people of your country."

"Don't say no so easily. At least meet with Leonard once—give him another woman's opinion! Now, we've got to go get ready!" Ernest leapt off the couch and offered Yuuri his hand.

"Wait, you want me to go outside now…?"

The shut-in witch had to muster a great deal of courage whenever she left the house. Going out that morning had drained her of energy as it was, but the sun would only climb higher as the day went on.

"That's why I tried to get here as early as I could. Don't worry, my carriage is waiting."

"P-Pardon?"

Ernest brought the empty glasses to the kitchen and grabbed Yuuri's parasol. Ever since that time she was sick, he lost all hesitation over entering her living quarters.

He grabbed the petite witch's hand and dragged her outside under the cover of her parasol.

🌱 🌱 🌱

THIS was only the second time Yuuri had been to the count's estate. The servants were kind and treated her with respect. Along with Ernest, they showed her into a parlor on the ground floor overlooking the stunning flower garden. It was a hot day with the intense sunlight tempered by fancy lace curtains that were occasionally swept about by the wind.

At twenty-seven, Ernest had attained the rank of count. Yuuri realized that was all she knew about him. Did nobility run in the family?

Were his parents alive? Would she get to meet them? What did they think of the unmarried couple visiting each other's homes at all times of the day? Her worries swelled to such great proportions that Yuuri could not keep them to herself.

"Lord Ernest, may I ask you something?"

"What would that be?"

"Well, uhm, are your parents…?" She couldn't find the right word to finish her question. Dead? Alive? Around?

If Ernest had reached the rank of count, it was possible that they were dead, but Yuuri had no clue how to broach the topic.

"You never ask me personal questions." Ernest's eyes widened.

"I'm so sorry," Yuuri said, instantly regretting her query. He knew a lot about her, but it was all things she wanted him to know. She wasn't sure if it was really all right to ask him about his family.

"It's all right. I'm glad you asked. My parents are well. They retired early and mainly spend their days lounging about. I have two older sisters, but both married into other noble families. Nothing special to hide, it's just never come up in conversation."

"So that's all…" Yuuri breathed a sigh of relief. At least now she knew she hadn't been rude by not greeting his family upon entering his home.

"My parents and sisters stop by occasionally. Next time they do, I'll introduce you."

She had no idea what she would say if she did meet them, so she could only nod and hope that it wouldn't happen anytime soon.

"The summers are cool and the winters frigid back at our family estate; it would suit you perfectly. Next time I go home, I'll take you along!" he exclaimed like it was a done deal.

"No, thank you! There's no reason for me to go."

"Really?" Did she imagine the hint of disappointment in his voice? "…Ah yes, we have some time before we meet Leonard. What should we do? The library and rose garden are about the only parts of this estate that are noteworthy."

"Rose garden?" The rose garden at his estate was so renowned that even Yuuri had heard of it. Ernest told her it was the perfect time of year to see the large-blossom roses in bloom.

"You can see it from here in the parlor."

He glanced over at the large windows. Yuuri approached and gently parted the lace curtains. It was just after noon and the sun's light was intense, blurring her vision.

The sight of the rose garden, a sea of large red, gold, and white roses in full bloom, would have been breathtaking for just about anyone. And Yuuri loved flowers. But it was so bright out, her eyes couldn't truly take it in.

"What do you think?"

"It is a lovely garden." Yuuri's words were wholly out of politeness.

Times like this made her painfully aware of how much she and Ernest could never share. They wouldn't be able to look at the flowers Ernest held so dear together. And the things she found beautiful were so dark, he wouldn't be able to see.

She forced a smile and he grabbed her cheeks, stretching them out to agitate her.

"Sorry, but I can see right through your lies," Ernest said, even though all Yuuri wanted was for him to smile and let it go. He could be so cruel. But she could see the concern in his eyes.

"I'm n-not..." she stammered.

His fingers should have still been pinching and pulling at Yuuri's cheeks. But instead, they were sliding down the contours of her face, lifting her chin so she had no choice but to look Ernest right in the eye.

Yuuri felt a strange sensation, one she had never experienced before with either alcohol or blood.

"Shall we visit the library?" he asked, releasing her face and grabbing her hand instead.

The library held ten times the amount of shelves Yuuri's shop did and was a tremendous sight. She was so taken with it, she stayed there voraciously reading the rare tomes until early evening.

❦ ❦ ❦

YUURI had completely forgotten the real reason for her visit by the time Ernest led her into another room. The shadows cast by nearby buildings and trees had grown long during her visit to the library.

"Could you wait here for a moment?"

It was one of the manor's guest rooms. Ernest escorted her into the room, but he lingered in the hallway.

"Why?"

"Well, I didn't think you'd want a man in here with you while you were getting dressed," Ernest explained with a wink.

"Excuse me...?"

Yuuri couldn't figure out just what she would be getting dressed up for. But judging from his playful attitude, this certainly didn't bode well for her.

"We're to meet Leonard at a dinner party this evening. And the timing couldn't be better, since you're already with me. But you'll need a dress for the occasion, so go ahead and change in here! Now, if you'll excuse me," Ernest said so quickly, Yuuri couldn't get a word in edgewise, and closed the door behind himself before shuffling away.

Yuuri stood there dumbfounded, only fully understanding what he said once his footsteps had receded down the hall. "W-Wait...!" Pulling herself together, she rushed toward the door and yanked it open. But where Ernest had stood before was now a plump, elderly woman.

"Is something the matter? I have been sent to attend to your preparations for the dinner party, m'lady. My name is Tarrah. We have drawn a hot bath for you, so follow me, if you please."

Tarrah was surrounded by four women all wearing the same standard maid uniform for Ernest's manor. Despite her confusion, Yuuri was led to the bathroom, stripped, and bathed. The scent of roses filled the bath, but in her anxious state, she couldn't manage to enjoy it.

"Ah, wait a second, please! I want to speak with Lord Ernest—"

"Please do not fret. You will have all the time in the world to speak with him after you have changed. You two must be very close, teehee."

"No, we're not!"

This woman made it sound as if Yuuri were so in love with Ernest that she couldn't bear to be apart for even a second. The unthinkable insinuation had Yuuri shaking her head furiously, her cheeks bright red.

"It's nothing to be embarrassed about. Now, please hurry."

The four maids blotted off excess moisture and rubbed cream in its place. Their hands were so deft that Yuuri couldn't even remember how to refuse. After her torso was dry, they wrapped it tight in a corset.

"Lady Yuuri, you're so slender, we really needn't pull the corset too tight. The bigger issue will certainly be..." Tarrah's eyes drifted straight to Yuuri's breasts.

"Let's try to pad those out just a bit, shall we? Just the slightest bit. Don't fret, my dear, every young lady does it for occasions such as this," Tarrah said, stuffing something into Yuuri's corset as she stressed the "every young lady" part in hopes of not hurting Yuuri's feelings. "Now then, let's pull it all together."

Yuuri's eyes seized upon a shiny blue dress one of the maids was carrying. It wasn't overly ornate or gaudy, merely draped in a second layer of lacy fabric of the same shade of blue. It was a lovely dress, accented with a flower motif.

"Will this do, m'lady?"

She nodded silently. Whether it was suitable or not was irrelevant; Yuuri could tell that she wouldn't be able to leave this room if it wasn't in that dress.

Compared to a normal Hylantian woman, Yuuri was petite with smaller feet. And yet the dress and matching shoes fit her perfectly.

"Our Master truly is a man of taste! He knew your size and what would look most stunning on you."

The design aside, how was it that Ernest knew her exact height and hip circumference? The more she thought about it, the worse her ruminations became, and she realized that was one rabbit hole she was better off not tumbling down.

❦ ❦ ❦

THE dull crescent moon slipped into the sun's place in the sky.

The myriad of lights at the viscount's manor kept Ernest and Yuuri from enjoying the stars. Other finely dressed couples were descending from their gilded carriages, greeting one another as they funneled into the mansion.

"Are you still cross? You must learn when to let things go."

"Why didn't you just tell me the truth?"

"If I had told you, you would have run away!"

Why did a bachelor like Ernest have a dress and necklace on hand? A dress and necklace that fit Yuuri like a glove. And why did he bring her to a fancy dinner party when she wasn't even his partner? Yuuri had all these questions and more for Ernest, but she kept them to herself. She wanted nothing more than to go back to being witch and client.

Looking dapper in a black suit, with his hair impeccably styled, Ernest reached out for Yuuri's hand, his mood sunnier than ever before.

"You really do look lovely this evening. So lovely, I would rather none of these other men have a look at you, but I suppose we've no choice there."

"Thank...you for the dress..." Yuuri said, her head down and her voice barely above a whisper.

"You're welcome. Now, aren't you going to tell me how dashing I look?"

"I could never say something so ridiculous!" she fumed.

Ernest's appearance and manners were sufficiently refined and he knew it. His confidence bordering on arrogance annoyed Yuuri.

"Haha, you're turning red!"

"I'm only doing this for the job! Don't push your luck!" Yuuri's dress concealed her foot as she used it to stomp on Ernest's toe.

"Well, Count Selden, I had heard that you might be bringing a maiden from a distant land to join us this evening," interrupted an older nobleman.

"Haha, it seems her reputation proceeds her. Please allow me to introduce you. This is Yuuri, the daughter of the president of Watoh Company. Miss Yuuri, this is Viscount Luniar."

Luniar was Leonard's family name. This man was likely his father.

"Oh, the daughter of the Watoh Company president? That's the company that trades primarily in Eastern goods, yes?"

"Yes. It is a pleasure to meet you." Yuuri dropped into a formal curtsy.

"Where might we find Leonard?" Ernest asked.

"Oh, he was on his way up to the balcony with Lady Riche. I tell you, those two are always going at it. He's the one who suggested breaking off the engagement, even after I told him an engagement that's been in place for so long can't be easily broken. And the worst part is, I know they haven't fallen out of love!" the older man exclaimed.

"I-I see. Those two are rather eas—"

"Indeed!" he spoke right over Ernest. "That's the biggest problem. It's as plain as day to everyone but them! If they truly were a bad match, I would not be so insistent! I cannot allow them to be driven apart.

And the wedding date is already set! It's easy for anyone to become tired in such a long-lasting relationship, but they've taken it too far. And honestly, those two—"

"Pardon me, Viscount, but I'm going to go check up on them," Ernest said, cutting into what would surely be another long-winded tirade. Yuuri's eyes had begun to glaze over, but she was grateful at least to get more information on Leonard and his fiancée.

Leonard and Riche stood alone on the sprawling balcony. Well, not quite alone. There had been others on the balcony who had fled at some point to escape their arguing.

Just as they were about to step onto the balcony, Ernest pulled Yuuri behind a pillar. He stood behind her, his arm around her waist to prevent her from running. Yuuri squirmed, trying to break free.

"Hold still," Ernest whispered into Yuuri's ear. Her heart thundered at the feeling of his breath upon her ear.

"Lord Ernest, you truly are horrible," Yuuri snapped, angered over being pulled into eavesdropping on a lover's quarrel that had nothing to do with her, angered by his wicked, mischievous grin. And yet, she did just as he asked.

Though having him close behind her made it difficult to concentrate, Yuuri strained to listen in on the pair.

"You did it last time too!"

"Last time? What did I do last time?"

It appeared that Riche was angry with Leonard. And from the looks of it, Leonard had brought his furious fiancée outside to calm her down.

"Did you forget all about how you flirted with your colleague's little sister?!"

"He asked me to dance with her and I obliged! I'm a nobleman—you can't expect me not to dance with anyone! You must learn to loosen up, my dear!"

From what Ernest had said, tonight was supposed to be about getting Leonard and Riche to reconcile. But that didn't seem likely to Yuuri.

"And another thing! I heard what you said to her! 'That looks stunning on you, Miss. Why it's the same shade as your sparkling sapphire eyes!'"

"I was being polite, Riche, as anyone would! ...Please, calm down!" Leonard's voice was growing louder, as if to keep pace with Riche's.

"Polite? Calm down? Leonard, when have you ever complimented me like that?!"

"What do you mean?! I'll compliment you right here, right now! Your dress is…ah…"

Before he could finish his sentence, Riche's palm landed hard against his cheek. Being complimented just because she asked for it was the last thing she wanted.

"You're the worst! I'm leaving!"

Riche fled the balcony with tears in her eyes. Leonard stood there, frozen, making no attempt to pursue her.

The balcony was steeped in silence.

Then, with a loud sigh, Leonard slammed his fist down on the handrail.

"Dammit! Why couldn't I just tell her she looked beautiful? I…I… Damn!"

After punching the guardrail several times and yelling increasingly more embarrassing epithets, Leonard ran off.

The reconciliation Ernest had hoped for fizzled into the night.

🦇 🦇 🦇

THE balcony had fallen completely silent after Riche and Leonard left. Unable to stand the silence for long, Yuuri felt she had to say something.

"…Uhm, don't you think we should just let them go ahead and break up?" Yuuri meant it. Between listening to Ernest and the viscount, Leonard meant well. But she failed to see his appeal.

"I don't exactly disagree. I mean, I have no trouble telling a beautiful woman she's beautiful, but he can't seem to manage it for the woman he loves most. It's embarrassing to watch."

They might have been friends, but Ernest and Leonard were polar opposites. Yuuri suspected their differences were what made them so close. Though being friends with someone so incapable of being genuine likely led to plenty of arguments.

"If they went their separate ways, I bet Lady Riche could find someone much better."

"Miss Yuuri, do I detect a hint of bitterness? Ah, well, he always seemed more in love with her than she with him. …Maybe that's why she always gets annoyed?"

If Riche, who was a noble on the same level as Leonard, wanted out of the marriage, she could easily break things off. But if she didn't love him, she wouldn't have cared so much that Leonard didn't compliment her.

For his part, the reason Leonard could compliment other girls and not the woman he loved was likely because he cared too much. He loved her so much, it was beyond what he could express in words. Though his failure ended in hurt feelings and misunderstandings.

It still didn't seem right, but at least now, Yuuri could see their problem.

"...So, can you finally give me some room to breathe?"

Realizing he was still holding onto her, Yuuri yanked herself free.

"Sorry about that. So, do you have any suggestions on how we might help Leonard and Riche out?"

"Not at all. I already tried to tell you I'm not well-versed in human relationships."

"Yes, but I thought you might have some insight into how Leonard was feeling, considering how similar you are."

Leonard loved Riche. And he had no trouble shouting it to the winds, as long as he was alone. He was indeed like Yuuri, who could never seem to tell Ernest how she truly felt.

Her defenses only ever seemed to drop when she was drunk on his blood.

"What about alcohol...?"

"No, that wouldn't work. He's uncannily hard to get drunk. And who wants to hear romantic overtures from a drunk man anyway?"

Yuuri had hoped giving him alcohol would do the trick, but things were never that simple. She was racking her brain for ideas when she noticed someone walk out onto the balcony from the shadows. It was a middle-aged gentleman with olive-brown hair. He had a woman with him, likely his wife, with flaxen hair and blue-grey eyes.

Any normal person wouldn't have been able to make out those details in the dark, but as a vampire, Yuuri could.

Why did they have to be here of all places...?!

They were two people Yuuri knew very well. They were, after all, her parents.

Her mother only acted unhinged when Yuuri was around. Beyond that, she was perfect at playing the part of the merchant's dutiful wife. So it was only natural that she would be in attendance at a party thrown by one of her husband's business associates. As long as her daughter wasn't around, she was the perfect wife and mother.

Yuuri began to sweat and clung to Ernest.

"What's wrong?" he asked, only worrying Yuuri more that her mother would hear them. What if her mother heard him say her rare Hinomotoese name? She was so afraid, she couldn't speak.

"...Is that them?" Ernest's grip on Yuuri tightened and he pushed her against the wall, completely blocking her view of the couple.

The Misfortune Devouring Witch is Actually a Vampire?!

"I'm sorry. I should have checked to make sure they wouldn't be in attendance," he said in a whisper so quiet only she could hear. He could see the fear in her eyes.

He had never met Yuuri's mother, but he was well-acquainted with her father.

Ernest was tall enough to keep Yuuri and her distinctive black hair hidden from view. To anyone else, they would merely appear to be a girl in a blue dress and a young man with blond hair whispering sweet nothings to one another.

Yuuri threw her arms around Ernest, trying desperately to calm down. What must he think of her, only opening up to him at times like this?

"My, how enviable it is to be young!" the woman remarked, her voice growing further away by the second.

The woman left without disturbing the young couple. Whatever she might think of such behavior, she was certainly more tolerant than if she had known it was Yuuri that Ernest was looming over. It was the first time Yuuri had ever heard her mother speak with such restraint.

Yuuri's parents swept into the hallway, leaving the pair in that position for several moments.

"Miss Yuuri, I'm sorry."

"As am I. I shouldn't have gotten so upset. I'm not a child."

The pair pulled apart enough that they could see each other's faces, but Ernest's usual confidence was gone. Yuuri didn't like the look that had seized his face.

"Please smile, Lord Ernest. I don't like to see you like that."

He forced a grin for her benefit.

"Shall we be going?"

"Yes."

As long as she was with Ernest, Yuuri could muster up the courage to manage an awkward smile. The thought warmed her heart.

🦇 🦇 🦇

IT was at Ernest's insistence that she spent the night at his manor, as it was far too late for her to go home alone and he would not take no for an answer.

She couldn't get the dress off by herself, so once again, she was surrounded by maids. With the restrictive dress gone and the jewelry and makeup cleared away, Yuuri felt lighter. At the same time, a wave of exhaustion swept over her.

"Are you ready to retire for the evening?"

Yuuri shook her head at Tarrah's question. They had left in the middle of the party, so it still was not her usual bedtime. And yet, so much had happened, leaving her exhausted.

"May I go to the library?" She was sure if she could borrow some books and read them snuggled up in bed, she might be able to drift off to sleep. As much as she hated her vampiric characteristics, she did relish the ability to read with only the tiniest amount of light.

"Of course. We will set your nightclothes next to your bed, then."

Back in the sundress she had arrived in that afternoon, Yuuri made her way to the library.

According to Tarrah, her room was on the second floor, while the library was on the first. There was just enough light in the library to find a book, not that she needed the light.

Yuuri preferred escapist fiction over practical books for her nighttime reading. After grabbing several books, she made her way back toward the guest room.

She caught a glimpse of the outside between the velvet curtains. The estate's garden proved especially alluring beneath the stars.

"The rose garden… I should be able to enjoy it now."

Yuuri set the books down for a moment and hung up the lantern she carried. She then made her way outside from the library.

With her vision, she would have no problem walking around outside in the dark. Unlike most humans, she had nothing to fear.

"It's lovely…"

Between the starry sky and the glowing roses with blooms bigger than her hand, the whole scene felt like a dream to Yuuri. The white roses, which stood out from all the rest, seemed especially beautiful. It made her long to have someone to share the scenery with. Someone like Ernest.

But with her grandmother gone, Yuuri knew no one could truly see the scenery the way she did. Even though Ernest knew what she was and loved her anyway, he could never see the world the way she saw it.

The Misfortune Devouring Witch is Actually a Vampire?!

Even if they sat side by side, they'd be seeing two different sights.

Any normal human would find it difficult to walk in such little light. They wouldn't be grinning like a fool the way Yuuri was.

"Miss Yuuri!"

"Lord Ernest! What's the matter?"

Ernest was rushing toward her from the manor. He actually seemed angry for once.

"Don't 'what's the matter' me! Why are you wandering the grounds this late at night without a jacket?! I was looking for you so I could bid you goodnight."

The temperature had dropped significantly since the afternoon and the breeze was gentle. That was why Yuuri was in better spirits than usual. But, concerned as ever about the Eastern witch, Ernest draped his jacket over her shoulders.

"It was just around your manor's grounds." Yuuri's face turned red, soaking up the warmth of the jacket Ernest had been wearing until only a moment ago.

"You can't be so reckless! What were you thinking?"

"I was just enjoying your garden. It's so pretty. I'm being sincere this time... It really is lovely."

Yuuri seemed completely different from that afternoon, as if she truly did love the flowers. Ernest glanced around a bit before lifting his gaze to the sky.

"The stars are lovely tonight."

"They are. And you, Lord Ernest...are so kind."

Just as she suspected, he could see little in the lantern light. But he was trying to show her that, even if their worlds weren't the same, there were still things they could share.

He took a seat next to her. For a while, they stared up at the sky in silence.

"Even if there were no stars, if you were the only one who could enjoy this scenery, I would still be happy just to know you were enjoying yourself." Ernest pulled Yuuri closer.

"...You would?" Yuuri wasn't sure if he was being smug or planning something more perverse, so she took his words with a grain of salt.

"I'm trying to make you understand that you don't have to temper your shine for me."

"But…"

Yuuri's heart thundered in her chest. She wanted to believe him.

"Don't hold back your love of the flowers or stars. I love you just as you are. The Yuuri who can see the true beauty of the night."

His face was so close, it took up her entire field of view. How could she enjoy looking at those things now?

Maybe it was easy for Ernest, who didn't seem too concerned about what others thought of him. But it was impossible for Yuuri to live as open and free as he did.

"I'm sorry, I can't…"

"Why not? Do as you like. That's what I'm doing…"

Yuuri nervously placed her hand on his chest. She did like Ernest. And if she could, she wanted to be with him for as long as possible.

And yet, Ernest cared so greatly for her that it scared her. She feared that if she truly internalized all the things he said, she would lose herself somewhere along the way.

Yuuri went to stand up, to put distance between her and Ernest. His hand loosened its grip.

He wouldn't force her. But the look in his eyes made it clear that he was disappointed. In the end, she felt like the one in the wrong. But why? He was the one trying to do something lascivious. So why was she saddled with such intense feelings of guilt? Whether she accepted or refused him, there was no doubt that he had stirred up intense feelings within her heart.

"Lord Ernest, thank you for today. For being here with me. It makes me so happy. So…" She wanted to show him, even just a bit of who she was, without being drunk on his blood. She leaned close to him, her lips inches from his cheek. "Good night."

She told herself over and over that a kiss on the cheek was just a normal nighttime greeting and flashed him a shy smile.

"Did you cast some sort of spell to free your true self or something?"

"A spell?"

He was implying that Yuuri had to use magic to be honest with him.

"Yeah. That or you drank some potion to reveal your true colors. Ah well, I suppose I should say my goodnights as well."

Some sort of potion? Suddenly, Yuuri had a brilliant idea and slipped out of Ernest's grasp before he could return her greeting.

"Never mind that! I think I've got an idea about that couple—"

"We can worry about them tomorrow..."

"It can't wait! It looks like my witch powers will be of use after all! Yes, I think a potion to unleash someone's true feelings like you said is just the thing we need!"

Yuuri set Ernest to work arranging another meeting with Leonard and Riche.

ACCORDING to Ernest, both sets of parents were willing to play along to get the warring couple back together. Their original plan had fallen through though.

Ernest gave Leonard a special "True Love Potion" which he said was a specialty of Yuuri's. He was supposed to use the potion at the next dinner party. Ernest was frighteningly convincing, it seemed.

Ernest invited the couple to a dinner party and it was the day after that an angry Leonard paid a visit to Yuuri's shop. Ernest walked in behind him. Naturally he was wearing a mischievous smile, a stark contrast to Leonard's scowl. But for once, Yuuri was the meddlesome count's willing accomplice.

"Are you the witch? That potion you gave me didn't work! Instead of being able to say how I really felt, I just ended up hurting her again!" Leonard bellowed, not even introducing himself.

"But the potion is working. After all, you just shared your true feelings with me." Yuuri declared with a surprising amount of confidence.

Though Leonard was essentially a stranger, Yuuri had a role to play.

"Beguiling witch! I don't care what I tell you! I love Riche! I've always thought she was beautiful from the bottom of my heart! I want to tell her! But when her beauty is before me, it's like a curse steals the words from my lips!"

These words, the ones Yuuri and Ernest wanted to get Leonard to say, were likely the same ones he wanted to say to Riche. Ernest broke in to bring Leonard down from his impassioned speech.

"...There you have it, Lady Riche. These are Leonard's real feelings. The witch's potion is as potent as ever, even if it took a while to kick in." Ernest called in to the back room of the shop.

The door opened ever so slightly. Yuuri opened it the rest of the way, revealing Riche standing there.

"…Wh-What is Riche doing here…?"

"I asked her to come," Yuuri said, having invited Riche in anticipation of Leonard's tirade.

The "True Love Potion" Yuuri had given Leonard was really just sugary syrup. Drinking it might warm the body, but it wouldn't really cause someone to reveal their true feelings.

In other words, it was a placebo.

Yuuri had two hypotheses: one, that he would drink it and, believing it was real, divulge his true feelings; in other words, the placebo effect. This was the outcome Yuuri hoped for.

The other possibility was that things would go as they were now, so either way, it was all going according to Yuuri's plan.

Ernest was also in on the whole thing, so he broke into a wide grin.

"Leonard…you really are something else." Riche stood in front of him smiling, her eyes blurring with tears.

"No, wait, I…"

Even though she now knew how he felt, he still couldn't say it. Leonard's affliction was indeed serious and it would take time to cure him, perhaps a lifetime even.

"It's all right. It's not as if I didn't know how you felt. It's just that I lacked confidence, and not being able to hear it from you made me uneasy."

"Riche."

"Listen. I love you, all right? And I suppose if you were the sort of man who could unironically whisper sweet nothings into my ear, you wouldn't be the man I fell in love with. And yet, isn't all this strange?"

The one person he couldn't express his love to was the one he loved most. But he finally let Riche know just how special she was to him. And with that, her anxieties were gone.

The case of the fumbling lovers came to a close for now.

Still blushing, Leonard turned to Yuuri.

"By the way, how much for the potion? I owe you, for that and for shouting at you earlier."

"Uhm…you've probably already figured this out, but that's just a standard vitamin tonic, so it's only five copper coins."

That was the same as a cup of tea at most ritzy teahouses.

"No. It was a witch's brew, and so I insist on paying the market price for that."

"In that case, for reward, I..."

The one who arranged this farce was that meddlesome count. So she didn't need Leonard to pay. Just as she was about to explain, Ernest waved her off.

"Leonard, consider it an early wedding present from me. After all, I'm the one who asked for her help, so I should be the one to pay."

The couple seemed insistent on doing something, but Ernest chased them off. He sure was an oddball, somehow anxious to offer up his "reward" to Yuuri.

🦇 🦇 🦇

THE "Shop Closed" sign still stood by the door. The Witch of the East's Apothecary had been closed temporarily. And even though it was midday, the curtains all around the shop had been pulled shut. Even if they wanted to, no outsider could see inside.

"All right, my little witch, time for your reward."

"Lord Ernest, wasn't I just playing the part of the witch in your little farce? If so, I don't need compensation for that."

Yuuri was angry. If the whole point was to get Leonard to where he could say his honest feelings, wouldn't the witch be unnecessary?

The cast really only ever needed to be Leonard, Riche, and maybe the meddlesome count, but that was all.

And staging a play without the cast knowing they were playing a part was sheer deceit. Yuuri's pride in herself as a witch had been deeply wounded. She was, in some ways, the one who had hatched the plan to give Leonard the placebo, but that wasn't completely the case. Ernest had likely come to Yuuri expecting her to do exactly as she had and in fact gave her several hints to push her in the right direction. That was what irritated her most.

"I may not have needed your skills as a witch, but I did take up your time, and for that I must pay you. Take all you want, if it means you'll forgive me," Ernest said, making himself comfortable on the only couch in the room. He wrapped his arms around her waist, bringing her to him. She gave no sign of resistance.

"Then please unbutton your collar."

"You go ahead. Or can a vampire not manage to undo buttons?"

He really was a cruel man.

Yuuri lifted his tie and swiftly undid it. She then attempted to unbutton his blouse but found it was much harder trying to undo someone else's buttons than it was her own.

"C'mon, you can do it! Or do you not want my blood?"

She ignored his provocations and, after a great deal of struggle, finally undid the four top buttons. She opened his collar, exposing his neck.

It was much larger than a woman's. His neck and built chest were bare. When she lifted her eyes, she realized Ernest was smiling down on her.

"...You're not afraid?"

Yuuri was afraid. Afraid that someday, Ernest would hate her for all of this.

"Go on. This is your reward, so drink up, my sweet little vampire."

"...All right. Thank you."

As the descendent of a vampire who had intermarried with humans, Yuuri was different from pureblood vampires. Yuuri's ancestors had much sharper fangs, where hers were merely considered sharp teeth by human standards. They weren't that sharp, but they could still draw blood. Ernest was a proud nobleman, but he still felt pain.

Thus, Yuuri couldn't really understand how he could accept this with a smile on his face, and the fact that she couldn't understand made it all the more terrifying.

And yet, she so desperately wanted the reward he was offering that, even as it made her hate herself, she couldn't stop.

Her half-parted lips hovered at the nape of his neck for a moment, hesitating before finally biting down. Ernest's body stiffened in response. Surely he was in pain. But the scent of her reward was already clouding her senses, leaving her powerless to fight against it.

It was like biting into fruit. She maneuvered her tongue to keep any blood from dribbling away.

The taste of his blood on her tongue was sweeter than any fruit she'd ever bitten into. That taste was finer than the finest tea and to

Yuuri, was better than any food or drink money could buy.

His breathing became ragged. Her breath was hot against his skin, her tongue lashing against the mark her fangs made. She was embarrassed, wondering what he must have thought of her. The spell that his blood had over her suddenly lifted and she looked up at him.

"You don't want to waste it, do you? Go ahead and keep going until it stops bleeding." Ernest's large hand began to caress Yuuri's head. Slowly, he guided her face back to where it had been before.

If he said it was all right, then it must be. Yuuri reassured herself and tried to let it go so she could enjoy her reward.

So they sat like that, with him pulling her into his lap and her wrapping her arms around him. His hand hadn't stopped caressing her head and so she assumed it was all right.

When the flow of blood finally did stop, Yuuri buried her face in Ernest's rumpled shirt. The euphoria she felt couldn't be explained away as simply feeling full or satisfied. All she wanted was to bask in that feeling just a little longer.

"Are you so full, you're tired?"

"…"

If she told him no, she'd have to pull away. She wanted to stay like this. So she pretended to be sleeping.

"I see. Are you really going to be all right not drinking blood for another two months? Maybe you should find someone else?"

She didn't need anyone else's blood. She doubted she could even stomach anyone else's. Why would he say such a thing? In another two months, he might forget about her. And she doubted she had the courage to ask him for blood without a job well done to justify it.

Yuuri was terrified.

"That's not for you to trouble yourself with. I'll worry about it."

I can't wait two months. I don't want anyone's blood but yours. Words that felt so unlike her were racing through her mind. Maybe she was suffering from the same curse as that man who couldn't be honest.

"You're a terrible witch. Maybe I should request a real truth serum. If you make it for me, I'll give you a reward. How about it?"

"No."

"You're turning me down because you know who I want to have drink it, don't you? You must know I just want you to be open and honest with me, right, my little Misfortune Devouring Witch?"

Misfortune Devouring Witch. That's what they called her grandmother. The original meaning was "let her eat your misfortunes, so only good fortune will remain", but the reason the name had been given was lost to time, leaving only the name itself. That's why she hated that name. She should hate that name. But Ernest had used it properly.

"If you keep eating all the misfortune in this town, I'm going to run out of cases for you to solve. So I need to find a way to get you to reveal your true colors before then…"

And so, within a month, he was back with a new task for her. He was, after all, an oddball count who sought all the world's troubles and strife and brought them right to her door, just so he could pay her reward.

Interlude: Hair Accessories for Her

ERNEST made his way to the Watoh Company headquarters, at the heart of the city's business district.

Though he hadn't told Yuuri, this was actually his third visit to the company without her knowledge.

The first time had been when he was trying to order books from the East. The second time, he had come to ask Yuuri's father about her. The third time, this time, he was there in response to a summons he had received following his recent antics.

Sitting in that conference room again, adorned with vases of striking colors, reminded him of that second time, when he'd come to ask Joh Watoh about his daughter.

❦ ❦ ❦

"MR. WATOH, what exactly do you know about your daughter's condition?" Ernest asked, beating around the bush. He wanted to see just how much the man knew about her life as a descendant of vampires, since the trait skipped his generation.

"Condition...? My Lord, you can't mean..." With just those words, Joh's face drained of color.

"Yes, she told me herself."

"Yuuri did? Really...?"

Joh didn't ask him to spell out exactly what Yuuri had told him. Nor did he launch into the topic himself. It was as if the men were competing to see who would use the words "vampire" or "blood" first.

"I suppose 'told' is inaccurate. 'Demonstrated' is probably more like it. Hahaha, it was quite the shock."

"Are you telling me she drank your blood?! I thought you just went to her to borrow books! How could this have happened? Could my daughter really…?"

Joh was clearly upset and unable to hide his anger at Ernest, who was of a higher status as nobility.

"I beg your pardon, m'lord," he apologized after rethinking his outburst. "…You are the victim here, after all. Please do not trouble yourself over my daughter. Please just leave her be."

Ernest could only speculate over what it was that had awakened Yuuri's vampiric instincts. But the fact still remained that she would, from now on, need to periodically drink blood. He knew enough about the vampires of yore to piece together that much.

With her antisocial nature, she was unlikely to easily find another to feed off of. So telling Ernest to "leave her be" seemed especially cruel, something a real parent wouldn't say. He furrowed his brow at Joh.

Ernest expected the man to try and do something for Yuuri amidst her mother's hatred, but he was discouraged to find that Yuuri's father was equally content to avoid her. What should he have expected of a man who had his daughter live in isolation? On the opposite hand, learning this about Joh helped free Ernest of any restraint about taking Yuuri from him.

"Mr. Watoh, would it surprise you to learn that I desire Miss Yuuri?"

"Inconceivable! My daughter is no ordinary human!" Joh shouted. Even from where he sat, Ernest could see sweat glistening on the merchant's brow.

"Haha, I suppose it is rather astonishing. But I am serious. That's why I've come today. To seek your permission."

"So you can keep her as a mistress?! A toy?! Some sort of exotic pet? My daughter isn't suited for such a life!"

"Hardly! If that was my intention, do you think I would even play at asking your permission? Please do not worry. I've already obtained His Majesty's blessing as well."

"You mustn't bring my daughter into your bloodline. What if your children inherit her condition?"

"It shouldn't be a problem as long as those closest to us understand and support us. Isn't that what love is?"

Yuuri's condition meant she could see exceptionally well in the dark, but not bear bright sunlight, and she had to begin drinking blood once she reached adulthood. Naturally, Ernest understood that any child inheriting those characteristics would have their share of challenges. But he wouldn't let those challenges scare him away.

Joh's mistake had been in not predicting the possibility of Yuuri inheriting those vampiric traits. If he had, he and his wife could have prepared for this circumstance. Yuuri's ancestors, her grandmother included, had intermingled with humans and married for love, blending into human society. There was no reason Yuuri should not have the same opportunity.

"But…"

"I will put her happiness first. What right do you have to hide her away and interfere in that happiness?" Those words silenced Joh. "I can promise you one thing: I will not hurt your daughter."

"My Lord…it is probably an inherited trait, but it is important you understand that we Watohs are a stubborn, awkward sort. I've kept Yuuri hidden away to protect her. I have no right to ask this, but, please…take care of my daughter." Joh bowed his head.

Ernest had been wrong. He assumed Joh had kept Yuuri at arm's length because he didn't care, but his words were sincere.

Ernest was finally beginning to understand some things about Yuuri. About her being a vampire and about the family she came from.

🦇 🦇 🦇

"COUNT SELDEN!"

The bang of the door and a loud voice jerked Ernest from his reverie about the day he came here so many months ago.

The short, chestnut-haired youth with a baby face and grey-blue eyes was mad before he even had a chance to say hello.

His looks, which he inherited from his mother, were no different from most Hylantians. It was his clothes that set him apart. He wore *hakama* as part of his everyday outfit. This was fitting for a self-proclaimed "Hinomoto fanatic" such as himself.

Yet remaining attached to his Hinomoto heritage also made him feel closer to his sister.

Ernest rather liked Simon's rustic simplicity, but Yuuri's brother did not care for him.

"Hi, Simon. It's a pleasure to see you again."

"Count Selden, what is this I hear about you showing my sister off at some dinner party and pretending she's your lover?!"

To think he was this angry that his sister had gotten so close with another man. These siblings who were supposed to be polar opposites had more in common than they cared to admit. Yuuri was like an aloof cat; Simon was like a dog fuming with jealousy.

Ernest smiled when he realized how both of them tended to get angry when he teased them, and just as quickly too. "Heh heh, 'pretending she's my lover'?"

"Don't deny it, you shameless cad!"

"Why Lord Simon, there should be no 'pretending' to it. I have your father's blessing. There's nothing for me to feel ashamed of, is there, Big Brother?"

Simon was gnashing his teeth, but he did not object any further.

Joh Watoh finally made his entrance shortly thereafter. Ernest expected Joh to blame him as well for bringing Yuuri to the dinner party with him even though they weren't an official item, but he didn't.

Her parents had been at the dinner party, making it a most anxiety-inducing experience for Yuuri indeed. They had managed to avoid her mother's notice, though he should have expected it. The Watoh family was among the Five Great Merchant Families of Hylant; it was only natural that they would make an appearance. But this wouldn't be the last time they might run across each other.

Mother and daughter would need to come to some sort of resolution. But Ernest wanted to give Yuuri a little more time for that.

❦ ❦ ❦

"COUNT SELDEN!" Just as Ernest was leaving, Simon charged after him in a panic. "...Uhm, I know I should give this to her directly, but please do it instead. It's a hair accessory, from me."

Simon handed Ernest a long wooden box with something engraved on it. It must have been intended as a gift.

"For Miss Yuuri? I don't mind, but are you sure you don't want to give it to her yourself?"

"Yes. I can't give it to her in the manner I normally would. It's a little embarrassing to talk about."

Ernest really did like him. So, without thinking about what he was doing, he patted the younger man's head.

"…What are you doing? I may not look it, but I am in fact twenty-four years old, sir!"

"Ah, my apologies, I hadn't meant to treat you like a child. I was just thinking, you and Yuuri really are perfectly alike."

"So you do the same thing to my sister?" Simon's eyes narrowed.

It was in that expression that Ernest could, finally, see the resemblance between the siblings.

Chapter 4: The Lonesome Peony

ERNEST was greeted in the King's office by Rodrick II and a surly soldier. Ernest knew the soldier, a man by the name of Derek Conquest who was two years his senior. At twenty-nine, he had attained the rank of major. They were about the same height, but Derek gave a far more imposing impression.

Perhaps "knew him" was a little too generous. Ernest had never actually talked to the man; he only knew his name and reputation. The green-eyed Conquest, with his short blond hair, showed not a hint of emotion. In all honesty, he was the most difficult sort of person for Ernest to deal with.

"Count Selden, I would like to request your assistance." He didn't look at all like someone asking for help. If this ended up being a personal request, Ernest would turn it down without listening to another word.

"We'd like to have you investigate an underground gentlemen's club. We have reason to suspect that illegal gambling is taking place there," Conquest explained without pausing to make sure Ernest understood.

A gentlemen's club was a private social club where the elite gathered to discuss everything from politics to the arts. The club in question was run by Marquis Groves twice a week out of his guest house. That was where the illegal gambling was happening.

Gambling itself wasn't forbidden in Hylant, but institutions running a gambling operation were taxed at a high margin. Something as minor as card games among small groups where the participants bet their own money were often overlooked. The difficulty was in determining where the line between "small groups" and "illegal gambling operation" fell.

The other problem was that illegal gambling dens were often a hotbed for other sorts of illicit activities.

It didn't sound like all of the club members were involved in illegal gambling. The investigation had only gotten as far as learning that some small subset was involved. But the whole affair was taking place on the grounds of the powerful Marquis Groves, which meant members of the highest tiers of the aristocracy could be involved. That was why this needed to be a secret investigation.

"Illegal gambling? Isn't that the military police's jurisdiction, Major Conquest?" Ernest pointed out the obvious.

"There is little we can do without proof. But a competent man like you should be able to slip in and find some for us."

That was it. They needed someone of high status to infiltrate the club for them. And if they were doing something illegal, they were bound to be hyper-reluctant about admitting someone involved with the military police. But refusing to admit a man from the upper classes would be equally suspicious, so they adamantly hid illegal activities from Major Conquest after allowing him membership. Sending anyone else affiliated with the military police or public security would have been equally fruitless. Thus, they asked Ernest.

"Well, I certainly am flattered you place such faith in me..."

"Faith? Is that what it is?" King Rodrick asked his longtime friend in feigned astonishment. Things were always casual between them, even though Ernest had served Rodrick since his youth.

"Why else would you ask me, Your Majesty?"

Though he was ever the loyal retainer, Ernest was uneasy to say the least. He prided himself on his gentlemanly nature, never chased skirts, and gave his all to his job in service to the king.

"Because you look just unassuming enough, that one would think if asked to join in on illicit activity, you would say yes just for the hell of it."

"Your Majesty, you wound me! I am a good and honest man."

"Of course I know that's who you truly are. But this is how others might perceive you. That's why we called upon you."

"How others perceive me? What a thing to say!"

"You never realized anyone saw you that way?"

"I have not! What do you think, Major Conquest?"

Though they were lord and retainer, this sort of playful back and forth teasing was normal for them, a sign of their close friendship. Major Conquest merely watched the exchange without batting an eye. He didn't laugh; rather, he seemed like he was ready to be dismissed. When Ernest tried to bring him into the discussion, he creased his brow in thought for several seconds before finally declaring—

"How should I know?"

—before returning to that same stoic expression.

Ernest and Rodrick immediately realized he was every bit as humorless as he seemed.

That'll teach me to try and joke with Major Conquest, Ernest dryly noted.

❦ ❦ ❦

IF he was going to investigate an illegal gambling ring in the gentlemen's club, Ernest's first task was naturally to get himself invited into the club by one of its members. He would then need to pay the initiation fee and gain acceptance from the other members.

He needed to get a member with considerable influence to invite him into the club without asking for it directly. He also couldn't allow his connections to the major be known, so he needed to make use of his own personal connections. But doing so was bound to take time.

And indeed, he became so busy with his secret mission, over half a month passed before he visited the witch's shop again. During that time, he only sent two letters through his servant Tarrah, telling Yuuri he was busy. While Ernest's letters were flowery, three-page love letters, Yuuri's responses were cold and to the point. What she couldn't convey in words, she conveyed with her gifts of tea leaves. Jasmine tea. Ernest's favorite.

As he got to know Yuuri, Xingkaese tea became a common favorite in his estate, and thus he had plenty of Eastern-style teacups, several of which were procured through Watoh Company. And though Yuuri had taught him and his servants how to make the tea, the taste remained incomparable to what he drank at Yuuri's shop. Still, his servants were some of the best around and conscientious to boot, so maybe it wasn't lack of skill, but lack of something else.

The Misfortune Devouring Witch is Actually a Vampire?!

For him, there was no greater tea than that consumed on the witch's comfortable couch, in the company of the expressive witch.

☙ ☙ ☙

WHEN Ernest finally did have a day off, he naturally paid a visit to Yuuri's shop.

Normally, he would just show up at the shop without warning, but this time he elected to send her a letter letting her know when he would be coming by. He had been so busy up to that point, and it was likely he would be equally as unavailable going forward; he wanted to make sure he caught her with what free time he did have.

In a stroke of good luck, it was a cloudy day, so Ernest could actually take Yuuri outside.

He strode down that narrow alley and gazed up at the brick shop, where he spotted a shadow just before it darted away. Yuuri must have been so anxious for Ernest's visit, that she had been taking occasional peeks out the window to see when he got there. Just the thought made Ernest's face break into a goofy grin.

"Miss Yuuri! Sorry to have kept you waiting!"

Ernest expected Yuuri to come running down the stairs and fly into his arms. Instead, she was standing in front of the shelf, trying to pretend like she was deeply involved in her work.

The days were still hot, so she wasn't wearing her usual *haori*. To keep her neck cool, her hair was pulled up high on her head with the hair accessories Simon had given her the other day. She began to turn slowly, but Ernest could not wait. He threw his arms around her.

"I wasn't really waiting, I ju—let me go!"

"Oh, come now! I've been so busy and tired!"

When Yuuri genuinely tried to push him away, Ernest always complied. But she didn't try as hard this time.

"Then why don't you rest up at your mansion? Why come all this way just to disturb me so early in the morning?"

Yuuri was worried his exhaustion was from lack of sleep and overwork, which Ernest was fine with using as a convenient ruse.

"I can think of no better cure for my exhaustion than having a cup of your famous jasmine tea."

"If that's what you want, please let me go."

This time he readily complied and headed right for his favorite spot. Yuuri disappeared into the back and before long, that gentle aroma was wafting his way.

"Is this a new cup? Is this camellia?" He had been drinking jasmine tea at the manor for so long, everything in Yuuri's shop seemed new once more.

The teacup was so dainty that Ernest feared too strong a grip would crack it. The inside was the brightest white, forming a stark contrast with the dark tea. The outside of the cup was azure blue, with red and white flowers painted around it. These flowers were the same as those on Yuuri's *haori* when he first came to her shop. Maybe it was just the strong impression their first meeting had left, but Ernest thought that color suited her best.

"It is very fragile. So please don't drop it."

"Were these a gift from Simon?" Ernest asked, causing her to furrow her brow.

"No! These were on sale at Watoh Company, so I bought them for myself!"

Ernest couldn't understand why their conversation was upsetting her so. Maybe she felt spoiled somehow because her brother was always showering her with gifts.

"...Uhm, Lord Ernest, I have a favor to ask."

"Well, that's unusual. It might even be a first. Go on, ask away." Ernest threw open his arms, as if to say, ask me anything, and it shall be yours!

"It isn't like that," Yuuri started, her jet-black eyes burning holes into him. Normally, getting her to be so forthcoming required a sacrifice of sorts, but that didn't seem to be what she wanted this time.

"Oh, I see. Too bad. ...Well, what is it then?"

"My brother gives me nice things, like these hair decorations. So I was wondering...what I could...give him in return? I have no idea...what boys like..."

Ernest had brought Yuuri the hair decorations from Simon last month. They were siblings, bound by blood, and yet they acted more like strangers than family.

Yuuri was merely asking him, if bashfully so, whether he would help her select a gift for her brother. It was a simple request. But Ernest felt a bit disappointed, perhaps because he too had given her gifts. The dress and jewelry Yuuri had worn to the dinner party last month, for one thing, were presents Ernest had bought specifically for her. He thought they might get in the way at her shop, so he kept them at his manor, but they were absolutely hers.

He was sure she must have known that, because of her small stature compared to the average Hylantian woman, he needed to have them custom-made specifically for her. He hadn't done so in anticipation of a reward, but now that Simon was getting one, he couldn't help but feel jealous.

"So you won't help me?"

"Of course I will! It will be like a date! But you know, Lord Simon will be jealous!"

Ernest was being honest with Yuuri, and yet it caused her face to cloud over. She shifted her gaze downward, staring resolutely at the table.

"...Hm?"

All that lay on the table were the camellia teacups. They featured the same flowers as Yuuri's *haori*, the ones he felt looked so perfect on her. The longer Ernest stared at the teacups, the stranger Yuuri seemed to act. He couldn't figure out why her face kept getting redder.

Huh? Have I done something wrong again?

Had she prepared these cups just for him, only for him to be completely oblivious?

"Stop grinning like that...like you know everything," Yuuri said in an almost whisper as he kept looking from Yuuri to the teacups and back again. He realized immediately he had been right.

"I'm not grinning like I know everything. Look again. I'm grinning like this because I'm genuinely happy."

"It doesn't look like that to me at all."

First, his king said he looked like unassuming noble and now the woman he loved was calling him a know-it-all.

"How strange..."

"What's strange?"

"Every morning, when I look at myself in the mirror, all I see is a good and honest man. ...But lately, I've been hearing the same things from my king as I have you. Tell me, what is it that displeases you about me, Miss Yuuri?"

"Your eyes, I suppose," Yuuri stated, not realizing her words landed like a cruel punchline. She was being serious.

Ernest could only hang his head in silent despair.

❦ ❦ ❦

THE sky was thick with clouds. In any other season, such weather would have depressed most people.

But this was at the height of summer and just about everyone was grateful for a break from the sun's blazing rays. Ernest and Yuuri were among those who welcomed the clouds.

Yuuri was different from most humans. But Ernest hoped that Yuuri, like her ancestors, could acknowledge her commonalities with humans in order to live among them.

Ernest grabbed his cane. Yuuri pulled on her hat, grabbed a parasol, and headed outside.

They made their way out of the narrow alley that led to Yuuri's shop and followed the street to the main thoroughfare, lined with bustling storefronts and restaurants. As they were just shopping for a gift for Simon, it seemed unnecessary to use a carriage.

"A gift for Simon, eh?"

Ernest knew the truth that if the gift was from Yuuri, Simon would love it no matter what it was.

Still, Ernest tried to give some thought to who Simon was. He was a collector of all things Hinomoto and the son and heir of a prominent trader. They could try to find something different from his usual inclinations, but it seemed better to stick with his interests.

When Yuuri went out, she never wore clothes from Hinomoto. On the other hand, Simon almost always wore his *hakama*. Since his features were more Hylantian, it seemed his clothes were a way of affirming his Eastern heritage and relationship with his younger sister.

"What about something that goes well with his *hakama*? Like a pocket watch or a bag...hmmm."

Ernest was deep in thought as Yuuri walked alongside him, smiling. Anytime he pointed out her smile, she stopped. So this time, he pretended not to notice, merely glancing over at her out of the corner of his eye.

"How about a hat? What sort of hats do people in Hinomoto wear?" Ernest asked, really just suggesting it because he had never seen Simon wearing one.

"A Hinomoto hat? I've heard Western-style hats are popular in Hinomoto right now." Eastern items were popular in the West, so it made sense that Western wear was also popular in the Far Eastern country of Hinomoto.

Ernest wasn't sure where to look for a hat that would go with Eastern clothes, but Yuuri seemed so taken with the suggestion that he felt it was the right way to go.

"So you're saying it wouldn't be weird to wear a hat with *hakama*?"

"Right."

"Perfect, I know just the shop! It's not far from here, so let's go!" He offered her his hand and, though she hesitated for a moment, she eventually accepted.

He was hoping the feeling that she was being more open around him wasn't just his imagination. Maybe it was because it had been over half a month since they had last seen each other.

🍎 🍎 🍎

IT was August according to the calendar, but the hat shop was already putting out its fall line of hats. The most popular women's hats were all subdued colors like olive or grape. The men's hats, however, didn't appear much different from season to season, though the fabric did shift from cotton to wool.

After just one lap around the shop, Yuuri picked up a hat with a tiny checked pattern.

"For daily use, would a hunting cap work?" she asked.

As these sorts of hats were traditionally worn when hunting, they weren't suitable for formalwear. But they were perfect for wearing about town, which seemed to be the same for Simon's *hakama*.

They didn't know Simon's hat size either, and since the hunting cap wasn't a tight fit, it was a safe choice. Ernest nodded and Yuuri gave him a shy smile. She hadn't been this genuine since they met. Ernest thought that perhaps he was finally earning her trust. Though it was a bit awkward that they were bonding over her buying a gift for another man.

"Were you this gung-ho when you picked out those camellia teacups?"

No sooner had the words left Ernest's lips than Yuuri narrowed her eyes on him. He knew his comment was unnecessary, but didn't realize how it had hurt her.

She might have seemed sour, but he took her silence to mean affirmation. She turned her back to Ernest, comparing several patterns of hats. In the end, she bought the first hat she had picked up and the two exited the shop.

"Looks like it might rain."

The clouds had thickened considerably since they left Yuuri's shop, and it looked like rain was soon to follow.

And indeed, soon after they started walking, rain began to fall, landing with a plop-plop on the pavement and leaving grey splashes in its wake.

Ernest took the hatbox from Yuuri and covered it with his jacket in the hopes of shielding it from the rain.

"We better hurry!"

He quickened his pace while still keeping an eye on her. The pair darted into a café that appeared to be transitioning into its lunch rush.

"Cold, isn't it? It'd be a shame for the gift to get soaked, so let's wait out the rain and have some lunch."

As they watched the sky from the café's large window, the clouds seemed to be sweeping through at a fast clip. After some time, the rain started to let up.

They leisurely enjoyed their sandwiches and washed them down with a coffee. By then, the rain had let up.

Afterward, Ernest escorted Yuuri back to her shop. As they were about to part, she grabbed his sleeve, as if she had something she was trying to figure out how to say.

"What is it?"

"Thank you for everything today...and, well, you will come see me again, won't you?"

This was the first time she had actually asked him to commit to another visit.

"Of course. But sorry, I'll probably be busy for the next month or so."

Yuuri nodded in understanding, but she seemed a little anxious to Ernest.

"If something happens, just come by my manor...all right?"

Yuuri had told him she needed blood at least once every three months. Up to now, he had been giving her his blood every month or two. And he knew there were times she would need it in between, such as when she caught a cold. But what would Yuuri do in such a situation without Ernest around?

"But—"

"You're a single woman living alone, so I can't exactly visit you in the middle of the night. But if you come to my manor, I can at least see you there after dark."

Ernest thought it best he not come over during the day. Now, if Yuuri weren't so skittish around him, if she really were ready, he would take their relationship to the next level in a heartbeat.

He thought meeting at night at his manor was the best compromise. His servants would be at the manor and able to vouch that he had conducted himself appropriately. But Yuuri couldn't read his thoughts, so she merely stood there silently bewildered.

"Miss Yuuri, remember, you promised me, all right?" Ernest said, leaving her with those words as he exited her shop.

But it was only a week before they saw each other again. And rather than Yuuri coming to the manor for his help, it was Ernest coming to seek the witch's expertise.

🦇 🦇 🦇

ERNEST had been to the gentlemen's club Marquis Groves was running twice since gaining permission to join. The gentlemen there, all united by similar interests, met twice a week and chatted the hours away amicably.

The men were diffused among the many rooms of the marquis' second home. Each room was adorned with a nameplate bearing the names of various flora and fauna. The largest of these rooms was the lounge known as the Rose Room. Billiards tables were held in the Butterfly Room. And the library was in the Oak Room.

Even though many of the members were there to relax and play cards or billiards, the club as a whole was much classier than Ernest expected.

Ernest finally chose a room with paintings that were from the East, though he couldn't be sure which country they were from. They were tall and made of a thin paper. The scenes depicting plants and animals were done in light colors. The first was a picture of barley swaying in the sun, the second depicted a long-legged bird, the third was a brown animal that looked similar to a mole, and the last was a flower reminiscent of a rose.

Ever since he met Yuuri, Ernest was having more and more opportunities to interact with Eastern culture. But artwork was still new to him.

"Welcome, Count Selden. How are you enjoying our club? I believe you'll find all the men here are of exceptional quality. I'm sure you'll have no trouble finding a conversational partner."

The plummy voice belonged to his host, Marquis Groves. He was plump and completely looked the part of an affable old man, but if there really was illegal gambling going on here, he was likely at its helm.

"Indeed, I have already had quite an illuminating discussion of the classics. You have my gratitude for inviting me to your soiree."

Ernest was a man of many interests, but had yet to focus on one in particular. Still, his focus today was not to stand out or give anyone reason to suspect him. He had picked topics of conversation in which he had at least a passing interest, but he wasn't here for intellectual competition. All he wanted was to wrap this case up and be done with it.

And now here he was, face to face with the man who held the key. He had to figure out whether or not it was pure coincidence that they were meeting like this.

After Rodrick told him he seemed like the type to do something illegal if it looked like fun, getting into the club had been easy.

Just bringing up gambling out of the blue would be dubious, so Ernest chose a different tactic: asking about the paintings.

"Are these paintings from the East?"

"Indeed. Which reminds me, there have been rumors circulating of a certain noble running around with an unmarried raven-haired woman."

Ernest had neither announced Yuuri as his partner nor attended very many social events. To the rest of the world, it was as if Yuuri had appeared at his side out of nowhere, and that was exactly the sort of rumor the members of high society loved. But Ernest had anticipated this.

"She is my lover. I hope to introduce her properly at a future event..." If his fears came to pass, that day might never come, but Ernest flashed him a convincing smile nonetheless.

"I take it you're also interested in books and paintings from the East as well, Count?"

"It is something I hope to explore further, but at this point, I'm little more than an amateur."

"And what of the Eastern girl? Perhaps she could teach you?" the Marquis asked, his eyes fixed on Ernest.

Ernest couldn't figure out why the Marquis would bring up a woman when they weren't allowed in the club. He must have an ulterior motive.

"My lover? She was born here in Hylant, so she isn't very well-versed in Eastern culture. She certainly couldn't keep pace with someone as knowledgeable about artwork as you are," Ernest said. The truth was, he didn't know how much Yuuri knew on the subject. At the very least, she was familiar with the items Watoh Company traded.

At any rate, the fact that the Marquis, who might very well be the leader of the illegal gambling ring, was interested in her concerned Ernest. It made him want to steer the conversation away as quickly as possible.

"I suppose that is understandable. Though such beauty is wasted on one with no interest in their own county's art and literature," the Marquis said, shifting his gaze to the paintings once more.

"Eastern artwork can easily be changed out to suit the season or occasion," he explained, pulling the attached cord. He then rolled the thin paper up into a tube.

"It's so different from Hylantian art."

"Indeed. Those exclusively familiar with Western art would deem these works barren and flimsy and overlook it, but it seems you are different, Count Selden."

The marquis seemed pleased with Ernest's reaction and he nodded to himself as he strode away. Ernest suspected he truly did love art as much as he said. And Ernest had had his first successful attempt at getting closer to the man behind everything.

After his conversation with the Marquis, he spent some time getting to know the other members before going home.

On his way home, he spotted Major Conquest, but carried on, pretending not to know him.

🐞 🐞 🐞

BEFORE retiring for the night, Ernest sat with a glass of wine, considering his next move.

"Mmm...what should I do? And then, there's that painting..."

Ernest had observed the marquis' shifting expressions the whole time. It was likely that the marquis had spoken to Ernest specifically because he had become aware of Ernest's interests in the East. But he seemed comforted upon learning that Ernest was not nearly as knowledgeable as he.

"I can't get Miss Yuuri involved..." he said, wishing nothing more than to end this annoying reconnaissance mission so he could go back to his carefree days of lounging around Yuuri's shop. "The problem is that it's a gentlemen's club. Ah well, I guess I should go ahead and ask her."

A week earlier, Ernest had told her to come find him if she needed anything, but it was he who was in need of her expertise. He would have to swallow his pride.

🐞 🐞 🐞

THE next morning, Ernest neglected his duties and headed for Yuuri's shop. He had been acting on the King's orders to investigate, so it wasn't as if he were skipping work and thus had nothing to feel guilty about.

Ernest threw open the door, prompting Yuuri to pop up off the couch and find herself eye to eye with him. She had been napping on the job again, certain no one would be dropping by. He suspected the reason someone as conscientious as her was always napping was because, like she had told him, the bright sunlight made her sleepy. Having superior night vision was usually characteristic of nocturnal creatures. Ernest suspected that Yuuri's ancestors were also creatures of the night.

"Hey! It's been about a week, hasn't it, my little witch?!"

"I-I th-thought you wouldn't be coming around for a while...!" she accused in a daze.

Ernest's shoulders drooped. He thought she would be happy to see him. "Yeah...I have something to ask you about."

"What might that be?" She checked her hair to make sure it wasn't messed up, likely remembering the first day they met. She cleared her throat then sat up, making room for him on the couch. He took his usual seat beside her.

"I'm on a secret mission right now, investigating an illegal gambling ring."

"Uhm, please don't tell me about your secret mission, I don't want to get caught up in anything dangerous."

This would be the second time she was being dragged into state secrets. This time, Ernest had prior permission, but Yuuri's face clearly showed her disdain.

"It's all right, you're already involved," Ernest said and then dove into an overview of everything that had happened up to that point.

"Those paintings stick out to me for some reason. Maybe they're some sort of password hint or hiding a hidden door or something? I feel like I've seen something similar offered by the Watoh Company. It's a painting on thin paper that can be rolled up and stored away."

"That's a hanging scroll. Both Hinomoto and Xingka have them."

Ernest had several sheets of paper on the table to show Yuuri. He had drawn pictures of what he had seen the night before at the marquis' second home.

"Are these supposed to be...a rough wave and a sunrise?"

"It's supposed to be the sun and a field of barley." Ernest's quick pen sketches weren't successful in replicating what he saw. After all, what Yuuri thought were waves was supposed to be barley dancing in the wind.

"And is that a dinosaur?"

"No, it's a bird! And this is the face of a mole peeking out from the grass."

Ernest was an even worse artist than he thought. He needed another way to get his point across.

"Lord Ernest, you're a terrible artist! Hehehe!" Yuuri laughed, unable to hold back any longer.

It was actually the first time he'd heard her laugh so openly.

"Why does that make you so happy?"

"I just think it's endearing to actually see you showing some weakness."

In other words, she needed to see he was human. He decided not to voice his discovery and let her enjoy the moment a little longer.

"So what do you think about these pictures? I tried to draw what I saw on the scrolls at the gentlemen's club. Do they mean anything to you?"

"I'm sorry, but I don't think Hinomoto has barley fields. I believe rice is far more common. And I've never seen any paintings of dinosaurs except in museums." Maybe she was just that amused by Ernest's art skills, but it was rare for her to do something as silly as keep calling the bird a dinosaur.

"Hey! I told you, it's not a dinosaur! It's a bird with a red head!"

"Bird with a red head? That's likely a crane. They're seen as good omens back east."

"All right, how about these flowers that look like roses?"

Yuuri stared at the pictures. "It seems like a chrysanthemum or something similar...but the shape of the flowers makes me think of peonies. Peonies are common on kimono. In fact, I think I have one. Wait a moment."

Yuuri disappeared off to the second floor and returned a moment later, carrying a *haori* he had seen her wearing back when the weather was colder.

"Ahh, that's it, that's it!" Ernest exclaimed, looking over the haori with large red flowers. The flowers looked exactly like the ones Ernest saw in the salon.

"Cranes and peonies are treasured motifs in Eastern art. So I can't really say if these pictures alone offer any obvious hints."

He couldn't say for sure if there was anything other than the peonies and the crane. And he could find nothing else of note in those two pictures.

"Miss Yuuri, would you be willing to have a look at the scrolls? I tried to draw them, but it seems that won't be sufficient."

"P-Pardon? Well, if it's just to have a look..."

"Yes, just have a look. You'd be all right with that, wouldn't you?"

The problem was how to get a woman into a gentlemen's club. Ernest looked Yuuri over from top to bottom.

"What is it?"

"Yes, I think this will work out just fine... I'll come for you at 2 o'clock, the day after tomorrow. I'll have everything you need then. All right?"

"All right."

There was a way after all. But if he told Yuuri what that was, he knew she would refuse. So for the time being, the deceitful count kept his plan to himself.

🦇 🦇 🦇

YUURI'S infuriated shrieks echoed all over the manor's guest room.

"You liar! You didn't say anything about this! I am an adult woman!"

Ernest stood just outside the door, trying to calm Yuuri's rage, or at the very least, prevent her from fleeing.

"It's all right. It'll look perfect on you. You'll be the cutest—nay, the best looking *boy* around! You really will be cute in that attire, I guarantee it."

"......"

"What a horrid thing to say to a lady! Your parents would be ashamed!"

This time it was Tarrah berating Ernest in Yuuri's stead.

If it were up to him, Ernest would have absolutely preferred Yuuri in a stunning dress. His desire for normalcy paled in comparison to hers.

"I...c-can't...breathe!"

"Miss Yuuri, please forgive me! Please bear with it a little longer!"

In order to make Yuuri look more like a boy, they needed to bind her breasts with cotton wraps and pad her height a bit. Just imagining what was happening on the other side of that door made the corners of Ernest's mouth twitch up.

"I bet you'll be the cutest page there is! Your master'll be pleased!"

Ernest opened the door in anticipation. Yuuri stood in her boy disguise, trembling in front of the mirror. The blouse trimmed with lace, the brass-buttoned vest, the culottes...and those long legs stretching out from beneath. Her hair had been plaited into a braid, with ribbon swaying from the ends.

"Miss Yuuri, you're so lovely. You're a convincing boy, from your head to your toes."

"You seem more excited about this than the dress you gave me," Yuuri intoned, her anger having subsided, leaving her eyes lifeless like a dead fish.

A page was a young servant tasked with assisting a nobleman and carrying their belongings. Many were expected to reflect the tastes of their lords, and so pages from foreign lands had become increasingly common.

Many of the members of the gentlemen's club brought their own attending pages and servants. Thus, Ernest thought this would be the best way to sneak Yuuri into the club.

The braid emulated a style he'd seen on an official from Xingka. Most Hylantians wouldn't be able to tell the difference between someone from Xingka and someone from Hinomoto anyway. At any rate, she looked the part of a page from the East.

"You deceived me," she hissed.

The problem now was that, girl or boy, Yuuri was no longer a child. She was a nineteen-year-old woman. It was only natural that she would be furious.

"Now, now, I did say I would have everything you needed. I didn't say anything about it being a dress. If that is your wish, then I can take you to all the fancy parties your heart desires!"

"What my heart desires is to go home!"

"Miss Yuuri, if you help me, we can finish this whole matter up right away. And I will reward you handsomely for your assistance!"

Yuuri couldn't hide her reaction when the word "reward" was brought up. After hesitating for a long moment, she found she could not avoid the temptation.

"Just this once, all right...?"

She decided this was her repentance for taking his blood.

But Ernest would have given her his blood without anything in trade. Their relationship had taken on a different shape from before. She liked their prior arrangement of witch and client though. It was simpler. So she willingly took on this foolish errand.

"I promise. Ah yes, and since you will be serving as my page, I will need you to refer to me as 'master,' got it?"

"M-M-Ma-Mas...te...?" she bit her tongue while trying to get the word out.

It was, after all, what Tarrah called Ernest. But coming from Yuuri, it sounded less like a servant and more like a subservient wife. Her face flushed scarlet.

"You can't make any mistakes when we're really there. So you'd better practice now."

"No! I'll say it when I have to."

Ernest and Tarrah then set to work teaching Yuuri the functions of a page.

With his deep connections to Watoh Company, no one would be suspicious of Ernest having a page from the East. And bringing along a new boy would be perceived as the result of previously failed pageships. Noblemen tended to swap out servants as much as clothes.

It was a good thing Yuuri didn't notice how much Ernest was enjoying having her tie his tie or put on his jacket like a new bride, or she might have fled.

🦇 🦇 🦇

"THIS way, Saizoh!"

Saizoh was Yuuri's fake name. They could have used her real name, as Yuuri was also a boy's name in Hylant, but there was a good chance that members of the gentlemen's club knew of her name. And if nothing else, they might find it in bad taste that Ernest employed a page with the same name as his lover.

Saizoh was Yuuri's great-grandfather's name. He had been the first head of Watoh Company, the one who had brought his family all the way from Hinomoto.

And yet, Ernest felt the name didn't fit her. To him, any name other than "Yuuri" felt unworthy.

"Yes, Master. How may I serve you?" she asked in boyish tones.

She was showing a great deal of bravery. As promised, she was fully committed to playing the part of a young boy now that they were here.

Many Westerners had little knowledge of common heights or features for people from the East, so they had no way of guessing Yuuri's true age or gender.

The pair made their way through the foyer and headed for the Rose Room, where the scrolls in question hung.

"There, Saizoh. Do you see? Are those not paintings from your homeland?" Ernest was unintentionally making a spectacle of himself. Of course anyone would recognize art that reminded them of their homeland.

"Wow! How lovely! Master, we call these hanging scrolls in my homeland!"

Yuuri was trying her best to play the part of an eager young page. She was adept at looking after Ernest and his belongings, but the rest was so clearly faked. Ernest sighed, hoping she would get the hint to tone down the chipper attitude.

"Oh, so you must know a lot about these, then! Tell me, what is that bird there?"

"Hehe, I haven't a clue, m'lord!"

"You don't? Hahaha!"

Yuuri tried to look like she was genuinely amused. The two of them quickly moved away from the scrolls before anyone became the wiser.

They mingled with the other members for a bit to avoid arousing suspicion before making their way to the Oak Room. This room housed the library, which included a great deal of books on artwork. It seemed their host had a great affinity for works of art. The pair wandered further in until they were out of earshot.

"Have they moved the scrolls?"

"Hey, not so close......!"

They couldn't risk being overheard, so Ernest thought it was obvious they would need to lean in close.

"We don't have much choice. Were you able to figure anything out?"

"Those pictures all share a similar motif: they're all images from Hinomoto playing cards called *hanafuda*. I used to play it all the time with my grandfather."

"*Hanafuda*, eh?"

That word had little meaning for a Hylantian like Ernest.

"Silver grass beneath the moon. A bush warbler by the sea. A sake cup and a chrysanthemum. And the peony with—wait. The one with the peony was the only one that wasn't right."

While the other images came in pairs, only the peony had been painted alone.

Marquis Groves had said it himself: in the East, scrolls were changed out to fit the season. Ernest believed that much was true. But if it was, why did he have the feeling the Marquis was still hiding something?

"So what about the mole and the bird that I saw?"

The Misfortune Devouring Witch is Actually a Vampire?!

"The crane is paired with the pine tree. The animal you called a mole was likely the boar with the clover. But isn't it strange? The bush warbler is meant to herald spring. It's out of season."

"I knew I could count on you, Miss Yuuri! We'll think about the rest later. For now, we need to kill some time here so it doesn't arouse suspicion when we leave."

For now, establishing the *hanafuda* connection, as well as the four matching prints and the two that were off was more than enough. They needed to leave the scrolls alone for now before anyone involved in the gambling ring started to catch on.

They returned to the Rose Room, and Yuuri left to fetch Ernest a drink. It was only then that he became aware of the eyes on her. Several pairs of them, in fact.

I shouldn't have brought her. I mean, it wasn't like I was trying to show her off, but still...

Her knowledge relating to the scrolls had been invaluable. But bringing her here had attracted a great deal of unwanted attention, and he regretted it. He lacked any sort of affection for young boys, so he hadn't noticed it earlier, but there were many unseemly stares in her direction. The looks on their faces filled Ernest with disgust.

Yuuri was stopped on her way back to him by someone as she balanced a tray with his glass on it.

"You there. Careful or you'll drop it. Here, allow me."

The man clearly had approached her with ill intent. Ernest knew that and yet he elected to watch the scene unfold instead.

Yuuri didn't only stand out when she wore the page's uniform. When she walked about town or even among high society, she always seemed to attract an abundance of attention. This sort of thing was bound to happen, and Yuuri needed to learn how to deal with it.

"Thank you for your concern, m'lord...but this is my job, so please, do not trouble yourself," Yuuri said calmly, giving a polite bow before attempting to pass.

"No need to be bashful. Give it here."

"Huh...?"

The man attempted to yank the tray out of Yuuri's hands. Caught off guard, she accidentally lost her grip on the tray and the glass toppled to the ground.

"What are you doing?! You're a servant! How dare you defy me!"

From how Ernest saw it, it was his fault.

Ernest never would have expected someone who had been admitted to an exclusive club acting so childish. For Yuuri, it was nigh incomprehensible. Unable to watch anymore, Ernest rose, attempting to come between them when—

"If you were trying to garner his affection, I'd say it was a genuine failure. And anyway, no man should be vying so for a child's affections."

A large, sturdy man managed to get there before Ernest did. It was Major Conquest, who had apparently infiltrated the club as well.

He dumped alcohol all over the man's head and then crushed the glass. The glass shattered with a smash and blood began to flow from Conquest's hand.

"Well? Have you cooled off now?"

"Hrk..."

One look from Conquest, his eyes pregnant with a silent rage, had the man quaking. Not only was Conquest a muscular military man, but the man had just watched him split his hand open crushing a glass barehanded with not a hint of pain.

Clearly outmatched, the rude nobleman turned and ran.

"Major, fancy meeting you here. You have my thanks for saving my page."

Even though he was undercover, Major Conquest had saved Yuuri. For the cool-headed workaholic Ernest knew him to be, this was indeed a surprise.

"Oh, Count Selden. If you're this boy's master, it's your responsibility to protect him from harm."

Saying he was just about to do so seemed unbecoming, so Ernest merely tried to laugh it off.

Ernest was suffering from his own poetic justice, as the part of the prince rescuing Yuuri was played by someone else while he rested on his laurels.

"Oh! Please let me treat your wound!"

Yuuri took Conquest's hand and stared at it.

"I'm rather thick-skinned, so it's not a major concern. See, it has almost stopped bleeding."

Any normal person would've needed stitches for such a wound, but as Major Conquest had insisted, his wounds had already begun to seal. Fortunately, it seemed as if the minor injury was almost healed.

"No, please let me have a look! You might have shards of glass in your hand."

Yuuri got water, a clean towel, and some tools and set to work treating his wounds. She really was an incredible witch.

"Yu—Saizoh is really skilled at rendering first aid. Ah yes, and Major Conquest, I'd like to do something to thank you for saving him. Please, come by my manor tomorrow, even if you cannot come until after work."

Ernest was attempting to pretend as if they had just met and that inviting him to his manor was a show of gratitude. If he wanted to tell the Major about the scrolls, it would be faster with Yuuri present. He could try to drag her to the palace, but he was positive she would shut down there.

"Very well. I am off tomorrow, so it will be in the morning."

"Shall we be off then, Saizoh?"

"Yes, Master. ...Major Conquest, thank you very much for your help."

Despite all the trouble, Yuuri had once again helped Ernest finish his task. As he thought about his promised reward, he led her out of the club.

❦ ❦ ❦

THEY were in the carriage, headed home.

Ernest thought back on the sight of Yuuri treating Major Conquest's bloody hand. Questions started to flood his mind.

Who knew she could handle treating wounds so easily?

From the first time Ernest had offered her his blood, to even the time when she had been sick, every time Yuuri caught sight of his fresh blood, her eyes flared with desire. It was as if she were intoxicated merely by the sight of his blood.

And yet, when she treated Major Conquest's injuries, she acted perfectly normal, without a hint suggesting that she was fighting back such powerful bloodlust.

As he turned the image of her drinking his blood over and over in his mind, a thought occurred to him. Maybe his blood had a special effect on her.

I'm sorry, Yuuri. This is all because I have a bad case of being mischievous when it comes to you...

Overcome with guilt, he bit the inside of his cheek. A metallic taste filled his mouth. He gazed over at Yuuri, who was likely steeped in her own thoughts.

She stared back at Ernest for some time and her eyes began to glaze over. Without realizing it, she reached out for him, before coming back to her senses and trembling in shock. She yanked back her outstretched hand and balled it into a fist on her lap.

Clearly struggling to calm herself, Yuuri looked everywhere except towards Ernest, from the curtains to her balled fists.

"Lord Er...nest...could we please open a window?"

"Why? You'd catch a cold from this chilly night air, so I'm afraid not."

He was being even more wicked than usual. He knew damn well why she wanted to open the window.

"Uhm...are you injured?"

"Hm? Oh, well, I just cut the inside of my cheek from all the shaking and swaying of the carriage. It's all right, it's not that big of a cut."

It was impossible to imagine anyone cutting themselves from the gentle motion of the count's carriage.

"Your cheek?"

"What's wrong? You don't look well."

Ernest pretended to not know what was wrong and sat next to her, trying to get a better look. Her breathing was ragged, as if she had just been running. And her eyes were dilated. In a way, it made her adorably pitiful.

"It's just...the blood..."

"Ah, I'm sorry Miss Yuuri, I didn't realize your ability to smell the blood of others was so strong."

He did realize it, but he decided to feign ignorance.

"I...have to get out! I can't...take the smell of blood any longer!"

Yuuri shoved Ernest away. It was a weak shove, likely because all of her strength was tied up trying to resist her baser instincts.

"You can have a taste. Come here."

Yuuri's body quaked in surprise. She was reaching her limits. Her quivering hand gently brushed his lips. Ernest, in turn, took her chin in his hand, trying to bring her face closer.

They were so close that either could feel the other breathe. Then, Yuuri took Ernest's hand in hers and—

"O-Ouch!" Ernest yelped.

Yuuri had bit the base of his thumb while he was distracted. Her will so eroded by the scent of blood, she made no attempt at being gentle.

"Yuuri...?"

Yuuri lapped up every drop of blood from his wound before it had a chance to spill. She glared up at him, tears welling in her eyes.

Had she figured out how he had tried to use her vampiric traits to bait her into a kiss?

Her angry eyes seemed to be saying, "this is all your fault!"

It was a painful lesson in not being so careless. But at least it reminded Ernest that being with Yuuri was never boring.

She gulped, clearing her throat, and her face became slack as she gazed lovingly up at Ernest.

He was food to Yuuri and he would do well not to forget it.

"Hey, how come you were okay looking at the Major's blood earlier?" Ernest asked, stroking her head and knowing that he wouldn't get an answer while she was feeding.

If something happens to me, then Yuuri will...

It was a realization that had been slowly creeping its way into his mind ever since the day he visited Yuuri's grandparents' graves. Yuuri's grandmother had followed her grandfather in death. Clearly, it was because she had lost her food source.

Ernest had intended to be Yuuri's prey, but somehow, it was the other way around. From the moment he allowed her to drink his blood, he took her life into his hands. He was her sole source of support.

"Oh, my little witch. This was all my foolishness. Please forgive me. I'll make it up to you. With something greater than flowers on a cloudy day or the starry skies. Perhaps we can pick up where we left off then?"

Stealing a kiss from the girl drunk on his blood was no fun. And kissing in the carriage with Yuuri still dressed as his page made it even less romantic.

Ernest lamented that he had such pride in being a gentleman. Yuuri had fallen silent for the most part. He knew if he did or said something she didn't like, she would let him know. But her silence gave him the freedom to reflect out loud.

"What do you think? Where shall we go?"

"Nowhere. I'm going to sleep. Good night."

Ernest wasn't sure at which point she had started paying attention to what he was saying, but her refusal was clear. She laid her head in Ernest's lap and closed her eyes.

She rejected Ernest so readily and then acted so sweet toward him. It was times like this that made him wonder just who was toying with whom.

"...That's too bad. Sweet dreams, Yuuri," Ernest said, trying out her name without the pretext of a title.

Yuuri gave no response and, soon after, the carriage filled with the sound of her snoring.

❦ ❦ ❦

YUURI showed up at breakfast the next morning wearing the summer dress Ernest had prepared for her.

It was a flowery dress with more frills than Yuuri was accustomed to. Ernest liked Yuuri in male attire, but in the end, he preferred to see her in something cute and girly. A silly grin stretched across his face as he internally applauded himself on his taste in clothes.

"Well, good morning there."

"Good morning. Why didn't you wake me up last night?"

"You seemed to be sleeping so peacefully. And you're light, so it was no problem. Still, you sure can sleep in, Miss Yuuri. You really are like a cat."

Yuuri had gone straight to bed the night before without supper and slept straight until morning. He had expected she would wake up hungry and so ordered his servants to make her a light snack, but Yuuri never touched her food.

"I was just tired from all of the excitement yesterday."

Yuuri refused to look at Ernest as she took a seat across from him. As she had missed dinner the night before, a large breakfast of pancakes topped with honey and apples had been prepared for her. The sweet smell enticed her appetite.

She dove into the pancakes like her usual self, cutting off big bites and shoving them into her mouth. As she did, her expression softened. Ernest could tell just how much she enjoyed the meal by looking at her face.

"Lord Ernest, is it really all right for you to skip work two days in a row?"

Her question didn't seem to be some thinly veiled jab or joke. She appeared genuinely concerned. So of course, Ernest was playful in his response.

"How rude, Miss Yuuri. Our toil yesterday was part of my job, as is my meeting today with Major Conquest."

Despite all the fuss, Ernest was taking his time, enjoying spending the morning with Yuuri. Thus her observations weren't completely unfounded.

🦇 🦇 🦇

MAJOR Conquest made his appearance at the appointed time, and not a moment sooner. When Ernest and Yuuri came to meet him in the parlor, he couldn't take his eyes off of her. He was shocked at his own shamelessness. Perhaps anyone might do the same, after seeing the face of a boy they had saved the day before on a girl.

"Thank you for everything yesterday. How are your injuries?"

Yuuri seemed oblivious to his shock, only worried about his injuries.

"...Count Selden?"

"Yes?"

"Now you're dressing your page in women's clothing? You're despicable!"

Yuuri finally figured out why Major Conquest seemed so uncomfortable: he still thought Yuuri was a boy.

"Oh, no. I'm not a boy. I had to wear that disguise because, as a woman, I wouldn't be admitted. This is what I normally look like, more or less."

"That's right. Her name is Yuuri Watoh. I thought you might have figured out that she was working with me."

Despite his misgivings, Conquest had not conducted the requisite background check on Ernest because the King held him in such high regard, and who was he to second guess the king?

"So you are Yuuri Watoh? Please forgive the misunderstanding."

Yuuri accepted his apology with a gentle smile.

"I'd like you to rescind your false allegations. I am not despicable."

"Count Selden, allow me to say this."

"What?"

"Forcing a woman to dress in boys' clothes is just as despicable, just as much a perversion, as forcing a boy to dress as a woman. How is it you do not understand this?"

Ernest thought that the major was every bit the boring man he suspected him to be. The two were unlikely to ever become friends. But he was well aware of just how awful what he had done was, so he wasn't angry with the major for pointing it out. Being despicable was still much better than being a bore.

"You're so harsh, Major. At least I chose clothes that looked good on her, right? And it was only because she was with me that I managed to find a clue."

"A clue?"

"Miss Yuuri, please explain these to the Major."

Ernest pulled out a set of *hanafuda* cards, the same sort he hadn't even heard of until yesterday. Yuuri's mouth fell open in shock.

"Wh-Where did you get those?"

"While you were asleep, I asked Simon to help me procure a set. I told him the game looked fun and he was all too happy to help. He has everything, doesn't he?"

"What a relief."

When Yuuri said "What a relief," what she really meant to say was, "What a relief that you didn't break into my shop and steal mine."

Ernest had his own magical tool for getting into Yuuri's shop. So he couldn't really complain. It was, after all, something he felt rather guilty about.

Yuuri laid the cards out on the table.

"There are four cards for each of the twelve months. Everyone has a different play style, but in general, these are the cards with the highest value."

The card with the highest value for January was the card depicting the pine tree and the crane. The second card depicted a thin sort of paper known as a *tanzaku*, on which poems or wishes might be written. The remaining two January cards had pine trees on them. The more simplistic the design on the card, the less points it was worth.

"Ohh. So the picture I thought was the sun and a field of barley was actually the August pampas grass card. It's perfect for this time of year, right?"

"The crane and the boar are January and July, and those are February and September."

"Could it mean the 17th and the 29th? In other words, those are the days of the month they gamble. The 17th has already passed this month, so maybe they were shifted to suggest the 29th instead."

Conquest had no idea about *hanafuda*, but with the cards as visual aids, he was finally beginning to understand. The first scroll was to indicate the month, the second and third represented the date. As long as one knew what the cards indicated, it was actually a fairly clever password.

"That's actually deceptively simple."

Many things from the East had ballooned in popularity, but *hanafuda* was still relatively obscure.

There were already so many ways to play with Hylantian playing cards that few people probably had the desire to learn a whole new game on a separate deck.

In the end, it was a unique way to display the information for those who knew what to look for. And it was befitting a man who loved art as much as Marquis Groves did. All he would have to do is tell those he wanted to include how to decode the dates.

"The only question that remains is the fourth scroll, that lone peony..."

Ernest turned the idea over in his head. The only thing on that scroll was the peony. What meaning was hidden within that image? June was the month of the peony.

If he stuck with the rules they had already decoded, then it must denote time. It was highly unlikely they would meet at 6 in the morning, so it had to be 6 at night. But there must be some reason why the butterfly didn't appear in the image.

"The one with the peony is the only one that doesn't make sense. It's all by itself. ...Where could the butterfly be?"

As Yuuri spoke, something finally clicked in Ernest's mind. The plates that hung alongside each room in the gentlemen's club! What was written there...?

"That's it. The butterfly flew away."

The billiards room in the marquis' second residence was called the "Butterfly" Room. That's where they were meeting.

And that was the end of Ernest's part in the investigation. Now that they knew when and where the illegal gambling would be taking place, the military police could handle the rest.

"I knew you would be able to help, my little witch!" Ernest patted Yuuri's head.

Part of it was that he wanted to praise her for her part in solving the mystery. But he also wanted to show off the special bond he felt they had. Of course he knew Conquest had no romantic interest in her. But still, he wanted to show that she was his, through and through.

"Please stop that! M-My part's over now, right? ...I would like to go home!" The scarlet-faced witch demanded, dodging Ernest's hand. She looked like she was ready to run out the door, so he grabbed on to her.

"Wait! I'll take you home!"

"Count Selden, I'd like to meet with you regarding our next steps."

"Next steps? But my part is over. I leave the rest to you, Major Conquest. The physical side of things is outside my realm of expertise."

"What do you mean? We need you to infiltrate and learn who else might be involved. That was your task, was it not? This is where the important work begins."

In other words, even if the military police raided the next meeting of the illegal gambling ring, they would only be able to take down those who were present. That was why the Major wanted Ernest to continue his infiltration and gain further intelligence.

"Seriously...?"

No matter how long Conquest spent in the gentlemen's club, he was unlikely to be invited into the illegal gambling ring. That's why he had no choice but to have Ernest continue investigating.

"I'll just be going then. Please excuse me, Major Conquest, Lord Ernest."

"I appreciate your help."

Yuuri gave a light bow before exiting the room.

Even knowing what the scrolls meant, it would be unnatural for

Ernest to just show up to the gambling game without being invited. But if he didn't see it through, then putting Yuuri in all that danger would be for naught.

Knowing he would be away once more, Ernest was glad he had given Yuuri her reward.

It would be another month before Ernest's life returned to normal.

Interlude: The Bond Between Brother and Sister

FOUR days after Ernest helped her pick out a gift for Simon, Yuuri paid a visit to the Watoh Company's main headquarters. She was there to deliver her herbal tea mixes and see Simon.

Simon was a gentle, kind man who cared greatly for his younger sister. He had some quirks, but they only helped define who he was. Yuuri understood that, but she still avoided spending time alone with him.

Thanks to Ernest's encouragement, though, she had come in hopes of repairing their broken relationship.

"Yuuri!"

Simon charged in as Yuuri was speaking with one of the employees. He was wearing *hakama* as usual, but this time, they appeared to be made from hemp. He was over the moon that Yuuri had asked him to meet for once.

"Hello, Simon," Yuuri said, dodging his embrace.

"I've made reservations for us. You are planning to stay for lunch, aren't you?" Simon suggested as soon as the employee walked away.

"Yes."

The last time she had come, she had rejected his dinner invitation outright. Today she intended to make that right.

"We're going to a Xingkaese restaurant. It's one I frequent, so I can assure you the food is delicious."

As Hylant was a coveted trading partner of many nations, there were plenty of restaurants operated by people from Xingka and some of the southern nations. And several had even popped up around the Watoh Company's main headquarters. Yuuri suspected her brother had picked a Xingkaese restaurant out of respect for her, so she wouldn't have to worry about standing out.

"Here, Simon, this is for you. To say thank you."

Yuuri decided to give her brother his gift. It was still a little early for lunch and the hatbox was too heavy to carry around.

"For me?"

"It's to thank you for the hair accessories you gave me."

Simon stared at her and, upon realizing she had her hair pulled back in the very same accessories he'd bought for her, threw both arms out and charged toward her.

"Yuuri—!"

Not wanting to suffer the guilt of avoiding him again, Yuuri accepted his very public display of affection. She didn't think it was appropriate for two adult siblings, but it seemed necessary if they were to repair all the years of discord between them.

The Misfortune Devouring Witch is Actually a Vampire?!

"I can't breathe!" Yuuri cried out, afraid if she didn't say something, he would never let her go. Spurred by a mix of embarrassment and pain, she pushed him away.

"Ohh, I'm so sorry."

"Go ahead and open my gift," she said, handing him the box.

Simon delicately untied the ribbon and opened the box, lifting out the item inside. "...Oh, a hat!"

The hunting cap she and Ernest had picked out the other day had a tiny check pattern, one that looked like it would suit Simon perfectly. Though the warm knit cap was out of place with the lightweight white jacket and indigo *hakama* he currently wore.

"It's supposed to be an autumn hat, so I guess it's a bit out of season," Yuuri pointed out, but Simon kept the cap on.

"No, this is great! Did you pick this out for me, Yuuri?"

"...Uh, well..."

".....

"Yes, I picked it out," Yuuri replied, selecting her words very carefully. Ernest had been the one to suggest a hat as a gift, but it was indeed Yuuri who chose the type and the pattern.

She wanted to buy it for him as a way of saying thanks. And yet, her face was guilt-ridden.

"Or was it that count who picked it out?" Simon asked, his previously sunny expression suddenly clouding over.

"Er—I mean, the count gave his input, but I was the one who picked out the pattern!"

"Oh, uh, I'm sorry, I'm not blaming you. I know I should keep my nose out of your relationships."

"Not at all. I know you're simply concerned about me."

Yuuri had told neither her father nor Simon about the true extent of her relationship with Ernest—namely the fact that she had drank his blood. Simon had figured out that Ernest was a frequent visitor, though, so it was entirely possible that he had an inkling about why that was.

It was a matter of life and death, so Yuuri knew she should bring it up eventually. But she was so estranged from her father and brother that she wasn't even sure how to broach the topic.

The impulse to drink someone's blood hadn't appeared right away when she became an adult. But once it did, it made her realize that she truly was a wholly different being from her father and Simon. It wasn't exactly something she wanted to talk to anyone about.

"Shall we be going?" Simon's eyes reflected a boundless kindness. But gazing into those eyes rekindled a colder gaze in the back of Yuuri's mind, and so she averted her eyes.

Still she believed that she could change, little by little, with Simon's help. She took his hand and off the siblings went.

Chapter 5: Summer Flower Forecast

DURING the period in which Ernest was otherwise occupied, Yuuri received a letter. More accurately, the letter was actually addressed to her deceased grandparents, Leon and Hana.

"Walt Aldridge? ...Of the Aldridge family?"

The Aldridges were merchants, just like the Watohs. They went back at least as far as Yuuri's great-grandfather.

So they should have been aware of her grandparents' passing. She couldn't figure out why they would be sending a letter to them now.

At a loss, Yuuri broke the seal and read the letter.

> *My dearest Leon and Hana,*
> *The cotton roses have begun to bloom in our garden once more. We hope you will bring that granddaughter of yours and pay us a visit.*

Those two sentences brought back a flurry of memories of being at the Aldridges' home.

The man who had sent the letter, Walt Aldridge, was an elderly gentleman who was a few years older than her grandparents. Yuuri could see him clearly in her mind, inviting her into the garden he mentioned and offering her sweets.

She had called him "Grampa Aldridge".

"The cotton rose...Grandmother's favorite... The flower she used to say looked just like me."

Going by what she remembered, it was not Walt, but his son, the current head of the family, who had attended her grandparents' funeral. Walt himself was too frail by then to attend. But if old age had robbed him of the ability to remember her grandparents were dead, should she really correct him?

Yuuri grew tired of turning the question over in her mind and decided she would ask Simon what he thought. Perhaps he or their father could reach out to the Aldridge family.

❦ ❦ ❦

SEVERAL days later, Yuuri and Simon paid the Aldridges a visit. Walt Aldridge was almost completely bedridden, but he had insisted on seeing the granddaughter of his dear old friends, and so his son Tracey had arranged for them to visit. His son said his mind had deteriorated so much that he had forgotten ever sending the letter.

"Yesterday he was completely aware that Master Leon and Miss Hana had passed. He still insisted on seeing you, Yuuri. ...I suppose time comes for all of us. He even treats his own family with suspicion, so I ask you to forgive him for anything he says that is less than kind," Tracey explained with a smile.

Depending on how Walt was feeling, some days he even forgot his own son's face.

"This morning, when I told him you were coming by, he insisted on getting out of bed and waiting in the sunroom. I told him you wouldn't be here for hours, but he wouldn't listen."

Tracey finally escorted them to the sunroom. The southern-facing wall was entirely glass, but it was covered with lace curtains. Thus, the light that filled the room was still gentle enough that even Yuuri's eyes could handle it. A man in a wheelchair sat next to a table, a wide grin stretched across his face. He was thinner and more wrinkled than she remembered.

"Grampa Aldridge, it's been so long…"

"Miss Hana! What good fortune that today is a cloudy day! I know how you hate bright light."

"Grampa?"

It took every ounce of strength Walt had to push himself up from his wheelchair. He swayed as he tried to stand. Yuuri and Simon rushed over to him, hastening to support him.

Seeing Hana—or rather, Yuuri—at his side put Walt's mind at ease and he slowly returned to his seat, gazing up at the young woman.

"Miss Hana, you're as lovely as ever."

Yuuri's grandparents brought her over often as a child, so Walt should have still had memories of an aging Hana together with her granddaughter. However, the image of her grandmother in her younger days likely held a larger place in the man's heart. Yuuri smiled awkwardly, not wanting to upset him.

"Father, this is not Miss Hana, but her granddaughter, Yuuri," Tracey corrected his father, unable to let him continue offending the lady.

Walt blinked several times, tilted his head, and then looked at his son, then to Yuuri, and back again.

"…Ah yes, that's right. Miss Hana and Leon are gone. I'm terribly sorry. I can't seem to remember anything anymore. You are indeed Yuuri and…Saizoh, was it?"

"I'm Simon, Master Walt. Saizoh was our great-grandfather's name."

"Simon, is it? You resemble a young Leon in a way. I can see it in your eyebrows. Can't you?"

Simon was always told he looked like his mother. Still, he had inherited some traits from his father's side of the family.

Walt's eyes were gentle as he talked about how Simon looked like Leon.

"Master Walt, were you close to our grandfather?"

Both Yuuri and Simon were certain that the one Walt was close to was their grandmother. After all, their grandfather had been a gardener, an unlikely friend for the son of a noble family like the Aldridges.

"Yes, of course. When I was nineteen, I worked and lived with the Watohs. However, my brother passed away and I was forced to return home, but still, we spent many afternoons puttering about the garden, just the three of us."

On Walt's command, Tracey opened the large glass windows in the sunroom. Just beyond them was a slope that led down into the garden. Yuuri was certain the lace curtains being drawn on a cloudy day was out of consideration for her. She wasn't sure how much Walt knew of her condition, but it was clear he had some knowledge.

"Shall I assist you out, Master Walt?" Simon asked, already making his way behind the chair and slowly starting to push Walt.

"Do you need a parasol?" Walt asked her.

"No, I'm all right. The sun's not nearly as bright today."

Yuuri walked alongside Simon as he pushed the wheelchair. Walt guided them to the same garden where the cotton roses from his letter were in bloom. The flowers were pink or white on the outside, and deep scarlet in the center. Many of the myriad of blooms were larger than Yuuri's palms.

The wheelchair moved along at an even pace, its wheels clattering against the stone walkway.

"Ahh, this takes me back. The scent of the soil and the grass. Oh, seeing you two makes me feel young again. I remember how Miss Hana and Leon would quarrel over every little thing... Since I was older, they never quarreled with me. I enjoyed watching them carry on."

"Grandmother and Grandfather did? That's hard to imagine. They always got on so well."

This man clearly knew a side of their grandparents that Yuuri and Simon had never seen. In Yuuri's memories, the married couple never fought. They had always been so close and loving, but it sounded like things were different when they were younger.

"The two of them fought because they were so close. As the adult, I could only watch over them. I cared deeply for both of them, even after they eloped..."

"Eloped? Our grandparents eloped?"

"This is the first I've heard of such a thing."

As much of a shock as it was for Simon, it was an even bigger shock for Yuuri, who had lived with them for so long.

"They never told you? Well, perhaps 'eloped' was too strong a word. After all, Leon was ultimately granted the Watoh name." Walt extended a hand and gently stroked a pink cotton rose. "I was an adult at the time, and more like a guardian than a potential rival for Miss Hana's affections..."

"...A rival?"

"As I've gotten on in years, I wonder what life would have been like if I'd gone down a different path. Would I have a happy family with her? Those feelings have never waned. But I suppose it's all right to dream, don't you think? There's so much I wish I could ask Miss Hana."

"That you wanted to ask my grandmother?"

Walt nodded sadly. No matter how badly he wanted an answer nor how Yuuri might try to give it to him, only her grandmother could truly give him what he sought.

Still the elderly gentleman gazed wistfully at the pink cotton roses in wont of an answer.

🍎 🍎 🍎

HANA arrived in Hylant from Hinomoto when she was seven. Her father was a trader and her mother a doctor specializing in herbal medicine.

Hana's father bought Xingkaese medicine to sell in Hinomoto, and her parents were brought together through their work.

When her father finally decided to expand his trading operation westward, beyond Hinomoto and Xingka, to a land called Hylant, Hana had no idea what lay ahead.

Their first year in Hylant, the family rented a home down by the pier. By their third year, they had amassed enough wealth to establish a manor in the city's wealthiest residential district. Ever since she could remember, Hana's parents were always busy, but she believed they did it all out of love for her. Once they moved into that enormous mansion, her parents became even more distant.

The mansion was so big, she could rarely tell when one of her parents came home from work. The lessons once given to her by her mother were now handled by a private tutor.

Though their life had become more luxurious, it also felt lonelier somehow. The house might have changed, but those feelings of loneliness remained. Hana wondered when, if ever, she would grow accustomed to their new home.

Hana found herself pondering that very question one early morning when she was ten, as she strolled through their beautiful garden. Both she and her father were the descendants of pureblood vampires. While bright sunlight didn't bring them to their knees in pain, it was uncomfortable for them.

Adults could push through such things if they had to, but as a child,

Hana was less inclined to do so. When she did go for walks, it was on cloudy days or in the evenings.

After about three days in the mansion, she remembered where just about everything was. But she couldn't seem to remember the faces or names of the people who worked there.

That day, she came across a boy around the same age as her. His hair and eyes reminded her of cinnamon, and the sharp angle of his eyebrows left the deepest impression on her. He wore an old shirt made out of hemp. It was a bit big on him, so the sleeves were rolled up multiple times. The vest and pants had been patched numerous times and were no better a fit than the shirt.

From the looks of his clothes and the fact that he was picking up leaves, Hana guessed he must be some sort of servant.

"Who are you?" Hana asked, happy to finally meet someone her age around the manor.

"Whoa!"

The boy had been so invested in his work, that he hadn't even noticed Hana until she called out to him. The shock caused him to fall back on his bottom.

But it wasn't the shock of her calling out to him. It was her appearance.

Her hair and eyes were an ebony that was exceedingly rare in this country. Her skin and the height of her nose made her look completely different from any Hylantian girl he had ever seen.

"Ah, I'm so sorry. I was just working here in the garden. Are ya the mistress of this manor?"

The boy was still clumsy with formal speech. Even Hana had a better handle on it than he did. Hana spoke less like someone born abroad and more like someone from a local region with a thick accent.

"I'm Hana Watoh. Nice to meet you. How old are you? What's your name?"

"I'm Leon. I'm, uh…twelve." The boy stood up, dusted the dirt and leaves off his pants, and introduced himself.

"Twelve? You're only twelve and you have a job?"

It was Hana's turn to be surprised. She couldn't fathom why someone so close in age to her would have to work. Even when they lived near the docks, her family had been wealthy enough to own a house nicer than most.

"Ah, yah, I got a job—I mean, yes miss, I am working. I apprentice under the master gardener here, so I can learn the trade."

"Okay, well, since I startled you, I'll give you a hand!"

"Huh? N-No, that's okay! It's my job, after all!"

"Why not? You'll get it done faster. Come on, I want to help!"

To the young Hana, someone offering to lend a hand was always a generous thing. She still had no sense of differences in social status or class.

"It's fine. I'm all right…but thank you."

"Aw, but I wanna help. Why can't I?"

"Because it's me job! If I let ya help, yer hands and clothes'll get all dirty and they'll yell at me!"

The more insistent Hana was, the more annoyed Leon became. He was so upset, his speech was lapsing back into an unrefined drawl.

"Hey! Leon! Why're you bothering the young lady of the manor? You can forget about lunch!"

A deep voice boomed through the garden. It was the master gardener, Leon's boss.

Hana looked around and saw the large man charging toward them. He was even larger than the seafaring men Hana had come to Hylant with, his grey hair accenting his sunburnt skin. He was tall, even for the comparably tall Hylantian people, and his size frightened her.

He was a boisterous, imposing man. Terrified, Hana hid behind Leon.

"I'm the one he's mad at though," Leon muttered in a voice soft enough so his boss wouldn't hear. Still, Hana was afraid, and clung to his back, squeezing her eyes shut.

"Boss, the young lady is afraid. Can't you see? Please stop."

"Hahaha, I'm so sorry about that, young miss." He roared with laughter and any hint of being angry with either of them seemed to disappear.

His body and voice might be loud, but it seemed that he was a good person on the inside. Hana finally peeked out from behind Leon's back.

"Uhm, I'm so sorry. Leon didn't do anything wrong, so please don't yell at him."

"He didn't, eh? Leon, you're lucky the young lady of the house is so generous!"

He was a good man. But he was so imposing, Hana found him too intimidating to talk to for long.

Hana still didn't understand the position she held, that she was actually the one with the most authority among them.

The master gardener tousled Leon's hair. It appeared to Hana to be a gesture of affection or even platonic love. Leon looked sullen, though he might have just been embarrassed.

"Miss Hana, there you are! Your breakfast is ready!" A familiar voice called from the manor. It was Walt, her father's personal assistant.

His suit was neatly pressed and his tie perfectly secured in place. Hana had never seen even a strand of his honey-colored hair out of place. Though he was a cool-headed, logical man, he bad always been kind to Hana, like an older brother.

He was only twenty. Hana had heard from her father that he was the second son of a company the Watohs did business with and so was training under him. Even though he had plenty of his own work to do, he often doted on Hana.

"Good morning, Walt. Is it breakfast time already?"

"Yes, your parents are waiting for you."

Hana silently accepted Walt's outstretched hand. Despite the fact that Hana was only a child, he always treated her like a lady.

"That's right!" Hana exclaimed, realizing as they turned to head back to the mansion that she hadn't said goodbye to the master gardener and his apprentice. "...Leon, Sir, I'm sorry about earlier. See you both later!"

Hana gave a vigorous wave as she made her way to the mansion, and the pair bowed as she passed.

"Did something happen?"

"Uhm, well, I was so excited to find someone else my age here, I asked if I could help, but he got upset with me."

The master gardener had yelled at Leon, who in turn had gotten angry at Hana, but she still didn't understand why he was so reluctant to have her help. She told Walt all about what had happened, hoping he could help her understand.

"Haha, so that's what happened? Miss Hana, do you know why he got upset with you?"

Hana shook her head several times.

"Leon said tending the yard was his job. But I don't understand why he wouldn't want me to help him. I thought if I did, it would make him happy because he could finish faster."

"But it is his job. It's how he earns his keep. And you, Miss Hana, are actually on the same level as his employers."

"So I shouldn't take away someone else's job?"

"Well, that's not always the case. For someone in a similar position as he, such as a servant, I think it would be all right for them to help."

"…But, how is that any different?"

Hana still didn't understand what Walt was trying to tell her.

"When that boy gets overly busy, other servants may choose to help him. And then, when someone else needs help with their work, he might return the favor. As long as both helper and helpee are on the same level, then it's beneficial."

"But I don't…really have anyone on my level I can help."

When her family had lived by the pier, Hana often played with the other children in her neighborhood. And though some children teased and bullied her for her appearance, those days still left her with many happy memories.

But ever since moving into this large mansion, her opportunities to leave the property had greatly diminished. Occasionally, she would play with the children of her father's clients, but as each of them was of a higher social standing, she was forced to show restraint.

"Are you lonely?"

"…Yes. Just a little."

During her conversation with Walt, Hana figured out what was causing her confusion.

Hana wanted a friend close to her age. She wanted to befriend Leon, but they weren't of the same social standing, and so she felt lonely once more.

"But I haven't done anything…so how come I'm better than Leon?"

That was the most difficult thing for Hana to understand. By interrupting Leon's work, she had been selfish. He was the respectable one; she was merely a useless child. She had been given everything by her parents, with nothing to offer in return.

"You really are something, Miss Hana."

Her parents, Walt, Leon—everyone here was working hard. Only

Hana, special little princess that she was, lacked something to contribute. And meeting Leon was the first time she had ever realized that.

❦ ❦ ❦

"...I'M going to plant a medicinal herb garden. So please help me, Leon! My mother thought gardening would be good for me and said you can be my...uhm...assistant?"

Hana was certainly assertive. They were only seeing each other for the second time and she had gone through the trouble of inventing a way for them to spend time together without anyone getting into trouble.

She was wearing a plain sundress, a work apron, and a straw hat. And she had all the tools they would need with her.

"Yes, mistress," Leon said, nodding, though he looked dissatisfied. Having to look after the young mistress of the house was one thing, but now he was going to miss out on learning pruning from his boss.

Discovering Leon was already working at age twelve set something off within Hana. She wanted to be known for something other than her parents' wealth and accomplishments. And now those feelings had only grown stronger. When she sat down and thought about who and what she wanted to be when she grew up, she realized she wanted to be a doctor, like her mother. But now her mother was using her knowledge to support her father's trading business. So Hana thought if she could succeed her mother, she could pick up the slack and become a doctor in her own right.

A child's mind made everything so simple, but Hana was especially sheltered. She didn't exactly have any steadfast convictions spurring her to succeed her mother. This was common in sheltered children, often pressed to choose their future from a narrow set of choices placed before them.

Hana was taking the same path as her mother. Her parents were overjoyed upon hearing this. While her mother taught her all about Eastern medicine, Hana studied Xingkaese under a tutor. Hinomotoese medicine was derived from Xingkaese medicine, so learning the language was a necessity.

Immediately after beginning her medical studies, one of Hana's first practical tasks was to grow medicinal herbs. While it was important for her studies, the main motive was to give her someone her own age to talk to. Walt had hinted at Hana's worries and loneliness to her parents. And so it came to pass that Leon became Hana's assistant.

For that first day, Walt, who had plenty of his own work to do, found himself with his sleeves rolled up and in his high boots, attending to Hana. The sight of the man, who was almost always in crisp suits, holding a spade seemed so uncanny, it made her giggle. Walt was so kind, even though he had his own adult matters to attend to; it made Hana wish he really was her brother.

Leon, on the other hand, looked like he had been sucking on a lemon. He found the prospect of babysitting some princess two years his junior annoying. But he of all people should have been grateful to have a girl his age to talk to. For that precious time each day when he helped her tend the herb garden, he didn't have to worry about his social standing.

Which, ironically, was why he could get away with having a sour look on his face.

"Don't worry! I can't handle the midday sun and my tutor comes every afternoon, so I'm not going to keep you here all day. Right, Walt?" Hana said, trying to illicit Walt's agreement to ease the pout on Leon's face.

"Indeed. We're counting on you to watch over the garden when we're attending to other matters, Leon."

"Fine, fine. I just think the lady of the house here is going to get bored and give up tending the garden eventually."

"It's not about whether it's boring or not. This is for my future dream. I want to help out around the manor so I can be a doctor like Mother!"

"Mm-hmm…"

Their first step was to till the flower bed and ready it for planting. For Hana, her time with a peer like Leon was precious. Between growing closer to Leon and getting adjusted to her new life, her loneliness began to fade.

She loved the time she spent with her new friend and the young man who was like a brother more than anything else.

BUT after several months, the herb garden hadn't grown anywhere near what they had hoped.

The books that held all the information on different seedlings and their characteristics were in Xingkaese. But even after Hana deciphered the books and readied the soil, Xingka and Hylant had different climates, as well as different diseases and insects that gardeners needed to worry about.

The garden was, after all, started by a child, so it should have surprised no one that many of the seeds failed to sprout, young buds withered away, and almost all the plants turned brown and perished.

"The only herb that's actually growing is the chamomile," Leon moaned early one morning. As a gardener himself, the fact that a garden he was helping out with was in such dire straits was discouraging.

Seeing him complain one second and work his heart out the next brought smiles to Hana and Walt's faces.

Little white and yellow flowers had begun sprouting in the flowerbed. Chamomile was a versatile medicinal herb that could be grown in the west or east, so it was the one herb that Leon knew how to grow properly.

Hana leaned close to one of those flowers that she had so painstakingly grown and inhaled its aroma. The books all likened the scent of chamomile to apples. A fresh, sweet aroma tickled her nostrils.

"It's all right. It's not a total loss."

They had cultivated the garden based on what the books said, but still, most had not bloomed. Essentially, they would need to select seeds that were better suited to Hylant's climate and soil. Hana reassured herself that this was all part of trial and error.

"Leon, Walt, did you know that in Hinomoto, my name actually means 'flower'?" Hana said as she gazed at the chamomile.

"What a lovely name."

"Wow. That's a pretty weird name. So that's what it means, eh?"

As an adult, Walt was always gentle with how he spoke to Hana. Then there was Leon, who was always anything but. Her name did sound strange when compared to the names of most girls from Hylant.

But he didn't have to go and say it out loud.

Hana puffed out her cheeks. "Meanie! Why do you always say things like that?!"

Leon merely laughed at Hana's anger. Maybe he was mean, but she loved seeing his bright smile. In a way, it was how he related to her.

"What flowers do you like, Miss Hana? I'll be traveling to Xingka with Lord Saizoh in the near future, so I would be happy to buy you some seeds," Walt offered.

"Really? Hmm, let's see, my favorite Eastern flowers...would be cherry blossoms, peonies, and chrysanthemums... They're all beautiful, and I'd love for you both to see them..."

Sitting in the garden reminded Hana of her life back in Hinomoto. They had lived near a lake and, in the spring, cherry blossom petals would flutter down to dance along the water's surface. She also loved the large blooms of chrysanthemums and peonies.

And the thing she remembered most of all was—

"Oh, yes! Cotton roses, too!"

"Why cotton roses?"

"Because they bloom in summer. I hate summer. But if I have something to look forward to out in the garden, then maybe it'll make me want to go outside, right? They have huge blooms, so big I could even see them from my window."

The next day, Walt and Saizoh set out by boat for Xingka.

And two months later, just as he promised, Walt sent Hana some cotton rose seeds.

❦ ❦ ❦

LEON and Hana took good care of the little seedlings Walt had sent over. The two of them often got into arguments. Even so, they would forget whatever it was they had been arguing about by the next morning and go back to tending the garden as usual. The days flowed into one another.

The garden that had been a dry patch of brown was now bursting with green. Two cotton roses stretched across the flower bed, three times the size they had been when they had been planted.

"They're still small, but I think those are buds, don't you?"

"Yes, definitely. Glad we didn't fudge it up again."

"It's because of all your hard work, Leon. If you become our gardener, you won't just be knowledgeable about Hylantian plants, but plants from the East, too!"

Hana had written down all she had learned about growing Eastern plants. If they could begin to grow what previously they could only import, it would greatly reduce the cost. Then, it would be easier to spread Eastern medicine to the common people. And if they increased the size of the garden, then Leon could tend that as well. That was Hana's dream.

"At first, I hated having to babysit you, but I'm a much better writer now, so th-th-th...nks, yeah?" He tried in vain to express his gratitude. His face turned bright red, but he could only manage to mouth a "thank you" without looking Hana in the eye.

Seeing that was enough to keep Hana's sunny smile on her face the rest of the day.

"I'm glad I came to the city," he muttered. His regional accent was becoming less noticeable.

The first day they met, Hana had her own thoughts on why Leon might have come to the city or where he came from, but she had not yet dared to ask.

"Did you come because you wanted to be a gardener?"

Anytime she had asked, he would push her away and tell her not to pry. Hana could tell he hated talking about it, so she had made a point not to bring it up.

Hana had already told him all about her family, her tutor, and what life was like back in Hinomoto. But he said nothing about himself. Finally, Hana's curiosity won out and she had to ask him. It wasn't mere curiosity or even gentle teasing; she genuinely wanted to get to know him.

"I came here 'cuz a man's gotta eat," Leon muttered so nonchalantly he might as well have been talking about a character in a book.

"Gotta eat? What?"

Hana's understanding of the Hylantian language was far better than that of her Hinomotoese, but she didn't understand this expression. She'd never heard it before.

"Guess a rich girl from a well-to-do family like yours wouldn't understand..."

Hana nodded. He was clearly being serious.

"It means I was extremely poor and cast aside by my parents."

"What...?"

"In the worst-case scenario, some children are sold into slavery to pay off their parents' debts, so I'm one of the lucky ones. My master is a good man and he pays me a living wage."

Hana had assumed he had taken on a job at twelve because he was an ambitious boy. And with his strict, but benevolent master, she took it as a given that he wasn't in a bad place in life.

But that wasn't the case. He hadn't chosen this.

"I didn't know…uhm…I!"

Hana was mortified over her past behavior. She could never have imagined this was why he didn't want to talk about his family or his past. But it was too late for regrets.

Her eyes overflowed with tears.

"I knew you would cry! That's why I didn't want to tell you! I mean, please, stop crying, m'lady!"

"You can't ever see your parents? I just…"

"It's not that I can't, I just don't want to! So stop crying! Be glad it's not your family!" His anger at his parents came through in his voice.

He wasn't angry at Hana, but to her, it felt like he was.

"I'm so sorry for being so insensitive and ignorant! I'm sorry, Leon!"

She had told him so much about her family. She'd had so few chances to leave her manor, as most daughters of well-to-do families did. But her world was so sheltered, it was suffocating. So she dumped everything on Leon: from her dream to follow in her mother's footsteps to the expensive things Walt and her father bought her to how strict her tutor was. All of it. With no concept of how much it hurt him.

"It didn't bother me. But I don't want someone treating me like some little charity case," he said, wiping away her tears as he spoke. His hands, rugged for someone so young, smelled slightly of soil.

"I really am selfish! I'm not even crying because I feel sorry for you. …I'm crying because I'm embarrassed about how ignorant I was. I don't want you to hate me…" Hana sniffled.

She wasn't weeping for Leon's misfortune. She was crying because she couldn't imagine being so poor, he had to travel to find enough work to eat. And then when she imagined what he must have thought of her, listening to all her meaningless problems while he was struggling just to survive, the tears wouldn't stop. Even her reason for crying was childish.

"You don't want me to hate you, eh?"

He stopped wiping her tears.

"Leon?"

Their eyes met and she realized he was smiling. It was a smile, pure and simple, bereft of his usual teasing and mischief. And it was clear that he didn't hate her. But she suddenly started to feel nervous. Her cheek was hot under his touch and that heat spread all the way up to her ears.

That embarrassment seemed to be contagious, as Leon's face began to turn red as well. They hadn't fought today, but Hana still felt if she looked away, she'd lose this round, so she kept her eyes on his.

"Agh, there's dirt on your cheek! Sorry, my hands are filthy," Leon exclaimed, yanking his hand away. But even as he did, the scent of the soil lingered. Her face was a canvas of soil and tears.

"…It'll come off when I wash up. I like the smell of soil."

Leon always smelled like soil.

Things were awkward between them the whole time they worked in the garden that day. This time, it wasn't because of some fight they'd had. They both remained redder than the flowers they tended—for quite some time. And even thereafter, the air between them was different.

It wasn't until Walt came to tell Hana that breakfast was ready that she started to feel normal again.

🌻 🌻 🌻

HANA was sixteen.

She and Leon were growing further apart with each passing day. He had become very conscious of the difference in their social status, and though Hana insisted it didn't matter to her, he only spoke to her when necessary, being sure to speak formally when he did.

He had stopped teasing her altogether. And he never tried to make her laugh the way he once had. It was only then Hana realized just how much she loved him.

She had been stuck inside for several days. But even though she awoke struggling to breathe, Hana popped out of bed and threw open her curtains so she could look out at the garden.

The cotton roses were in bloom again this year. And standing right next to them was Leon.

"Leon!"

"Yes? What is it, m'lady?"

"The cotton roses are in bloom! I'd like to put some in my room."

"Very well. Please give me a moment," Leon said and looked away immediately after.

Hana's heart thundered in her chest. She was the one still acting like a child, not Leon. Her chest was in excruciating pain. And she was so thirsty.

No! Not Leon...

Her father had told her how the blood of vampires coursed through the veins of the Watoh family. And of how they were destined to burden the one they loved most with their secret as they partook of their blood.

Hana was forbidden from marrying the one person she truly loved, so at sixteen, she still had no fiancé.

Leon would not be able to marry Hana. As she had no siblings, it was her responsibility to marry someone with strong business acumen who might become the heir to the Watoh Company. Leon was working-class and could only read and write enough to get by. He certainly didn't speak any foreign languages.

No matter how hard he worked, he would not be able to succeed the Watoh name.

Hana, clever as she was, had long since figured out why her father had brought Walt to train under him. He had hoped that, over time, Hana would fall for Walt on her own. And she wanted nothing more than to please her father.

The truth was, she did love Walt. But it was in the platonic way a sister would love a brother.

Leon was the one she had romantic feelings for.

She loved everything about him, from his rugged hands to his suntanned skin to the earthy scent that followed him everywhere.

But if they were all bonded to their first love or forced to face death, vampires would've gone extinct by now. Hearts can change. She didn't need to drink blood just yet. She still had time.

In which case, it was probably better for her not to see him, but the harder she tried to come up with a reason to avoid him, the more she wanted to see Leon. Love was a wretched disease.

Hana sat down on a bench to watch Leon, who had grown into a young man in his own right. She felt like she only ever saw him from the back nowadays, and the thought made her chest hurt.

"Ouch..."

Leon let out a soft groan. He had either pricked himself on a thorn or cut himself with the clippers.

In an instant, Hana's vision went red. She could no longer control her body and was quickly losing the ability to form a rational thought.

The sound of her parasol hitting the ground seemed so far away.

"Are you all right, Miss?"

"Miss Hana! Miss Hana!"

Please stay away—! She wanted to scream those words, but found she couldn't speak. The last thing she remembered was Leon, and then Walt, charging in from afar, calling out to her. Then, the scent of the earth, and the grass. And then the scent of blood, strong enough to overpower both.

🦇 🦇 🦇

HANA awoke in her bed.

"Did I...pass out?"

It had been because of Leon. She had smelled his blood and collapsed. She remembered it clearly now.

"That was close. I almost..."

If she drank his blood, she could never turn back. If she hadn't lost consciousness, she would have reached the point of no return.

Oddly enough, she wasn't thirsty anymore. Her head felt so much clearer now that she thought hours must've passed since she collapsed. She patted her chest, proud that she had overcome her urges.

She rang the bell on her bedside table and a servant appeared. The servant called for her parents.

Saizoh asked her if she was still thirsty and she responded, "No, not at all."

This was the truth. Her thirst was completely gone. However, Hana was avoiding what her father was really asking: "have you fallen so in love with someone, you crave their blood?" In other words, was she maturing into an adult vampire?

Hana understood that it was serious, a matter of life and death even, but she couldn't tell her father the truth. She knew that, no matter how much she loved Leon, her parents would never approve.

After her parents left the room, Hana allowed her mind to wander. A servant entered with a bouquet of flowers.

"Miss, did you ask the gardener to prepare this bouquet for you?"

The flowers were scarcely worthy of being called a bouquet. They were wrapped in simple white paper and bound with a hemp cord.

The Misfortune Devouring Witch is Actually a Vampire?!

Before she had collapsed, Hana had asked Leon to set aside some cotton roses for her. And so he had.

"Where shall I put them?"

"Just get me a vase, please. These flowers are special, so I'd like to arrange them myself."

"That sounds like a lovely idea, Miss."

The servant brought Hana the vase, some water, and scissors before leaving her. Hana reached for the hemp cord, intending to set right to work on arranging the flowers.

"Huh…?"

As she removed the paper wrapped around the flowers, another piece of paper slipped out. Hana set the flowers down and picked up the paper.

I've ben woryed.

If u're feeling beter, open the windou and let me see that u're doing ok.

The writing on the crumpled page was sloppy. The sentences were brief, with multiple misspelled words. It was definitely from Leon.

After Hana diligently arranged each cotton rose Leon gave her, she took out a pen and sheet of paper and replied to his note.

I'm going to come see you before bed tonight. Wait for me by the herb garden.

She opened the window of her second-floor bedroom and looked for Leon. His white shirt swept in and out view beyond the branches of a large maple tree. He had been worried about Hana, and spotted her immediately. She gave a wave and Leon made his way back to the house. He moved his lips without using his voice:

Are you okay?

Hana read his exaggerated lip movements and gave a big nod in return. The midday summer sun was far too bright. As she gazed down on Leon through half-lidded eyes, the world around him appeared to be twinkling. She wanted to be with him, day or night, without being afraid of reproach.

What she was doing was wrong.

Nothing would come of it. But still, she folded her reply and tossed it out the window. The wind carried it along and dropped it near Leon, where he picked it up. Hana strained to see the look on his face. Her heart was a sea of fear and anxiety, dotted with specks of hope.

Idiot.

She could see his lips whispering those words. She expected nothing less.

❦ ❦ ❦

AFTER that, Hana and Leon began meeting in secret at night in the herb garden.

In the beginning, they hadn't specified a time, but just knew as a matter of course that the other would be waiting there. If it rained, then they would meet the day after. This unspoken rule was how the lovers were able to be together.

They kept up appearances during the day. Leon would only look upon Hana with a sullen expression. But at night, they clung to each other, unleashing every ounce of emotion they had withheld during the day. Leon couldn't see Hana's face in the pale moonlight. But thanks to her impeccable night vision, she could see his gentle expression all too well. His words, deeds, expressions; everything about him was kinder at night.

Over the next half a year, Hana had two more episodes, both times leaving her comatose. She was so overcome by thirst that she became unable to move. She was sure that if she were able to drink Leon's blood, she might come around.

The day after each episode, she would feel fine. Her thirst abated and she found she could move once again.

It was at that point that she learned she just needed to wait for the desire to pass. Or perhaps waiting it out was just her excuse to continue her secret meetings with Leon.

She did nothing more than hold Leon's hand when they were together. After all, Leon was not Hana's fiancé. Perhaps that was why the thirst abated. She did not want to betray her parents or Walt.

That was the excuse she repeated over and over again in her mind.

Whenever Hana went out to the sort of social gatherings befitting the daughter of a wealthy merchant with close ties to the nobility, it was always Walt who accompanied her.

Her parents and Walt would never force her into anything. Because they all only had the best of intentions, and because she loved them so, she refused to do anything to disrupt their plans for her.

The nights she went out with Walt, her heart was racked with guilt. Perhaps she should have stopped seeing Leon then and there, but she couldn't keep away.

Just once more.

Just through the rest of autumn.

Just until I turn seventeen…

Hana was still telling herself these lies as they began to spend their first winter together.

"Aren't you cold, Leon?"

Hylantian winters were frigid. Even though no snow had fallen, when night fell, it was as if the air itself froze over. Hana could still feel it even though she was bundled up in a wool coat and gloves. In Leon's threadbare clothing, he must have been freezing.

"Of course I am."

"I'm sorry. You're out here because of me."

Hana came from a wealthy family; she could have whatever she wanted. But she had never even considered buying Leon a decent coat.

"I wouldn't be out here if I didn't want to be… Here, this should warm me up."

Leon put his hands on Hana's cheeks. The stinging chill of his touch didn't last and soon, they were sharing their warmth. They leaned in closer to the other.

"Yes. Same for me."

The feeling of his hands on her cheeks gave her strength. His eyes were so intense, Hana could tell exactly what he was planning to do, and closed her eyes.

Leon clumsily pulled Hana close and kissed her gently.

Their lips barely touched. But Hana was so happy, she could feel a heat building in her eyes. As tears began to roll down her cheeks, Leon pulled away from her lips and planted a kiss on her cheek, as if trying to dry her tears.

"…Come with me?" Leon was acting so strange tonight. Hana didn't know how to respond. "Let's run away and live together. We'll be poor. I have money saved up, but it's not enough to create the sort of life you're used to. But as long as we can be together, that's all I need…"

His eyes were intense. She could see he wasn't joking.

Her family, or him. Hana would have to choose.

Hana might have been brought up in the lap of luxury, but she believed she could give it all up in a heartbeat if it meant she could be with Leon. Naturally, she was naive about just how hard their life might be. But still, being with Leon was all she dreamed of.

But she knew they couldn't. Leon was a gardener. And if he eloped with Hana, he would lose his job. His potential employers were all wealthy people. If he wanted other work, he would need a recommendation from the Watohs, and there was no chance they would oblige if he had run off with their daughter.

"I'm glad I came to the city."

Leon took pride in his work as a gardener. He had worked so hard on tending Hana's herb garden. Surely there was work for someone so knowledgeable about Eastern herbs and produce.

"I can't. I'm so sorry. I just…can't…so please, don't leave me. I'm sorry, Leon. There's so much that's precious to me here… And I don't think…I could live in poverty."

She didn't want to say that Leon wasn't enough for her to give up everything else. So she placed the blame on herself and her family. After all, there were so many other people she cared about. This was true.

She could think of ten or twenty reasons why they shouldn't be together, but couldn't think of one justifying her leaving with him right here and now.

"I see. I guess you're right. That's probably the only way we can both be happy. I won't lose my job. Sorry, I forgot that you actually have a family to care about, unlike me."

For Leon, there was only one person he wanted to be with.

The realization hit Hana hard, making her feel as if her heart were being ripped out.

"This is goodbye, Hana. …This is the last time I'll meet you like this."

This was the first time he had called Hana by name.

She only understood once morning came just how much finality he had felt when he kissed her that night and said her name.

He had fled the manor through the night.

He cleaned out his room completely, leaving to his master only a note that said, "I quit" before disappearing into the night.

The Misfortune Devouring Witch is Actually a Vampire?!

🦇 🦇 🦇

LEON should have had an easy career path as a gardener now that his and Hana's relationship was no longer a concern. But he threw it all away and disappeared.

It was likely that he left in order to make a clean break with her.

Lost without him, Hana told everyone what had happened.

It would be impossible for a sixteen-year-old girl to search the city for him by herself. It made her painfully aware of how naïve and powerless she truly was.

Her parents were more disappointed than angry when she told them. They only agreed to help her find him once she promised to give up on being with him.

As long as she didn't drink his blood, he would not officially become her partner.

Her parents didn't take their naïve, ignorant daughter's feelings seriously. To them, her feelings for Leon were nothing more than a passing fancy.

But this feeling is so powerful... Will it ever go away?

Hana had only ever known one love, so she couldn't be certain. But even without Leon on the grounds, she couldn't forget him, and that intense feeling of thirst began to torment her once more.

Not a thing had changed. Not her feelings toward him or her bloodlust.

They still couldn't find him after two weeks, so they called off the search.

Walt worried over the increasingly listless Hana and invited her out for shopping and to the theater to cheer her up. She never refused him, hoping to satisfy her parents. But every time they went out, she kept her eyes peeled out the window of the carriage in hopes of seeing the young man with cinnamon hair.

She knew what she was doing was cruel to Walt. But she could not stop herself from looking for Leon each time they went out.

And then, finally—

"Stop!"

The carriage was heading down a road she had never been to before. They were neither in the wealthy residential district nor the merchant's quarter.

Just after that strange feeling swept over her, Hana finally found him. The young man she had been searching for.

Her pulse throbbed.

She couldn't mistake the way he looked from behind.

"Miss Hana, you mustn't! Remember your promise to Lord Saizoh? He will be heartbroken." Walt sighed, seeing just who Hana's eyes had landed on.

Hana threw open the carriage door, keeping an eye on Leon the whole time. "I'm so sorry, Walt. But if you won't stop the carriage, then I'm going to jump! I am serious!"

Hana was leveraging her position for everything it was worth. If she missed her chance now, it may never come again. She didn't care whether or not Leon actually wanted to see her. She had to see him, no matter what.

"You've always been obstinate about the strangest of things," Walt said, a sad smile coiling on his lips.

Who was it that had sent the coachman on this path that they normally never would have taken? And in a city as large as this, how could it be by chance that they had finally found the one person she had sought for so long?

"Walt…I'm so sorry, but thank you. From the bottom of my heart."

"You'd better go now or you'll lose sight of him."

Hana gave the man, who had been like a brother to her, a deep bow and leapt from the carriage. She ran with every ounce of strength she had, desperate to catch Leon, who was slipping into the crowd.

"Leon! Leon!"

He stopped for a second, then started to dart away. Hana, who had never run a mile in her life, knew she had little chance of catching him. She was the one who had refused him. She couldn't blame him for never wanting to see her again. And yet, she ran.

"Kya!"

Her high heels weren't made to run in. She toppled over and skinned her knees. She could stand the pain, but the thought of losing Leon brought tears to her eyes.

"Dummy…"

You're the dummy, Hana thought with a smile. He had tried to run away, yet all it took was her tripping to get him to rush back to her. He was such a kindhearted fool.

"But I didn't want to lose you. You should have known I wasn't just going to forget about you after you left."

"So, what do you want?" he asked, an icy gleam in his eye.

But Hana hadn't jumped from a carriage and run all this way just to end things here. She hadn't chased him through the streets just to say goodbye.

She took several deep breaths and finally told him how she felt. "I want to be with you, Leon. That's all. I just wanted you to know that no matter what happens, I want to be by your side."

She had chosen her former life over him once before, so she wasn't sure he would forgive her. But she didn't care how selfish it seemed; she just wanted to be with him.

"You really are a dummy."

He reached out to Hana, who was still on her knees, and pulled her up into his arms. This was his answer.

☙ ☙ ☙

THE space Leon was renting was located above a bar. It could only be reached by climbing a rickety set of stairs.

It was a dank room with little sunlight. The door was shorter than him, and Leon's bed was only half the size of Hana's. A stove and counter rested against the wall with a plain wood table nearby.

Hana had never seen a kitchen and a bedroom combined into one room before now. Leon smiled bitterly as she spun around, taking everything in with a sense of wonder.

"Are you surprised it's so small?"

"Yes, but you know I like places with little sunlight."

"I'm glad, though that's not exactly a compliment."

If she ever returned to the manor, they would never let her out again. This was Hana's new home if she truly wanted to be with Leon.

"Leon, there's something I've been meaning to tell you."

"…What?"

"I'm not a normal human being. I'm the descendent of vampires. … See? My teeth are sharp. That's why I can't handle sunlight…" She had no idea how to break the news to him without him thinking she was crazy. It didn't feel like she had done a good job explaining it, but she wasn't sure what else to say.

"I've known for a while."

"You have?"

"Either you've forgotten or you blocked out the memory, but back when the cotton roses were in bloom, you drank my blood. Both times you collapsed, I snuck into your room."

Hana gulped. He was right. The taste of his blood was coming back to her. The unpleasantness of the headaches and the cold sweats returned. At the same time, a haze broke in Hana's mind.

"Hana...? I'm sorry. You probably forgot about it because I freaked out. But I didn't hate you for it. Everyone's scared of what they don't understand at first, right? ...But I'm not afraid anymore. I understand now, so it's all right."

It's gonna be all right.

Those words brought all of Hana's memories rushing back.

The memory of that hot summer morning, while the cotton roses were in bloom, when she finally chose the single most important person to her.

🌷 🌷 🌷

SOMEONE was calling Hana's name.

The air around her was tepid and she had broken into a cold sweat.

"Are you all right, Miss?"

"Miss Hana! Miss Hana!"

Leon's voice was so close, while Walt's was so far away.

The intense smell of blood broke through her mental haze and she struggled desperately to get free from Leon's grasp as he tried to scoop her up.

She wasn't sure if she could resist any longer. If she stayed with him just seconds more, she might suck his blood.

"...Miss Hana, do you want some blood?"

How could Walt have known that?

Confused, Hana continued trying to get away,

"No...you have to get...awa...noo."

Her breathing had become ragged and the world around her was enveloped in an orange haze, making it difficult to find something to focus on.

It made her crave Leon's warmth even more. And his blood. But she was terrified that she would lose all sense of rational thought and turn into a monster if she gave in.

"Miss Hana, it's all right. I know all about it. Here…"

Something was being pushed into her lips. It felt like a man's finger. A metallic scent filled her nose.

No! No! I want Leon's blood!

Something similar but all too different from what she wanted filled her mouth. Her body convulsed, trying to reject the foreign substance.

Hana could no longer suppress her urges. She pulled herself up and grabbed on to Leon's shirt with all her might. She bit down on his neck, hard.

"Wha—Miss! Stop! What are you doing?!"

She had craved Leon's blood for so long, but it tasted like a mix of sand and tears. She had wanted his blood for so long, finally having it failed to meet her expectations. The tears belonged to her, flowing down her cheeks and blending with his blood.

Leon tried to pull away, but Hana threw her hands around his back and bit down harder.

"Let me go…! Let me go! Stop. This isn't right." Leon yanked himself away, tossing Hana to the ground.

"Leon! Calm down, please! Miss Hana…wasn't supposed to…"

Hana had no sense of the pain flowing through her body. The only thing she knew was that Leon had rejected her.

Tomorrow he wouldn't even want to be her friend.

The first time a vampire drank the blood of the one they loved was supposed to be a happy occasion. But she had ignored his objections and now she was sure he would never forgive her.

Hana's thirst had been satisfied and yet, despair encircled her heart.

She was exhausted and released her grip on consciousness. She wanted nothing more than to fall asleep and forget all of this.

LEON told Hana all about that first time she drank his blood.

She could see it in her mind and still hear the two young men's voices clearly. But the sense of something akin to despair that accompanied those memories clenched her heart.

"So that's what happened... I repressed the memory somehow..."

Leon nodded. "That was when Walt told me about your family. After that, I started sneaking you my blood. I thought it would just be better for you if you didn't remember. But in reality, I guess I also wanted you to forget how upset I was and how I pushed you away."

Hana understood why he wouldn't want her around after all that had happened. So the fact that Leon had asked her to live with him even though he knew she was a vampire brought her untold joy.

"I just reckoned if I left, if I wasn't there for you to think about... that you would just find someone else's blood to drink. But I was wrong. I'm sorry. You must have been in so much pain."

Without realizing it, Hana had chosen Leon as her partner. There was no going back now.

Leon had left under the assumption that Hana could just pick a new partner. But he told Walt where he would be going, just in case Hana had another fit.

"...I was also wrong about so many things...so, shall we call it a draw?"

Leon had rejected Hana out of fear once, as she had him.

Hana laughed as she pointed out the tie between them. Leon smiled bashfully.

Walt had likely heard about the family's vampiric ancestry from Saizoh, and so he understood Hana's condition on some level. It was he who explained her condition to Leon and he who facilitated their reunion. He knew all about their secret meetings. He had always been watching over them. Hana had no idea how she could ever repay him.

That night, Hana climbed into bed, comforted by the warmth of the man she loved. But it was hard to get used to sharing a bed with another, let alone for that person to be someone she felt so strongly for. Her heart raced and she found she could not sleep.

Choosing Leon should have made her happy, and yet she couldn't just forget her parents or Walt. She didn't feel at peace with her decision at all.

"Give it a little time, then we'll go apologize. Together. Just because you chose me doesn't mean you gotta cut your parents off forever."

"Will they ever forgive me for being so selfish?"

"You're their little princess, I'm sure they'll understand."

"…I hope so."

Shortly thereafter, Leon found another gardening job and Hana slowly adjusted to her new life. Her parents were more upset over the fact that she left without telling them than the fact that she chose Leon. They wouldn't forgive her so easily.

Walt served as the arbiter between parent and child. Eventually, it was decided that Leon would take on the Watoh name. Any children born to the couple would become Watoh heirs and were required to be educated as such. This was at Leon's insistence. He wanted his children to have the benefit of a good education. He felt he lacked refinement and didn't want his children to suffer the same fate.

The pair then found a new home. Hana opened an Eastern medicine clinic on the first floor of that shop. While trying to think up a name for her shop, Hana thought about how the neighborhood children called her the "Raven-haired Witch", so she took on the name "The Witch of the East". It was meant to be a light-hearted name that she used sparingly in the beginning, but over time, she came to love it.

The name "Misfortune Devouring Witch" would come several years later…

🦇 🦇 🦇

THE cotton roses on the Aldridge estate were those that had been grown in the Watohs' garden. With Leon and Hana gone, the task of tending the herb garden fell to Walt.

And with the passing of his older brother, Walt was forced to return to his own home and take over his family's estate. Over time, Hana, along with the days he spent at her family's estate, became a part of his past.

"You always said that…you were grateful to me?"

All that time spent reminiscing was causing Walt to mistake Yuuri for Hana again. Simon and Yuuri could tell that this elderly man still had unresolved feelings for the younger Hana and so stopped correcting him.

"I forced my blood on you so I could marry into the Watoh family. Even after my attempt failed, I still deceived you. You had finally chosen a partner and yet, I kept it from you and everyone in the manor!"

His quivering, wrinkled hand reached for Yuuri. She gently took his hand in her own.

"I was the one who made Leon think he wasn't bright enough to handle all the complexities of the trade. I persuaded him to leave. … If you hadn't eloped or just told Lord Saizoh the truth from the start, things might have turned out different."

Hana's leaving without telling her parents was what caused the chasm between her and her father, one that took years to heal.

She hadn't realized at that point that she had already chosen her partner, so she forced herself to obey her father's wishes for her, all the while contradicting her nature. If she had known all along that she already tasted Leon's blood, she could have convinced her parents without needing to run away.

Walt had always regretted not telling her. But Yuuri's grandparents had seen it differently, and were grateful to Walt. Hana must have shouldered her own guilt for repressing such an important memory.

So Yuuri tried to give this man the words she was sure her grandmother wanted him to hear.

"But you were the reason I was able to be with Leon, right?"

"…You were growing weaker by the day. I could bear to watch you suffer no longer. That was all."

"What is it you want from me? To be forgiven or to be punished?"

The man shook his head. "…I am not sure myself."

"Neither is possible. I am stubborn and will never change. Even after everything you've told me, my gratitude toward you will never fade."

Hana and Leon had left this world feeling grateful to Walt. And Yuuri believed that was how things should stay. Yuuri knew her grandmother to be stubborn; her grandfather even more so. But both of them were compassionate people.

"Miss Hana…"

The man had a peaceful expression. And so, Yuuri and Simon decided to join him in gazing at the cotton roses in silence.

The Misfortune Devouring Witch is Actually a Vampire?!

❦ ❦ ❦

DURING the carriage ride back from the Aldridge estate, Yuuri confided in Simon.

"While things…aren't that serious, I do believe he loves me for who I am…"

"He? Do you mean our esteemed Count?"

Yuuri nodded. She took a big breath, trying to pull herself together and finally tell him something she should have long ago.

"You've probably already figured it out, but I drank Ernest's blood. He knows…that I need blood from time to time. But I haven't…told him everything about what it means to do such a thing for a vampire."

"Father and I already knew. He told us himself."

"I see…" Yuuri wasn't surprised. It seemed like the sort of thing Ernest would do.

"Listen, Yuuri…I know you know him better than I. He seems flippant, but he really is a considerate man. He cares about you."

"He does."

She had never doubted that. He was always showing up just in the nick of time. Lately, he would even offer his blood before Yuuri had to ask.

Ernest truly was kind. But it was his kindness that frightened Yuuri. She was afraid that if she let herself lean on him too much, she would become weak and unable to take care of herself. That was why she had always been so reluctant to accept his attempts to reach out to her.

But she desperately wanted to lean on him, and that made her doubt if she ever was strong to begin with.

"Father and I want to do whatever we can for you. So please, talk to us. About anything. Well, almost anything… Just open up to us about what you want to say."

"Thank you, Simon… Hehe, don't cry."

At twenty-four, Simon still cried openly. Yuuri handed him a handkerchief.

Vampires and their descendants could be awkward, foolish, and fragile. It was why they were on the verge of extinction. They may have even already died out in Himomoto. Yuuri might even be the last vampire left on the planet.

As foolish as it was though, even vampires deserved happiness.

That was why Simon wept openly before her.

Yuuri vowed that, as soon as Ernest finished his current job and started coming back to her shop, she was going to change things, once and for all.

Final Chapter: The Way to a Witch's Heart

ALL of the newspapers jumped on the arrest of Count Groves and the illegal gambling incident at once. It was a rarity for every paper, from the most trusted news source to the sleaziest tabloid, to report relatively the same thing on the same topic:

"The Fall of a Noble Dynasty. Was it All in the Art?"

"The Underbelly of an Exhausted Hylantian Gentleman. Marquis Groves Arrested for Illegal Gambling!"

Surely, Yuuri had read the papers and learned that Ernest's classified mission was over. He was making his way through his mountain of paperwork as fast as possible so he could finish his work at the palace and go see her.

Though he was being used for odd jobs lately, his original job had been to serve at the King's side and help him process approvals on various documents.

"Ernest, you seem distracted..." King Rodrick II said to his subordinate with a subdued expression from across the room, where he sat pressing his seal to a mountain of documents.

"You must be imagining things, Your Highness. There isn't a purer soul among the nobility than I."

"How impudent to misrepresent yourself so. Aren't you going to see the young lady of the Watoh family?"

"Once I've cleared this mountain of paperwork. I would hate for anyone to accuse me of being lax in my duties."

Ernest had been trying to hide the fact that he was anxious to see her, as the King had suspected. If he were being true to his heart, he might have said, "please let me leave on time today. Please don't ask why and please don't interfere."

But the intuitive, honest king had rightly guessed what was on Ernest's mind and called him on it.

"I need your help with a certain matter."

"Anything you desire, Your Highness."

"It's about the new roadway and the construction on that bridge over Rhinwest River."

He was referring to a multiyear initiative to build a bridge over the river that formed the western border between Hylant and their neighbor, Fosdan. Rhinwest River was wide, and the cost of building a bridge over it was enormous. In the interim, there was much debate over whether people should use the existing bridge or travel by boat to get across. They were trying to figure out which option would best allow trade to continue between their most prominent cities.

There were many things to consider. With the bridge benefiting both nations, how should the costs and labor be divided? Should any changes be made to the current tariffs in place? There was also the matter of small agrarian communities near the bridge and how they should be restructured to best benefit from the bridge.

"Would you be willing to travel to Fosdan as our plenipotentiary ambassador?"

A normal ambassador was dispatched to an allied nation to serve as a government liaison and advocate for citizens from his or her home country. But a plenipotentiary was expected to carry out negotiations and even sign off on policies on behalf of the king, essentially acting as his proxy.

Thus, King Rodrick intended to place the full burden of negotiations for the bridge over Rhinwest River on Ernest's shoulders.

"Your Highness, don't you think you're working me a little too hard these days? I really could use a vacation…"

"I certainly do, but there's a shortage of men of your caliber, my friend."

Several prominent government officials had been arrested in the illegal gambling shakedown. It wasn't enough of a scandal to shake the foundations of a nation with as rich a history as Hylant's, but it did mean that some of its civil servants would be tied up for some time.

"…This really does pose a problem."

Ernest's hesitance wasn't merely because he was in wont of a vacation. If he took the position and relocated to Fosdan, he could be gone for months or even years.

What would happen to Yuuri if he were gone for that long?

"Well, you won't have to leave today. I can grant you three months to put your affairs in order."

"Three months…? I see. Would you permit me to bring my bride with me then?"

If he couldn't be sure when, if ever, he was to return, then obviously his only option was to bring Yuuri with him.

Rodrick was so shocked by the suggestion that the document he had been reading over fell to the floor. He furrowed his brow. "If memory serves, Count Selden, you are still single, yes?"

"I was hoping to wait a little longer, but I suppose if it's in service to my most esteemed King, who am I to refuse? I will just have to move "happily ever after" up a bit on my calendar!"

"Most esteemed, huh? And do whatever you like! As long as the 'bride' in question is amenable."

Ernest thought of the moody, raven-haired witch. He suspected the reason she kept her heart closed was because of their difference in status and her shame over her vampiric characteristics.

Even if he asked her to come along and told her he would be away for a long while, he doubted she'd agree. He could try to persuade her to come along as an employee, such as a servant or a private doctor, but that was a last resort. If he gave her the choice of being his employee, she would likely settle for that as the final destination for their relationship. He'd already tried to ease the awkwardness of her sucking his blood by saying it was a reward or compensation.

This was his chance. He couldn't let it slip away.

"I don't know if she'll actually accept. That's my concern. …This all really is too sudden."

"She isn't willing to marry you?! Then why not just free the poor girl of your advances?"

"As if I could, Sire! I'll bring her with me."

His mind made up, Ernest wanted more than before to finish his work at the palace and hurry to Yuuri's shop. He straightened up and set right to work on the documents before him.

❦ ❦ ❦

THE worst of the summer's heat might have passed, but Yuuri couldn't tell. Maybe it was the heat, maybe it was her anxiety over Ernest's absence, or maybe it was just her unquenchable thirst. All she knew was that, for several days now, she had a desperate craving for blood.

But her symptoms were light. She could hold out a little longer. Yuuri tried to appease her thirst as much as possible with tea, hoping that Ernest would return soon.

Occasionally, she received letters from him. The letters usually featured overtures so melodramatic that she was sure he had stolen them from the lyrics of some opera. She thought back to the love letters Joel Weller's father had left behind. These were worse. She giggled at the thought that the deceased baron was so ashamed of his innocuous poetry while Ernest reveled in his own.

Yuuri blushed at the idea of anyone sending her love letters. She quickly resealed the envelopes. What he wrote might have been his true feelings, but she was too embarrassed to do more than skim it. It felt like some sort of punishment to her.

Ernest was intelligent and good with people, or at least that was how Yuuri saw him. But she had put him down, mocking his art and saying his writing style made him sound creepy.

That was only because she didn't like the way his words threw her heart into chaos, not for lack of skill on Ernest's part. She was both amused and mortified that someone could write such embarrassing things.

Yuuri's responses were cold and matter-of-fact. She only reported events and sparse details, like how she was slowly becoming comfortable around Simon again.

She could never write something as sincere as, "I miss you, please hurry back to me."

He hadn't written anything regarding the position in Fosdan, so she was left to assume he was merely busy with work.

With her days steeped in loneliness, Yuuri was only just learning that the illegal gambling ring had finally been brought down.

On her way back from the bazaar that morning, the headline "The Fall of a Noble Dynasty. Was it All in the Art?" caught her eye and she purchased the newspaper. The article gave all the details of the final takedown.

Was Ernest on his way right now? Or was he still caught up in paperwork?

I shouldn't get my hopes up.

Yuuri repeated those words over and over, but her heart's desires would not be silenced. Before she knew it, she was running around, meticulously cleaning her shop and insuring (multiple times) that she had plenty of his favorite tea.

She usually fell asleep reading during the day, but she tried to keep busy enough so he wouldn't catch her napping.

It was only once the sun was at its brightest that the man she had been so eagerly awaiting opened her door and stepped inside.

"Hey, Miss Yuuri! Sorry to keep you waiting! I bet you've been dying to see me!"

After a long month apart, Ernest walked right over to Yuuri, who was standing by the couch.

"Welcome."

Ernest pulled Yuuri into his arms. Normally, he would hold her until he sensed she was genuinely trying to pull away, then let go. But this time, Yuuri made no attempt to pull away. She wanted to make up for all the time they had been apart.

"…I see. So absence really does make your heart grow fonder."

Yuuri wanted to stay like this as long as she could manage. So she said nothing, merely listening to the beating of his heart. What normally frightened her was all she wanted today.

"Miss Yuuri? What is it? What's wrong?" Ernest asked in a soft voice.

Yuuri's sudden display of affection had shocked him, and she liked that. When she had finally had enough, she pulled away to get a look at the expression he wore. His baffled face pleased her.

"I knew it. The one time I don't push you away, you're completely flummoxed…"

He knew how uncomfortable she was when he tried to hug her and teased her mercilessly for it. He was always the one in control. But today, she had taken control and taken him by surprise. But she was content to let him think she was merely acting on impulse.

"I'm not flummoxed."

"Oh, so you're just a poor loser then."

"...Not at all. Why don't you put your little theory to the test?"

He was such a cad. Now that he knew what she was thinking, he definitely wouldn't give in.

"No, because I can see that look in your eye. You're plotting something."

"You're as perceptive as ever, my little witch."

Ernest gave up and took his usual seat. Yuuri went into the back to prepare some tea. She swiftly filled the camellia teacups she hadn't used in his absence.

Unlike tea prepared in Hylant, the tea was transferred from the small teapot to the cups partway through the preparation process. If this step was done in a timely fashion, it allowed the flowery aroma to become even stronger. It also gave the tea itself a smoother, less bitter flavor.

She set two teacups and the teapot on the tray, along with some teacakes. She placed a cup in front of Ernest and took the seat next to him.

In the past, when she took that spot beside him, she always had to come up with some excuse. But over time, her feelings toward him, as well as their relationship, had begun to change.

"Oh, how I've missed the taste of this. It's a bit different than what we have at my manor. I wonder why? Perhaps it's only good if I drink it here?"

He was close. It likely wasn't the place one drank the tea, but whom they drank it with that was important. One cup in the company of a special person was more delicious than a hundred cups anywhere else. But Yuuri couldn't bring herself to say that out loud. So she silently sipped away, happy he enjoyed her company as much as she enjoyed his.

"So I see you and Simon have been getting along well in my absence."

"Yes. After I gave him the hat, we paid a visit to the Aldridges, some family friends of ours, to see their cotton roses."

The only thing Yuuri had done in his absence that was out of the ordinary was going out with Simon. That was why most of her letters were about her brother.

"Your letters are so concise. All you told me was that you went."

"I'm not very good at letter writing. And I could never write those flowery, mushy sentences like you do."

"I merely write from the heart. But I know you have a hard time being open... So tell me all about what you have been up to in my absence."

Yuuri did have a lot she wanted to tell him. About their meeting with the elderly man who had been her grandmother's good friend. About the stories he told them. About how she had finally learned to look Simon in the eye.

About how Ernest's words were what had made her feel optimistic for the future.

But the thing she wanted to tell him most, she was too embarrassed to say.

He listened intently to everything she had to say, even as he interrupted from time to time to tease her.

🦇 🦇 🦇

YUURI was stricken by an intense thirst as they chatted.

To drink his blood though, she would need to complete a task for him first. And she didn't know if she could last long enough for him to find something for her to do.

She had realized he sometimes brought her tasks he could have solved on his own, just to give her something to do. But she couldn't ask him to try and come up with something just after he had finished such a massive investigation.

She desired to ask for his blood outright, not under the pretext of being a reward or compensation. Because she desired it. And because only Ernest's blood would do. That was all.

"Lord Ernest, I have a favor to ask," she turned to him, finally resolved.

"Hm? You know I would grant anything you asked. What is it?"

"I...uhm...well, I'm a bit thirsty."

"Oh? And?"

He was going to make her spell out exactly what she wanted.

"Please let me drink some of your blood. ...Not as a reward, but because it's what I want."

"All right. ...But only if you agree to do something for me. Fair enough?"

Ernest ran his index finger along Yuuri's lips. It was his way of showing her that he expected something in return. Embarrassed, Yuuri had to look away, but the heat that filled her cheeks was already pulsing its way up to her ears. The last thing she wanted was for Ernest to see how easily he could have this effect on her.

"You understand what I mean, don't you?"

"Can we do it later? Please let me drink your blood first?"

She was happy that Ernest wanted her. But she was afraid, and she had pushed her timid heart just about as far as it would go for now. She needed his blood to give her the courage.

"I'm afraid not. I can see you're trying to weasel out of it."

He had seen through her, yet again. Yuuri had no other choice. Her heart began to race as he wrapped his arms around her. Tears formed at the edge of her eyes. She squeezed them shut in hopes of keeping her tears from spilling over.

"Are you afraid?"

"I'm not afraid. P-Please, just hurry!"

Yuuri was terrified that if she waited any longer, she might lose her nerve. She had grabbed onto Ernest's shirt without even realizing it. Ernest took that as his cue and placed his lips against hers.

The tears that Yuuri had fought so hard to hold back ran down her cheeks.

Her mind was heavy with anxiety. What did she want to do? What did the future look like for her and Ernest, days or months from now? She could scarcely imagine it in years.

Right now, all she wanted was his warmth.

She didn't care that he was the king's right-hand man, a dignified noble who knew far more about the ways of the world than a naïve shut-in like herself.

She funneled the intensity of all her worries and fears into that kiss and Ernest gave it right back to her, refusing to hold back just because it was her first. As long as that was the intensity of his love for her, that was all that mattered.

Finally, slowly, Ernest pulled away. It actually made Yuuri a little sad when he did. Some part of her was afraid to let him go.

"Are you all right?"

"…Yes. Just a little surprised."

"Oh? Well, come here then, Yuuri."

Her heart skipped a beat just hearing him call her name, with no formalities, no "Miss" or "Little Witch". Just Yuuri.

They had been sitting side by side the whole time, and yet they felt even closer now. Yuuri slid into his lap without hesitation this time. She told herself it was so she could better drink his blood.

Ernest deftly removed his tie. Yuuri stroked his exposed collarbone over and over again.

"Come on. That tickles."

Her lips trembling, Yuuri suddenly straightened up and kissed him in lieu of thanking him, then quickly pulled away. She then bit into his neck.

"You might look like a girl, but sometimes, you really are as enchanting as a witch. Do you know just how wicked you are?"

Euphoria had seized Yuuri's mind and she couldn't manage an answer. The last thing she thought as her consciousness fluttered away was, "no, I'm not."

The Misfortune Devouring Witch is Actually a Vampire?!

THE morning sun had begun to pierce the curtains by the time Yuuri opened her eyes. She had vague memories of Ernest carrying her to her bedroom on the second floor after trying to entice her to go for dinner.

"I'm full. I already ate my dinner."

"That wasn't dinner though. All right, I'll take my leave then. I won't ask you to invite me in for the night. I'll behave myself for just a little longer."

She thought the conversation went something like that, but couldn't remember clearly.

Yuuri leapt out of bed, feeling better than she had in a long time. She always felt this way after drinking blood.

Her clothes had become wrinkled after sleeping in them, so she hung them up to smooth the wrinkles out.

She took a different dress out of the closet and fixed her unkempt hair.

She made her way downstairs and headed for the kitchen, but stopped when she noticed a letter and a paper bag on the dining table. She picked it up.

To My Sweet Yuuri,

You were as sweet as a daisy and as beautiful as a rose last night.

I want nothing more than to arouse you from your slumber and ask how is it you can unseat my heart so.

But I must suppress the urge for now.

You look like a kitten when you sleep.

"Eeek!"

Yuuri let out a shriek, unable to continue. She knew what his letters were like, so why was she so surprised now?

She slumped down in a chair and grappled with her embarrassment.

She focused on calming herself, breathing in and out. Only once she had did she finally try reading the letter once more.

She skimmed the rest of it, saving herself the torture of reading overwrought descriptions of her sleeping face, until she reached the last two lines:

I bought some pastries and apples for your breakfast, so make sure you eat up. I'll be taking a few vacation days soon, so you be a good girl and wait for me until then.

—Ernest

"I just wanted the facts."

His words were even more self-assured than usual. He had called her his before, as if he owned her, but until now, Yuuri had written it off as a joke. Now that it was here, preserved in print for her, there was no mistaking it.

And so, Yuuri found herself with another letter she could not bring herself to read.

❦ ❦ ❦

YUURI was particularly active that day, invigorated from drinking Ernest's blood. She finished preparing her orders for Watoh Company and even had lunch at a restaurant before delivering them.

She told them in advance that she was coming, so there should be no reason she couldn't just leave everything with an employee and—

"Miss Yuuri, your mother is here today," one of the senior staff members informed her.

The two of them could barely handle seeing one another. That's why she always picked the day she came in advance and, if her mother planned to be in that day, she would change her plans,

Isn't this why I always ask Simon or Father to make these arrangements for me?

"I see. Then I shall be on my way."

Even just hearing about her mother caused Yuuri's hands to ball into fists and sweat to break out on her forehead. She turned to make a hasty retreat.

"She commanded me to bring you to see her should you come by, m'lady."

Her mother wanted to see her? If she wanted to reconcile, why didn't she just say so? Yuuri tried to think about it logically, but dared not take a step.

"...And what of my brother and father?"

"They have business away from headquarters today, I'm afraid."

She would have felt better if one of them were with her. But she understood. If the two of them had been there, they would have tried to prevent this meeting. Her mother was only asking for her because they weren't there.

"I can't! I'm sorry…I'm in a hurry, so I really must be going."

"I see. Then I shall inform her."

"I'm sorry, but I have a private matter I must attend to."

Her mother was unlikely to be mad at the employee for failing to stop Yuuri. But still she apologized for mixing business and personal matters.

"Understood. Please allow me to prepare a carriage for you."

Yuuri was on the verge of making her escape when—

"Miss Yuuri."

Just as she was taking the stairs down toward the building's entrance, a woman's cold voice called her name. Yuuri didn't have to turn around to know that it was her mother.

"…!"

"It has been awhile, my dear."

Her mother was stone-faced. For Yuuri, that was still better than the usual anger and disdain with which her mother normally treated her.

"Y-Yes…"

"I have just one thing to tell you."

"……"

"I've heard you've become close with a gentleman. And that the two of you attended a dinner party together."

"I have. Is there a problem with that?"

It was considered improper in Hylant for an unmarried woman to be running around with a man without her father's express permission.

But Yuuri's own mother was the reason she had been living on her own and beyond their sphere of influence. Yuuri strengthened her resolve. If her mother was going to pick Ernest of all things to suddenly complain about, then she would give it all right back to her.

It was the first time she had ever felt like she could stand against her mother.

"I see. Well, that isn't what I really wanted to speak to you about. …While I was at a tea party with some members of the nobility, Duke Harcourt inquired about you. Do you know him?"

"No, I've never met him. The only members of the nobility I've interacted with are Count Selden and his acquaintances."

All of the members of the upper class who Yuuri had interacted with were those she came to know through the cases Ernest had brought her. If this man had business with Ernest's witch girlfriend, he should go through Ernest.

"You stand out far more than a pureblood Hylantian. Remember that," her mother warned in clipped tones.

"……"

"I haven't accepted you as my child. And I *never* will. But that is due to my own intolerance. Your father and Simon are well aware of that. Even so, some things can never be changed. But if you are happy where you are, and keep your distance from me, then I will not attempt to intercede."

"What is that supposed to mean?"

"It means you need to be cautious. You have made far too much of a spectacle of yourself as it is."

"I see. If you have nothing else to say, I'll be on my way," Yuuri said, turning her back toward the woman who gave her birth and walking as quickly as she could to her carriage.

Even after she was in her carriage and then the comfort of her own home, Yuuri still couldn't calm down. That was likely the last time she would ever speak to her mother. And she was angry with herself for letting the opportunity slip away.

Perhaps her mother's warning had been out of genuine concern. If that was the case, she wished she had been a little kinder to her.

But then her mother said she could never accept her. Yuuri had been foolish to ever expect otherwise.

Yuuri's mother had taken hold of her mind. No matter how she tried to distract herself with reading or housework, a sense of malaise swept over her.

The sound of a bell caught Yuuri's attention from the back of the shop. There could only be one man who would dare visit her. She rushed to the front to greet him. In his letter, Ernest said he wouldn't be back for several days, but she had no idea why.

It didn't really matter. The only one who could lift her spirits was Ernest.

But Yuuri's hopes were immediately dashed.

The Misfortune Devouring Witch is Actually a Vampire?!

It wasn't Ernest standing in the doorway, but a redheaded woman around twenty with her hands on her hips. Her face tightened into a scowl when she saw Yuuri.

"You're not 'The Witch Who Preys Upon Misfortunes' are you?"

She made no attempt at hiding her displeasure in either her expression or speech. Most people first addressed Yuuri with that old nickname, but few ever did so with such resentment.

"I don't care for that nickname! Who might you be?" Yuuri asked, giving the girl a scowl of her own. This girl clearly wasn't a potential customer. And it was clear from her clothing that she wasn't a member of the nobility either. Yuuri did not have many connections or political power, so she was unlikely to get in any trouble if she returned this woman's hostility with her own.

"Does the name Rosie ring a bell?"

"I don't recognize that name. Rosie who?"

"Dan's fiancée, Rosie, that's who!"

"Dan who…?"

Yuuri was even more confused than ever. This was her first time ever meeting this woman and she had never heard the name Dan.

"Don't play dumb! You homewrecker!"

"Homewrecker? I'm sorry, but could you come back another day when you're in a better place to calmly explain what you're talking about? I don't know who you or Dan are. …And I don't deal with people who can't listen."

"Hmph! V-Very well… If you insist, I will spell it out for you."

Rosie kept her scowl fixed on Yuuri the entire time as she moved to the sofa, where she helped herself to a seat.

"Not there. Wait a second."

Yuuri felt that seat belonged to Ernest and Ernest alone. So she grabbed a chair from the dining area and set it at the counter.

"Here."

"Fine." Rosie was clearly displeased with the fact that she was being forced to sit on a hard, wooden chair when a couch was right there. She pouted, reluctantly settling into the seat.

This woman wasn't a customer, merely a nuisance to Yuuri, so she cared little for her displeasure.

"You might think Dan is your lover, but he and I are engaged!"

"…Like I said, who is Dan?"

The idea suddenly pulsed through Yuuri's mind. What if Dan was an alias Ernest used?

Lovers—? Yuuri wasn't sure exactly what she and Ernest were, but he was certainly the closest thing she had to a lover.

Still, no matter how hard she tried, she couldn't picture him being with this boisterous woman. Ernest seemed to prefer more subdued women.

"I'm talking about Baron Thewlis' chef, Dan!"

"Oh. What does he look like?"

"His hair is brown, as are his eyes."

The only two brunettes Yuuri knew were Simon and her father. At the very least, she could breathe a sigh of relief knowing this woman wasn't talking about Ernest. While hair color could be changed, eye color could not.

"He does not sound like anyone I know."

"Lying trollop! Dan said he was leaving me because he was seeing the witch who lived here…"

"He just told you that? Do you have anything other than his words for proof?"

"Are you saying he lied to me? Why would he do that?!"

As she watched Rosie, Yuuri began to suspect Dan had another reason for leaving her. Still, she lamented the fact that someone so hardheaded would come to her.

"…I can't speak for someone I don't even know. Why don't we do this? Ask this Dan when exactly he met me. Get exact dates and times. If he gives you ten and I can prove even one of them was a lie, then perhaps all of it is, right?"

"Are you stalling? Trying to run away?"

"Run away from what? This is my home. I have nothing to prove here. I'm merely offering to help you because I don't like people suspecting me of wrongdoing."

"You certainly are cocky. Fine, I'll be back soon."

"I'd be just as happy if you didn't come back."

Just when she was hopeful that she finally had a genuine customer, it turned out to be unwanted trouble. Perhaps because yesterday was such a good day, today had to be bad to retain the balance.

"'Life is a balance. We must take the bad with the good.' I believe there's a proverb like that from Xingka."

Her mind mired in depression, Yuuri couldn't be sure. Overcome with exhaustion, she leaned back on the couch and heaved a sigh.

❦ ❦ ❦

THE next morning, Rosie returned, but this time, she brought a young man with her. It was immediately obvious this was the Dan who was supposed to be Yuuri's lover.

"I'm so sorry!"

Yuuri heard him shout. She didn't stop what she was doing long enough to notice that he was bent over in a deep bow.

"Why did you use my name?"

"I figured a foreign witch with such a bad reputation wouldn't mind one more little sin on her pile. And I was so afraid of my girlfriend. But I never expected her to barge in on you like this!"

Yuuri regretted ever trying to make sense of the irritating couple.

The nickname, "Misfortune Devouring Witch" was supposed to be a compliment, as her grandmother would seek to resolve that which ailed the people of this town. But then the name took on a life of its own, becoming "The Witch Who Preys Upon Misfortune" instead. Yuuri hated that new name because it dishonored her grandmother's memory. Despite that name, not one bad thing about her grandmother had ever been said.

"Why did you want to break up with me then?!"

"Well…"

Rosie now directed the anger she had for Yuuri yesterday at Dan. Dan approached her, his eyes moist with tears.

"Would you two mind taking this outside? I really don't care…"

"No, please, you must let me explain myself. The truth is…"

And then, despite the fact that Yuuri wasn't even listening, Dan launched into the story of his life.

He was born in a town about half a day's ride from the city. His parents and brother managed a factory, but he chose to come to the city to look for work.

As luck would have it, he was taken in by the baron's estate, and found himself with a stable lifestyle.

And yet…

"I became the guarantor for my family's debts. I was afraid that, after we got married, someone might show up, looking to collect…and you would think I was pathetic…but I was so embarrassed I couldn't tell you. I was just afraid anyone coming to collect may go after you, Rosie."

"Don't you think involving a complete stranger is even more embarrassing?"

A woman could never truly understand a man's pride. Somehow, having his fiancée think he had cheated was less shameful than her knowing he had debts to his name.

Yuuri definitely didn't get it. She thought the former was far worse.

"I'm sorry. But everything's all right now. Someone came to the baron's home to collect and, when I explained everything to the baron, he paid the debt on my behalf."

"Dan, that's wonderful!"

"He's going to take it out of my monthly pay, but he agreed not to charge me interest."

For them to come all the way to his workplace, it sounded like these lenders weren't legitimate. They were likely the sort to charge a high interest rate and no matter how much the borrower paid, the principle total never went down. For the baron to pay down Dan's debts, he must have truly been a generous man.

"That is good."

Yuuri had no reason to fret over the collectors, as she had only just met Dan. Moreover, she resented him for dragging her into his personal problems. But at least the incident had resolved without issue.

"Uhm…actually, I hate to trouble you further, but I have a request."

"…What now?"

"Rosie and I have very little education. But we're about to go sign our promissory note and we were wondering if you would stand in as our witness?"

Yuuri was shocked. She thought the whole ordeal was over.

"I don't want to be involved any further."

"I understand. But what got my family into this mess was not understanding things like interest. So as embarrassing as this is, would you please come along and help us?"

The Misfortune Devouring Witch is Actually a Vampire?!

Dan had dragged Yuuri into this, so there was no real reason for her to help them. But something deep down wouldn't allow her to abandon people who needed her.

And they weren't asking for much. They didn't seem to be bad people either.

"All right. I'll help you."

"Really? Thank you, Miss Witch!"

"It's Yuuri."

The three of them set off for Baron Thewlis' estate.

The couple assured Yuuri that their carriage was waiting just off on the main road, so she left her parasol in the shop, electing to walk in their shadows instead. As they were walking, Yuuri sensed someone behind her. She glanced back and noticed two tough-looking men heading her way.

"A-Are those the bill collectors? Why are they here?!" Dan's voice wavered.

"I don't know. We'd better run the rest of the way to the carriage!" Rosie grabbed Yuuri's hand, even though she wasn't the one they were after, and they took off running.

"Wait! You there. Miss Yu—"

They burst out onto the main road, the men's voices drowned out by the hustle and bustle of the crowd. Yuuri was out of breath, but somehow, she made it to the carriage and jumped in.

"I thought the baron paid off your debt?" she questioned.

"I thought so too! Those aren't the usual collectors though. Maybe not all of their collectors were informed? Either way, we'll be safe at the manor!"

I knew I shouldn't have gone along with this. Yuuri lamented as the carriage rolled on toward Thewlis Estate.

🦇 🦇 🦇

THEWLIS Estate was a gorgeous, stately manor. Artwork from around the world adorned the hallways and the parlor. Yuuri understood that it was all valuable, but none of it was anywhere near her tastes. Next to a contemporary piece by a popular artist was a bronze statue from a southern nation and a Hinomotoese ink painting in a gilded frame.

There seemed to be no unifying motif or taste behind the artwork.

The baron had paid off his employee's debts, so Yuuri figured he must be a nice man. But a nice man with horrible taste in art.

She felt apprehensive as they sipped tea in the parlor. The employee, his fiancée, and Yuuri, the odd one out.

There, someone (likely a steward, Yuuri thought) was explaining the matter of the promissory note. The promissory note itself was fairly straightforward. Naturally, it spelled out just how much would be deducted from his current monthly pay, as well as what would happen should he need to leave the position, or how unexpected illness or death would be handled.

She explained the contents of the note to them, ensuring there were no discrepancies or disputes, and took the time to look everything over. Finally, Dan signed the note and the task was completed without incident.

"Yuuri Watoh. I apologize that one of our employees has caused you so much trouble. My lord would like to express his apologies in person, so please wait here for a moment."

"No, that isn't necessary," Yuuri declined, but the steward had already gone to summon the baron.

A few moments later, the baron appeared with two male servants. Just like everything else in the manor, they were overdressed for a midday tea.

Finally getting a good look at his face, Yuuri's eyes grew wide.

Baron Thewlis was the man who had tried to pick a fight with Yuuri when she was disguised as a page at the gentlemen's club.

"You're still here? You're dismissed. The only one I have business with is that Eastern girl over there," the baron said coolly to Dan and Rosie.

Yuuri broke out in a cold sweat. There was no way this was pure coincidence.

"Heh heh, so it is you. I've searched high and low for you. ...Never did I think to look for a young woman." The baron approached Yuuri, a lascivious grin creeping onto his face.

His interest in her hadn't waned since that day at the club, and he'd been searching for her ever since.

"What's going on?"

The Misfortune Devouring Witch is Actually a Vampire?!

"Huh…? Do you two know each other? My Lord, did you fall in love with her in town somewhere? Is that why you wanted us to arrange a meeting? I mean, not that there's anything wrong with that, but—"

Dan and Rosie had absolutely no idea what was happening. The baron shot Dan a look as he rambled incoherently.

"Keep your incessant thoughts to yourself! Or I'll cancel my promise to pay your debt! Now get lost!"

"Then I'll just be taking my leave as well. I've completed my business on Dan's behalf," Yuuri said, offering the baron a small bow before nonchalantly taking a step toward the door. The baron took a step toward her, blocking her path.

"You Eastern women are so frigid. So Yuuri is your name, is it? It sounds rather masculine, but it does have a certain ring to it. Yuuri… Yuuri… Bahaha!"

"The only ones who may call me by that name are my family and Ernest. I really will be leaving now!"

When Ernest first called her name without formality, it had filled her heart and tickled her ears. She was happier than she had ever been. But when the man before her did the same, it rotted on his tongue, polluting the sound she had previously cherished.

She became increasingly angrier, her tone grew tenser. She kept chanting, "calm down, calm down" in her mind.

"Ernest? …Ahh, Count Selden? Well, I regret to inform you that, though I am only a baron, my father is a duke! I outrank your sweet count. I can drape you in finery that fool could only dream of."

Yuuri immediately realized he must be the "duke's son" her mother had mentioned.

"I despise cowards like you. And I can buy my own finery, thank you."

There was no point in trying to reason with this man. From what he was saying, this sounded like retaliation. Retaliation against her, Ernest, and Major Conquest.

"I do relish that defiant look in your eyes. Taming you promises to be a most amusing challenge…"

He had never intended for Yuuri to stand on equal footing with him. His one goal with her was always subjugation.

"I pray that your father is the just sort of man who would punish such an insolent son. I would never waste my time on some sniveling child who thought social ranking granted him the right to do as he pleases." Yuuri emphasized the phrase "insolent son". She knew angering him was dangerous, but he repulsed her so much, she couldn't keep her mouth shut.

Baron Thewlis' eyes bulged on hearing a girl younger than him mock him so. He grabbed her by the wrist.

"Impudent wench! I can see it's time to teach you your place!"

He slapped Yuuri across the cheek. Unable to pull away from his grip, Yuuri took the brunt of the blow. There was pain, then the taste of blood in her mouth.

Yuuri could do nothing, save fighting back tears and vowing never to forgive this man. Using her vampirism to her advantage at this point would be too dangerous.

"Aaaah!" Dan screamed, leaping at the baron. The baron released his hold on Yuuri as he and Dan toppled to the ground.

"How dare you attack your betters!"

"Run! Both of you, go! Rosie, hurry, I can't let anyone else—ungh!"

The steward and the two servants leapt in, pulling Dan off the baron. They dragged him off and punched him in the stomach over and over.

Yuuri crumpled to the ground, unable to watch the violent spectacle any longer.

"Let's go!"

"After them!"

Rosie yanked Yuuri up off the floor, desperately trying to steady her on her feet. They darted for the door. However, the servants and the steward were faster, stopping them in their tracks.

"Ugh, let us go! It's illegal to keep us here…"

Yuuri had been knocked onto the cold, hard floor and was being held facedown by one of the servants.

Baron Thewlis' cackle as he closed in on her made her skin prickle. She was so terrified and felt so ill that tears began to flow down her cheeks. She had to stop herself from giving in to her vampiric instincts and attacking him, for fear of how that would end for both of them.

"That's enough!"

The door burst open and a cold voice cast a chill over the room.

Yuuri tried to lift her head just high enough to see who the voice belonged to. It was someone she knew very well, yet never expected to see here.

"Lord…Ern…st?"

It was definitely Ernest who stood before her. And at his back, Major Conquest and several men who were likely members of the military police.

"Get off of her."

That deep growl was one Yuuri had never heard before. The servants, terrified of Ernest's white hot rage, released Yuuri immediately.

"Who ordered this?"

"…Baron Thewlis."

"Ohh. Did you hear that, Major? Catching him in the act means you can arrest him, doesn't it?"

"Unlawful imprisonment and assault are serious crimes. Seize him. …And see to that man's wounds."

On Conquest's orders, his subordinates rushed the room and took the baron and his men into custody. Dan was clearly in pain, holding his stomach as he tried to talk to the soldier attending to him.

"F-Fools! How dare you trespass upon my estate?!" Baron Thewlis shouted, kicking and trying in vain to break free.

"I announced myself at your door, so I see no problem here. But I have no interest in arguing with criminals. So butt out. Yuuri, let me see your wounds."

"Ohh…I'm so sorry."

Ernest loomed over Yuuri, who was still on the ground. He was so frightening, so different from the Ernest she knew, that she couldn't help but apologize.

But as she got a closer look at him, she could see beads of sweat glistening on his forehead and his strained, uneven breaths.

She still wasn't completely sure what was going on, but it was enough knowing that he had come to her rescue.

"Doesn't look like you've got any broken bones or lost teeth. How did you manage to give my guards the slip?"

"Guards…?"

"It's so stuffy here. We'll talk more once we're back at my manor."

"Those two tried to help me too!"

Rosie and Dan hadn't known what Baron Thewlis was planning, nor had they intended to lure her into a trap. Once they figured out the baron's plot, they had tried to help her escape.

"But they're the reason you were caught up in this mess. You're far too trusting."

"...But..."

Ernest was so different from his usual self. While his words and tone weren't any harsher than usual, it was clear that he was upset. Yuuri found it difficult to argue with him like this. She couldn't be selfish in the face of all he had done for her.

"All right. Major Conquest, we'd like to be going, is that all right?"

"I'll need to hear her testimony later. But until then, I leave her in your care. We'll take this man with us and see to it he gets the optimal medical care."

"Let's get out of here. A gentleman like myself can scarcely stand to breathe the same air as this degenerate," Ernest said, scooping Yuuri into his arms.

Yuuri was used to always seeing Ernest smile. But now he was expressionless. His steel blue eyes were emotionless and cold.

"I'm so sorry..."

"I'm not upset with you." Sensing Yuuri's fear, Ernest flashed her a brief smile. His smile was fake and did little to calm her apprehension.

Yuuri couldn't help but feel guilty for making him worry and causing him to wear such an expression.

🐦 🐦 🐦

BACK at the Selden estate, Yuuri decided to have a bath and change her clothes before speaking with Ernest again. She only realized how much danger she had been in once she saw how red her cheek was in the mirror. Imagining what could have happened had Ernest not come to her rescue made her eyes well up with tears.

After Tarrah finished helping her get ready, Yuuri made her way to her usual guest room, where Ernest was waiting.

"Are you hungry?"

"Not really..."

She had missed lunch due to all that had happened, but she found she didn't have much of an appetite.

The Misfortune Devouring Witch is Actually a Vampire?!

After some time, black tea and baked goods were delivered to her room. Ernest urged her to at least drink something, so Yuuri drained a cup of tea blended with plenty of sugar.

Ernest took a seat next to Yuuri, just as he did back at her shop. She felt uneasy though. It wasn't that Ernest had done anything wrong. She just didn't want him to see her swollen cheek up close. Not only that, but her wrist where the baron had grabbed her felt dirty even after her bath. She felt embarrassed to even be sitting next to him.

"Do you feel up to talking? I thought maybe I was just paranoid, but I had a couple of my personal guards stationed around your shop, just in case."

"Why?"

"Because it was made public that I was the one who had infiltrated the illegal gambling ring. You're...my weakness. I was afraid someone might take you hostage, you know?"

Ernest had to sneak into the illegal gambling ring in order to bring its illicit dealings to light. But when he was the only one not busted, it quickly became clear that he was the mole.

He couldn't avoid the fear that someone would seek revenge, so he sent guards to those closest to him just to be safe.

"So the people I ran away from were actually the guards you sent to protect me?"

"I should have told you. I'm sorry. And I never expected he of all people would target you."

Yesterday, all Ernest knew was that Yuuri had a visitor. He hadn't learned the visitor's loose connection to Baron Thewlis until this morning. By the time he thought to have her brought to his manor for safekeeping, she had already left the shop.

That was when Ernest went to Major Conquest and asked him and his subordinates to help him "pay a friend a visit".

"Normally, a warrant would be required to investigate someone's home, but if serious crimes like kidnapping or assault become apparent during a routine visit, the military police are able to take drastic measures."

"I really was careless. I'm so sorry."

Ernest had scolded her for her recklessness many times. And yet, Yuuri had trusted Rosie and Dan so readily and in turn, been tricked.

"You need to be mindful of those around you... You especially need to heed your intuition when it comes to other men. This time was my fault though, so I won't badger you about it further."

Baron Thewlis had become infatuated with a page by the name of Saizoh and sought to have him for himself. He was quickly able to determine that the page had some sort of connection to Watoh Company because he served Ernest.

No matter how he searched, he could find no information on a black-haired, black-eyed boy. But Yuuri likely did come up over the course of his search.

The baron didn't care if Yuuri was Saizoh or vice-a-versa; either would do. He saw Yuuri as a rare raven-haired doll to be put on display for the amusement of his peers.

"Where's Rosie?"

"It seems she knew about her fiancée's debt all along and agreed to play along. It wasn't mere happenstance that she found her way to your shop. She bore you no ill will, but she wasn't exactly upstanding either."

One condition of Baron Thewlis paying off Dan's debt was that they would bring Yuuri to him. It was the baron's steward who had penned this illicit farce, with Dan and Rosie aware of their parts well in advance.

But the two of them had no malicious intentions. They were merely under the impression that they were facilitating a meeting between Yuuri and the baron. So when they saw what the baron was really planning, they tried to help her escape.

"It's precisely because there wasn't a hint of malice in them that you were so easily deceived," Ernest said, his eyes fixed on the witch as the truth finally dawned on her.

He was far from his usual lighthearted self. That lighthearted nature made him seem so gentle and kind. Because everything was a joke with him, it gave Yuuri a way out if she was feeling uncomfortable. But there wasn't a hint of that gentleness now. He was letting her feel the full weight of just how much trouble she had caused him—and just how much worry.

He had lied when he said, "I'm not angry with you." He was angry.

"You poor thing, your cheek's all bruised."

Yuuri knew that, as much as she might want to, she couldn't pull away from his hand nor avoid his gaze.

"You don't want me to touch you?"

"You're a little scary right now. But…"

"But what?"

"But you're here with me, so I don't want to waste a second of my time with you… I hated it. You're the only one I want to touch me or call me by my name…that's why…that's why…"

Yuuri buried her face in Ernest's chest. As soon as she did, it felt like all of her horrible thoughts and feelings had been swept away.

"That's right. You're mine and mine alone," Ernest proclaimed, asserting his claim on Yuuri once more. It was terribly arrogant of him.

But Yuuri was his, for she was so fragile that she would die without him.

Was it really because of her vampirism? Or because of her feelings for him? She couldn't be sure. But she wanted to give him everything he ever wanted. And at the same time, she wanted all he was to be hers as well.

She decided that it was time. There should be no secrets between them anymore.

"I have something I've never shared with you before…can I tell you now?"

Without him to give her blood, Yuuri would die.

She had been terrified to tell him of the burden that rested on his shoulders. But she felt like a traitor for keeping it from him for so long.

Ernest had always been so forthcoming, so considerate of Yuuri. He always made sure she knew exactly how he felt. Yuuri resolved to do the same for him.

"All right."

He flashed Yuuri his usual grin for the first time that day.

"For those of us descended from vampires—"

Just as she was about to tell him, she sensed someone was in the hall. Tarrah knocked on the door, informing them of a visitor.

"We'll talk tonight."

Major Conquest had arrived to interview Yuuri and Rosie.

Ernest had promised they would speak that night, but Yuuri was afraid her courage would wane long before then.

YUURI and Ernest headed for the parlor on the first floor to speak with Major Conquest. As they entered, they saw a woman with glasses seated next to him. She wore a uniform similar to that of the military police and introduced herself as military secretary Ashleigh Lind.

"I was asked to accompany the major in the hopes that having another woman in the room might make you more comfortable. We thought being stuck in a room with Major Conquest alone might be a little too much to ask."

"Thank you for your consideration."

Yuuri wasn't afraid of Major Conquest exactly. But after such a harrowing experience, she was grateful to have another woman present.

Especially since the major was being his usual taciturn self. Ashleigh took over and filled Yuuri in on everything, including Dan's condition. He had a few cracked ribs, but his life wasn't in danger.

Meanwhile, Rosie was in another room in Ernest's manor, talking with another member of the military police. Those involved with the incident at Baron Thewlis' manor had been taken into custody.

"Even if they go to jail, they will likely be out soon. You would do well to exercise caution, Count Selden."

"I'm well aware. But his father at least should have enough sense to keep him on a short leash for a while...and don't worry, I won't make the same mistake again."

"That's all that matters."

The one who should have exercised more caution wasn't Ernest, but Yuuri.

She thought back to everything that had happened up to that point, especially the moment when she told him her welfare was none of his concern.

But even Major Conquest could see the truth that she could not.

She knew that she never wanted to go back to being witch and client.

It made her sick to think that a complete stranger had realized how important she was to Ernest before she had. She just wasn't ready yet.

As they were talking, a servant arrived with an urgent summons, calling Ernest back to the palace immediately.

"Sorry, but there's a lot going on right now. Can you handle it from here?"

"Yes. Have a safe journey."

"Major, Miss Lind, I leave the rest to you."

After Ernest departed, they asked Yuuri about the events that led up to her being taken to Baron Thewlis' estate. Major Conquest was aware of everything after the baron entered the parlor.

Yuuri told them about how Rosie and Dan had visited her shop and how she had become embroiled in their quarrel. She also revealed that she had agreed to serve as a witness to their promissory note without due consideration.

They finished questioning Yuuri there, intent on hearing the rest from Dan.

"Still, that Count Selden certainly is a bold man, marching into the Major's office and demanding use of his troops like that. I couldn't believe the Major just relented immediately."

"Be quiet! I did not cave. I just felt I should be flexible with him was all."

The way Miss Lind told it, Ernest forced Conquest to lend him his men. But that was against the rules, so they framed it as a "friendly visit". After all, the military police couldn't act in a case like this without proof.

"Uhm, did Lord Ernest cause you a lot of trouble, Major? It sounds like he made a lot of unreasonable demands?"

"He did!"

"I'm terribly sorry."

"There's nothing for you to apologize for, Ms. Watoh. The count is lucky I don't have to re*COUNT* his actions."

"Major, your jokes are terrible."

"I have not told a single joke in my life."

"Uh-huh."

Major Conquest was normally a taciturn, humorless man. But with Ashleigh here, he was different. His speech patterns and attitude might not have changed. And yet today, he seemed gentler somehow. She seemed to serve as the straight man to his understated antics. Watching them made Yuuri feel better.

Yuuri watched them with a smile. The two demonstrated the perfect boss-subordinate pairing.

"Well, we should be going. Are you planning to spend the night here? If you need to return home, we can escort you."

"Ah, uh...mm, I should wait here until Lord Ernest returns."

Yuuri didn't live in this manor, after all. And it wasn't normal for an unmarried, unrelated woman to be staying overnight the way she did. But she couldn't just leave while Ernest was away without saying anything.

"That's right. Count Selden has been busy making preparations for his journey, settling all his affairs and so on. I hope he comes back soon."

"Preparations for what journey?" she asked instinctively.

Conquest and Ashleigh grew pale as if they had just said something they should not have.

"...Ah, well..."

"Settling what affairs? ...Is he leaving for an extended period of time?"

This was absolutely not the sort of thing she should have heard from strangers. If Ernest declined to tell her, maybe it was because he didn't want her to know.

She understood, yet he wasn't there for her to ask.

"We thought you knew. It was a gaffe on my part."

"Where is he going? Is this for another secret investigation?"

"No, this is a public matter."

"Then it shouldn't hurt for you to tell me, right? You shouldn't need his permission to tell me." Yuuri wasn't asking; she was pressing them to go on with it.

"...I, uh, suppose you're right. Count Selden is being relocated to Fosdan to serve as our ambassador there. He'll be leaving in three months' time."

"I see. For how long?"

"It depends on how negotiations proceed. He likely won't be back for at least half a year."

Half a year without drinking Ernest's blood was a death sentence for Yuuri. She hadn't told Ernest that she couldn't drink another's blood or even that she preferred death to being away from him. This must be her punishment for not being open with him.

"Thank you for telling me. I will miss him, but there's not much that can be done if it's for work. But not telling me…he can be so cruel…. how sad."

Yuuri wasn't sure what story her posture and expressions told, but she hoped her words at least were enough to be convincing.

She saw the major and secretary as far as the entrance to the manor.

"You look unwell. Are you all right?" Ashleigh asked, peering into Yuuri's face.

"Do I? I suppose I'm just tired from everything that's happened. But I really am all right."

As soon as she let her guard down, all of her doubt and anxiety had found its way onto her face. Yuuri tried to pull herself together and forge a smile.

"Please, get some rest."

"Well, we'll be off now."

After they left, Yuuri took a break in her usual guest room. It had been a trying day, and she felt at ease under the watchful eye of Tarrah and the other maids.

Once Ernest returned home, she joined him for dinner. He figured out right away that something was wrong. But she refused to reveal the anxieties that weighed so heavily on her heart.

Instead, she said she was just distressed from the events that had taken place at Baron Thewlis' manor. Yet the truth was that she had almost completely forgotten about the day's events in favor of her worries over losing Ernest.

To calm her fears, Ernest insisted that she was out of danger once and for all. She could return home without fear. Baron Thewlis was in a place where he could never harm her again. Since the sun had already set, she would stay the night at Ernest's estate and return to her home the next morning.

Ernest asked Yuuri to resume their conversation from earlier, but she lied and said she was far too tired.

❧ ❧ ❧

UPON returning to her shop, Yuuri curled up in her bed and closed her eyes.

Normally, she slept quite well, but last night, she barely slept a wink.

It was because reality had come crashing down before her without warning.

She just lay there, chasing the eternity she and Ernest thought they would have through her mind.

She dozed on and off, to the point where she became unable to tell when she was asleep and when she was awake.

Ernest had always been honest with Yuuri. But she had been fearful, distrustful, and kept her true feelings from him.

Maybe I should get a job, like as a servant or maybe a counselor, and travel with him...?

That felt unfair to Ernest. After how honest he had been with her, was she really just going to pretend that was the way she wanted things to be between them? And as kind as he was, he likely wouldn't complain.

I don't have any choice though.

What if she told him and he rejected her? What would he think of her, knowing she feared being apart from him or dying of thirst? But he would be heartbroken if she never told him and he only found out after the fact. That possibility hurt Yuuri most of all.

She had intended to tell him last night, but had lost her nerve. To think that doubt could be the weakness of creatures as powerful as vampires.

She lay there, steeped in worry just beneath her covers, when a knock came from outside. From the front door of the shop, to be precise.

"Yuuri! Are you home?"

It was Ernest. Ernest, who was supposed to be busy preparing to leave the country.

Yuuri pulled the quilt up around her face. She hadn't adequately gathered her thoughts just yet. If she saw him now, she wasn't sure what she would say. She lay completely still, listening to him call her name, just hoping he would go away.

"Are you ill again? ...Sorry, but I'm coming in," he called.

She heard the door clatter open.

"How?!"

She heard him coming up the stairs and toward her door. She had absolutely nowhere to run and so just stayed under her quilt as Ernest entered the room.

"Aha, I knew it! Pretending to be out, were you?"

"H-How did...you get in?"

Her new lock was supposed to be much more secure than the old one. So how did he get in?

"Certainly not with this," Ernest drawled as he twirled the key on the chain playfully. It was exactly like the key he had given her.

"That's my..."

Her eyes shifted to the wall. Her key was hanging on the hook, where it belonged.

"No, this one's mine. I figured you wouldn't mind me having one, but I guess I was wrong. I'm sorry."

The old lock had been crude and insecure, so Ernest had hired someone to change it out for a better one. Both on that day, the day she had been sick, and that night three nights ago, he had locked Yuuri's home when he left, ensuring she would be safe and sound. He wouldn't have been able to do that without his own key.

She should have realized it sooner, but somehow it was almost too obvious.

"Please don't just barge into my house!"

"Were you crying? ...You look awful."

"No!"

Yuuri tried to sound threatening, but Ernest approached her bed, undeterred. She tried to pull away from him and ended up against the wall.

"I hear Major Conquest was running his mouth about things he shouldn't have last night. He's usually so taciturn, but that's because when he actually does open his mouth, he's usually got his foot in it. I thought you had been acting strange last night. ...His attendant, Miss Lind, was the one who told me."

"They only told me that you were going to Fosdan. Was I not supposed to know?"

"You weren't. Not before the right moment."

Ernest grabbed Yuuri's quilt and yanked it off.

"The right moment?"

He drew close to her, the frightening intensity gone, and gently kissed the back of her hand. He then lifted his head and looked her in the eye.

"Yuuri Watoh, will you marry me?"

"Huh?"

"Is that your answer?"

Yuuri gave the question a full twenty seconds of thought.

"But I ca—!"

Ernest placed his hand over her mouth before she could finish.

"Don't. If you refuse me so effortlessly, it'll break my heart. Just answer me this for now: you love me, don't you?"

Yuuri shook her head vigorously. Love needn't equate to marriage.

"I was going to tell you about Fosdan only after we had properly dated and you accepted my marriage proposal. I'm sorry we're having to do this backwards. I wanted to spend so much more time getting to know you, but I wasn't given a choice. I want to take you to Fosdan with me, as my wife. ...So, what's your answer?"

Ernest slowly pulled his hand away. He told Yuuri he didn't want her to reject him so easily, but what other answer was there?

"You already know how I feel! But, I can't! The relationship between you and I is unbalanced. ...I would feel guilty."

"Our social standings are irrelevant. His Majesty gladly gave his permission, seeing as you're the daughter of renowned merchants from abroad."

"But, what about my condition...?"

If they married and she bore him a child, it was likely that child may inherit some of her vampiric traits, introducing it into his family line. It would be difficult for them to live a normal human life, as it had been for her.

"You mean the condition that makes you single-minded, awkward, and extreme when you're in a lovey-dovey mood? Do you think those things make you unlovable somehow? Yuuri, your grandmother and your ancestors before her got on well enough with humans to bring you into this world. And yet you think there's something wrong with you exclusively?"

"But..."

Yuuri had been certain it would never work because Ernest was a nobleman. It was why she had rejected him so intensely.

She had always been afraid they would eventually be pulled apart, yet it was never what she wanted. But now his words were swaying her. Could they really be together?

The Misfortune Devouring Witch is Actually a Vampire?!

"You've been mine and mine alone since the moment you first drank my blood. If we're torn apart, you'll die, right?"

"You knew? Since when?"

"I more or less figured it out that day we went to the cemetery. I was sure after I saw how you didn't react to seeing Major Conquest's blood. Weren't you going to tell me about it last night?"

"...Lord Ernest, you're always one step ahead of me."

Normally, she could never tell when he was joking and when he was serious. But right now, it was clear that he was completely serious.

Somewhere along the way, Ernest had completely figured her out. His kindness was all-encompassing, but she was afraid that, if she gave into it, with how weak her confidence already was, she would stop being the self-sufficient girl she always had been. But she couldn't bear to be apart from him either.

Yuuri had no choice but to admit defeat.

"So, your answer?"

"I love you, Lord Ernest. You are the only one I want, now and forever. It's true, because of the bond forged in your blood, I could never be apart from you, but that is only because I accepted you. The bond only forges after we have chosen who we are truly in love with. ...I belong to you, and you alone."

He kissed her cheeks, which were stained with tears. Then her forehead, just above her eyelid. When his lips finally found their way to hers, her heart pounded so furiously, she feared it might burst.

She still wasn't used to kissing him. And she feared that, without being intoxicated on his blood, she may never get used to it.

🦇 🦇 🦇

AFTER that, Yuuri became very busy with preparations of her own.

She would be accompanying her husband, the ambassador, to Fosdan, after all. There was much she had to learn, so she was given a room at Ernest's manor.

She returned to her shop intermittently to gather her things and clean up. Thankfully, Simon was taking ownership of the shop, so Yuuri wouldn't have to say goodbye to the home she had shared with her grandparents just yet.

She was exhausted. Her mornings were filled with lessons on everything she needed to learn to be a good ambassador's wife. Her afternoons were filled with dancing lessons.

Ernest found her in her room, sipping tea, happily free from the day's obligations.

He had been scrambling to try and pull together a respectable wedding in only three months. Most noble weddings took anywhere from six months to a year to prepare. And gaining the proper acceptance and permission to marry into the nobility took some time.

"No ordinary man would be able to pull all of this together in such a short time. I suppose I'm just that amazing," Ernest boasted, though the truth was he had been planning this well before he even asked Yuuri. He had even been meeting with her father, ever since she first drank his blood.

"I wish you had told me, rather than done so much behind my back."

"Shame on you, you wicked witch. I was so madly in love that I couldn't contain myself, and there you are, holding back and letting me make a fool of myself."

"You're the wicked one."

This time, it was Yuuri's teasing words that hurt Ernest. But he merely laughed it off. Having her call him "wicked" actually made him feel proud somehow.

She took a sip of tea as a sign of defeat, just as a knock came at the door. A maid entered a second later.

"M'lady, a letter has arrived for you!" a woman in a polished servant's uniform announced, far louder than most servants would.

It was Rosie, wearing one of the manor's maid uniforms.

"Please stop addressing me that way. What are you doing here, Rosie?"

"The count hired me! We're coming with you to Fosdan too!"

Yuuri had heard that Ernest had hired Dan after he could no longer work at the baron's estate. But why Rosie too? Yuuri gave Ernest a quizzical look.

"Just for insurance. I didn't want anything to happen to her if that creep ever got out and tried to take revenge. ...We'll need servants when we go to Fosdan, so why break them up?"

Dan had received reparations from the baron over his injuries. But they weren't enough to cover all the debt the baron had paid off. And Dan was unemployed.

Ernest took over the remainder of the debts, with the caveat that Dan would pay a little back from his salary each month. But as Dan would have to come to Fosdan, he couldn't just force the man to leave Rosie behind.

"All right, I'll just set your letter here then."

Yuuri wasn't sure if she should correct Rosie on her boisterous manner.

She felt someone watching them from the door and looked up to see Tarrah standing there, seething.

"Rosie, come along now. …Master, I beg your pardon, she is still learning. Please excuse us."

It was inappropriate for Tarrah to wear anything but a smile in front of the head of household. But it was clear as day that Rosie was in for quite the lecture.

"It never is boring here, as you can see. Is it from your family?"

"Yes. I wrote to them regarding the wedding…and…"

With everyone gone, Yuuri could read the letter in peace. But her face clouded over and Ernest could guess what it was about.

"Is it your mother?"

Yuuri had asked her father if her mother would be attending her wedding ceremony.

"He said why let someone who cannot share our joy sour our special day?"

"Are you all right with that?"

"Yes. I suppose I knew she would choose this all along. After all, she did say she would never accept me."

It was so strange. For most of her life, the fact that Yuuri's mother had shunned her was like a millstone that she struggled to carry through life, weighing heavy upon her heart.

Children revered their parents above all others. So if her mother hated her so, then she must truly be a despicable creature. A monster.

But the words from the man she loved were even more powerful. Knowing how deeply he loved her, that she was in fact lovable, set her free.

Her mother was neither right nor perfect. And she could finally admit it. So she no longer needed to be bound by what this heartless woman thought of her.

"Are things different now?"

"...Yes."

To Yuuri, Ernest's words were her truth. Because he told her she was not a monster, though she was "determined, awkward, and extreme in her expressions of love," she felt free.

"Ohh. And just why have you become so positive all of a sudden? Care to tell me?"

"No."

"I see. Too bad. I have an idea anyway. By the way, this is your room, for you to use as you see fit...for now."

"Thank you very much."

Why was he bringing up the room all of a sudden? What was he really getting at?

"......"

Ernest gave her a wounded look, though she wasn't sure what she had done to upset him. She had merely thanked him for letting her have use of the room.

"That's not what I was looking for. This is a guest room and you are no longer a guest, so you won't be able to stay in here forever. Just prepare yourself for that."

This room had an expiration date? What would happen then? He certainly wasn't going to run his fiancée out of the manor, so where would she go? After he said "prepare yourself," she had a good idea of what he was implying.

Ernest lifted a lock of Yuuri's ebony hair to his lips. Startled, she tried to scoot away, but found herself trapped by the armrest. He was always so intimidating when he closed in on her like this.

Surely, it was his right as her future husband, but still, she wanted to wait just a little longer.

She was trying to squirm away, but she ended up on her back. She didn't want him any closer, so she grabbed his shirt, and gave a mighty shove.

"Ohh, you're being so aggressive today!"

No matter what happened, Ernest had the uncanny ability to rewrite every situation in his favor.

The Misfortune Devouring Witch is Actually a Vampire?!

Yuuri was trying to push him off of her so she could evade his advances, but Ernest was treating it like she was trying to take his shirt off.

"N-No, I wasn't! ...Stay back or I'll bite you!"

"Go ahead."

His lips curled into a mischievous smile as he swiftly undid his tie.

"Never mind, I think I'll pass for now!"

No matter how Yuuri's eyes filled with tears or how much she glared at him, he only smiled brighter. He usually gave her an out. But this time was different. Was it different because he was more serious than ever... or because this was exactly what she wanted as well?

Ernest gave Yuuri no time to think it over.

🦇 🦇 🦇

COUNT Selden's wife, Countess Yuuri, was known as the "Misfortune Devouring Witch". Anyone who had problems that needed solving could visit her at the manor. But in order to gain the witch's help, there were two rules one need follow.

One: All requests for aide were to go through the count himself first.

Two: No one was to request jasmine tea from the countess.

The count could be rather jealous and couldn't bear to see anyone else drinking jasmine tea his wife had made.

If you can manage to follow those two rules, the kindly witch from a distant land will happily devour your misfortunes too.

But what becomes of those who have their misfortunes devoured—?

The End

After Story: Dyed in His Color

WHILE preparing for their move to Fosdan, Yuuri occasionally returned to the shop to pack up.

After she left, Simon would take it over, but she still wanted to bring her clothes and mementos of her grandparents.

Ernest and Simon often came along to help.

"Wow, look! This brings back memories." Simon held up a box he had found while organizing the supply closet.

"The spinning tops? Those really do bring back memories."

It was a toy from Hinomoto. The box contained several different tops and the cords necessary to spin them.

One day, Simon had snuck away from home and come to play at his grandparents' house. He had left his tops there that day and there they had remained.

It had only been half a year since the siblings had started to repair their relationship. Their mother's adverse reaction to them spending time together had pushed Yuuri away from any kind of relationship with her brother and father. That icy gaze her mother gave her had forced her to seal away her happy memories with Simon, as he shared their mother's grey-blue eyes.

Her relationship with her mother had not changed, and it never would. But her relationship with Simon was slowly but surely getting better. While the memories of her pain would never fade, she at least had stopped associating everything her mother did with Simon.

That was all thanks to Simon's kindness and Ernest's presence.

The Misfortune Devouring Witch is Actually a Vampire?!

"Oh, that looks fun! How do you play?"

Ernest had been sitting in his usual spot, reading the paper. But now his eyes shifted to the spinning top Simon was holding with great interest. He had genuinely intended to help with the cleanup, but his curiosity kept getting the better of him and he would get easily distracted. He had questions about everything he found and ultimately, Yuuri deemed him a nuisance.

But to him, the witch's shop was like a fantastic toy box, full of treasures from a far away land. It was of course different for Simon, who had spent a lot of time in Xingka and Hinomoto, and Yuuri, who had received so many gifts from the East over the years from him.

"We compete to see who can get them to spin the longest. Alternatively, you can have the tops fight to see whose top can knock the other's over."

Simon wound the thin thread around his top and let it go with gusto. The harder one pulled the string, the faster the top spun.

"That's interesting. Here, let me try!"

Ernest grabbed a spinning top and cord out of the wooden box and copied Simon's movements. He let the top fly. But his top barely got one good spin in before toppling over on the floor

"Just because this is a child's toy doesn't mean the game is easy. Here, watch me. You can't just let it fall like that."

His face awash with pride, Simon patiently gave Ernest a thorough explanation of how to play the game.

"You have to wind it up good like this. It's like you're winding up a clock. If you don't put enough force behind it, it's going to fall over."

He wound his own top as he explained. When he let it go, it swept about the floor in whirlwind patterns.

Ernest listened intently to Simon's instructions and then picked up the top again. He released it much quicker this time, letting the top fly.

"Like this?"

The second time was a success. His top slammed into Simon's, which was still spinning even as they clashed.

The two men completely lost sight of why they were even here.

"Oh, Simon, not you too. I thought you came to help me? Or did you just come to play with toys?"

Yuuri wondered how grown men could still be so childish. But the sight of them both crouched on the floor, spinning tops, made her smile.

Her grandfather had been the same way. He had been fascinated with the very top that Simon was playing with now. Memories of her childhood came flooding back.

Not long ago, Yuuri would have tried to shake off any memories of her grandmother and grandfather. They brought nothing but sorrow and longing for a distant past. However, knowing that she had someone by her side who supported and loved her enabled her to change, slowly but surely.

She knew she had the two men who were gleefully spinning tops to thank for that.

"Sorry, but we have to finish this match first."

That match was unlikely to end anytime soon.

From the very first time they met, the two young men in her life had been at odds. Or rather, Simon had a one-sided grudge against Ernest. But it made her happy to see that her brother was getting along so well with the man who was to become her husband.

"What is it, Yuuri?" Simon noticed her gaze and tilted his head quizzically

"I was just admiring how well you two are getting along. You really are like brothers."

"Simon was just being protective because you had brought another man around. It wasn't personal."

"I still hate your flippant manner. Argh, why do I keep losing!"

Maybe they weren't exactly as close as Yuuri hoped. Then again, brothers tended to fight. Either way, she went back to cleaning and packing.

The first floor was almost completely cleaned out, so all that remained was the second floor, where her bedroom was.

The only clothes left in her bedroom were her winter clothes. But she knew that eventually, she would need them, so it was best to grab everything and store it at the Selden manor for now.

She opened the paulownia bureau and checked inside. This bureau had been brought over from Hinomoto, so it also contained many things Simon had given her.

She took out each item, one by one, and remembered that the bottom drawer had some of her grandmother's things. Her grandmother normally wore Hylantian-style clothes, but in the drawer were several of her grandmother's Hinomotoese kimono.

"These are…"

Yuuri picked up a black piece of fabric and froze.

It was a long, jet black kimono with vivid red flowers and folding fans painted onto it. The flowers and the fans were connected by yellow thread that would grab anyone's attention. And that raw ebony material was second to none. Black fabric was highly valued in Hinomoto, as it required a great deal of skill to produce.

Cheaper black fabric ended up having a red tint, as the color had not completely set in.

But her grandmother's kimono truly was black as the night. Her grandmother wore it only on rare occasions, so its color had not faded over the years.

"Grandmother's black *furisode*…"

Remembering what her grandmother had used the kimono for, Yuuri stood in front of the mirror and tried it on.

She looked like a younger version of the woman who had raised her. Surely, the kimono would look just as nice on her as it had her grandmother.

Her grandmother was likely the same age she was now when she had worn this. How had she felt back then?

Yuuri was happy that she had found someone who felt the way about her that her grandfather had felt about her grandmother. Though the fact that she was descended from vampires and was destined to cause pain and suffering to her beloved always lingered in the back of her mind. Her grandmother had likely felt the same.

Human hearts might change. But Yuuri and Ernest were bound by blood. She could never be with another. Just as the kimono had been permanently dyed black, so too had she been dyed in his blood. No other color, no other person, could erase him from her heart.

She loved him unconditionally. There was no question there. But she was still racked with guilt over the fate she had saddled him with. He held her life in his hands. She would die without him. It was as true emotionally as it was physically.

And yet, Ernest showed no signs of running away.

The *furisode* was the deep color of night. It was perfect for her, for many reasons.

"Yuuri! What are you doing in there?"

Yuuri jumped at the sound of Ernest calling her. He had left the spinning top game at some point, snuck upstairs, and was now standing in her doorway.

Their eyes met in the mirror and she looked away out of embarrassment.

"It's my grandmother's kimono. It was a rare find."

It seemed Yuuri was just as guilty of getting distracted as Ernest and Simon had been, yet there were no complaints.

"Black? That's such a rare color."

In Hylant, black was the color of mourning. But the kimono Yuuri wore was covered in bright red flowers and gave off a more festive feeling.

Ernest was used to seeing Yuuri and Simon in most Hylantian-style attire. Seeing Yuuri in the *furisode* made it even more special somehow.

"But it looks nice on you. A bit different from those *haori* you usually wear."

He stood behind Yuuri, staring at her reflection draped in the black robe.

"Long-sleeved kimono are called *furisode*. They're worn by young women in Hinomoto who aren't yet married."

"I see. Soon enough, you won't be able to wear that anymore."

"That's right."

Yuuri put her hand on her chest in relief. It was true, *furisode* were meant for unmarried women. But she had one last surprise for Ernest. She was content to let him think she was just trying it on out of curiosity for now.

But then—

"Wasn't that the kimono Grandmother wore on her wedding day?"

Simon blurted out. He had followed Ernest up to the second floor and robbed Yuuri of her chance to surprise him.

He knew far more about Hinomoto than Yuuri. Even if he never heard his grandmother mention it directly, he knew what the kimono had likely been used for.

He was right. This was the kimono Hana had worn on her wedding day and a gift from their great-grandfather.

Yuuri tried to imagine her wedding with Ernest and slipped the kimono on once more.

"A wedding outfit? I thought you said it was only for unmarried women?" Ernest looked back and forth between the siblings and tilted his head.

"That's right, but some women wear their *furisode* on their wedding day as well."

Yuuri had gone quiet in order to hide her embarrassment, so Simon explained in her stead.

"Really......?"

"Black is the color of mourning here in Hylant, but in Hinomoto, thanks to the difficult dyeing process, it signifies that the wearer won't be 'dyed in the color of another', so many brides go for the black *furisode*. Some do choose white for weddings in Hinomoto, but I prefer black myself."

Ernest already knew very well how Yuuri felt about him, so there was no need for her to be embarrassed about the kimono. But this was who she was. Obstinate, awkward, and unable to show her true feelings. So she had wanted to keep the color's significance a secret, at least for now.

"So you won't be 'dyed in the color of another' except for mine, eh? I like the sound of that!"

Yuuri was turning red and couldn't even bear to look at him in the mirror any longer. He could always see right through her, and he knew it vexed her so.

"I wonder if that's what the ebony color of your hair means too, my little witch? That you were always fated to love me and only me?"

He played with her hair. He was telling her that this was their fate. He didn't need special clothes or words or other symbols to know that.

"...This is the hair I was born with. That's all."

"Oh no, you're just saying that because I've figured you out. Just as you need blood to live, I need words."

He was right, as usual. His human heart might easily be swayed, but it was useless to worry and suspect his motivations. Yuuri knew exactly what he wanted.

She wanted to be with him forever. Not because he was her food source. But because she loved him. And it was selfish to expect him to intuit that was how she felt without saying it.

"Uhm...I..."

It wasn't a matter of sex or lineage. She loved Ernest and wanted to be with him. That would never change. And if he needed to hear it, then she would tell him, right here and now.

"Count Selden, you would really push my sister into public displays of affection right in front of her brother?!" Simon broke in, ruining the moment, his face redder than his sister's. Yuuri backed away from Ernest.

As much as she knew he wanted to hear her words of affection, now didn't seem to be the time.

"You're the one ruining a perfectly good moment! You have no sense, Simon!"

"I was busy packing in here anyway, so please leave!"

Yuuri chased the two men out of the room. Her face was feverish, her cheeks red from embarrassment.

"See! You pushed her too far and now you've upset her! You better learn not to push your luck or else it'll bite you in the butt!"

"As long as Yuuri's doing the biting!"

"Oh gosh, spare me that horrible image!"

The two of them continued bickering all the way down the stairs.

Yuuri was suddenly overcome with exhaustion and flopped down on her bed with a sigh.

After her grandmother had passed away, Yuuri had been all alone. Her whole world had fallen into a hopeless silence. She merely existed from day to day.

But then Ernest had crashed into her world, shattering the silence once and for all.

Her home had become a bustling, warm, and comforting place once more. One that, no matter where she went, she knew would follow, so long as she had Ernest by her side.

Her life with Ernest was far from peaceful. After all, he, more than any other, possessed the ability to rattle her heart.

Their life together may not be a quiet one, but it would certainly be far from boring or bereft of love.

Afterword

GREETINGS. I am Kiiro Himawari, the author.

I hope you enjoyed reading *The Misfortune Devouring Witch is Actually a Vampire?!*

This was a fantasy story set in a fictional world. However, I intended for the homeland of our heroine's ancestors to resemble Japan, and so this story features several items prominent in Japan several centuries ago.

For example, the black *furisode* kimono from the After Story being depicted as wedding attire was an actual custom taken from ancient Japan. I hope those aspects of the story were interesting for you.

I write novels here in Japan. I started writing in earnest after finding a website where you can submit your own novels three years ago.

Though I loved light novels and manga before then, I had never thought about trying to write my own. But it's because of a site where I could easily write and release my work for readers that this book was able to be published. It's also thanks to that site that I can continue to write for a living while raising my child.

Before that, I always thought I knew where my life was headed. I studied hard, graduated from college, found a job, got married…it was probably a pretty standard life. I love books, but never did I think I would see my own work on a store shelf.

But through one chance finding, one unconscious decision, I gained newfound courage and took the first steps to changing my life in a way I'm still realizing today.

Kiiro Himawari

I owe so much gratitude to that site, "*Shousetsuka ni Narou*" (Become a Novelist) and to Cross Infinite World, who proposed and are handling the English publication. I'm very excited that people in the US and other English-speaking countries will be able to read light novels.

There are likely those who believe that Japanese pop culture isn't for adults. But I want my works to impact readers across their lifetimes.

So I hope to keep releasing works that I would want to read myself, for my readers to enjoy.

And I hope someday, I could provide someone else a life-changing chance of their own...

Thank you so much.

-Kiiro Himawari

THE MISFORTUNE DEVOURING WITCH IS ACTUALLY A VAMPIRE?!

BY KIIRO HIMAWARI
ILLUSTRATED BY KIBIURA

LITTLE PRINCESS IN FAIRY FOREST
STORY BY: TSUBAKI TOKINO
ILLUSTRATION BY: TAKASHI KONNO
STANDALONE | OUT NOW

Join Princess Lala and Sir Gideon as they flee for their lives from the traitor who killed the royal family and wants to wed Lala! Gideon is willing to do anything to protect his princess, even if it means engaging the mighty dragons in combat! Tsubaki Tokino's fairy tale inspired Little Princess in Fairy Forest!

ANOTHER WORLD'S ZOMBIE APOCALYPSE IS NOT MY PROBLEM!
STORY BY: HARU YAYARI
ILLUSTRATION BY: FUYUKI
STANDALONE | OUT NOW

Just when I thought navigating high school was bad enough, I woke up to a rotting, post-apocalyptic world!

THE ECCENTRIC MASTER AND THE FAKE LOVER!
STORY BY: ROKA SAYUKI
ILLUSTRATION BY: ITARU
VOL. 1 OUT NOW

Yanked into another world full of dangerous magic and parasitic plants, Nichika does the one thing she can to survive: become the apprentice to an eccentric witch!

THE CHAMPIONS OF JUSTICE AND THE SUPREME RULER OF EVIL
STORY BY: KAEDE KIKYOU
ILLUSTRATION BY: TOBARI
STANDALONE | OUT NOW

Mia's a supervillain bent on world domination who lacks tact in enacting her evil schemes! Will the lazy superheroes be able to stop her?

THE WEREWOLF COUNT AND THE TRICKSTER TAILOR
STORY BY: YURUKA MORISAKI
ILLUSTRATION BY: TSUKITO
VOL. 1 | OUT NOW

"I don't care if you are a man, let me court you."
Rock's whole life is shaken when a werewolf shows up at her shop in the middle of the night...asking for more than just clothes!

OF DRAGONS AND FAE: IS A FAIRY TALE ENDING POSSIBLE FOR THE PRINCESS'S HAIRSTYLIST?
STORY BY: TSUKASA MIKUNI
ILLUSTRATION BY: YUKIKANA
STANDALONE | OUT NOW

After being dumped by a dragon knight, Mayna sets out to prove that fairytale endings aren't only for princesses! See how this royal hairstylist wins over the dragon kingdom one head of hair at a time!